Black Out

A Make You Mine Romance

KIMBERLEY ANNE

www.kimberleyanneauthor.com

First published in Australia in 2023 in conjunction with The Erudite Pen Independent Publishing.

Please be aware that this novel has been written in **Australian English** and uses Australian language, spelling, grammar and punctuation conventions. These are notably different to American, Canadian and even British language conventions.

Cover design by Judith San Nicolas
Typeset in Avenir Next LT Pro 26pt/Centaur 11pt
Printed and bound in Australia by IngramSpark
Prepared for publication and edited by Dr Juliette Lachemeier @ The Erudite Pen: theeruditepen.com

A catalogue record for this book is available from the National Library of Australia

Blackout: A Make You Mine Romance - Book One in the Acoustic Series
First ed.
ISBN 9780645784503
E-ISBN 9780645784510

Dedication

To my family and readers. Without you, none of this would be possible.

A Make You Mine Romance

Book One

Acoustic Novel Series

Prologue

April, 2013

It was a rare night off. A night to let down my hair, have a few drinks, blow off some steam and maybe check out Jam, the recently opened karaoke bar. A night off definitely did not come around very often, especially now that I was managing the business my family owned, James Family Bakery. So, tonight was all about mustering up just enough courage to step outside my comfort zone and try to make the most of a good time.

Making my way through my wardrobe, I dressed for comfort, not wanting sore feet at the end of the night. I settled on jeans, a singlet and a pair of strappy flats. With a small amount of make-up and my champagne hair falling in soft waves down my back, I reached for my purse and slung it over my shoulder.

I stood in the bedroom that I occasionally slept in at the front of a terrace-style house my grandparents had gifted me at the same time I started managing the family bakery. This bedroom was just like the rest of the house, which had been minimally furnished when I moved in. I guess it was up to me to purchase whatever I wanted to make this house a home, but when I spent hardly any time here, I didn't see the point.

My clothes and toiletries were the only items I had unpacked as they were items I used every day. Everything that I had brought with me from my grandparent's house was still in a few boxes in the front bedroom with the door closed. I needed to make this house my own, but I didn't want the reminder every time I walked past that I hadn't got around to doing it.

As I stared at myself in my full-length bedroom mirror, I was satisfied with the outfit I had chosen. Taking a deep breath I headed for the front door, turning to lock the door of my quaint Victorian terrace and pocketing my keys beside my phone, cash, debit card and driver's license. I then walked the short distance to The Royal, a corner pub just a street over from my house.

The Royal was a small inner-city Melbourne pub in the suburb of Fitzroy with a lot of dark wood and a bar that sat in the middle of the room. Stools covered the three sides of the bar; there was also one pool table and a stage big enough for an acoustic session or two, with tables and chairs scattered throughout the rest of the floor space.

I had ventured to The Royal a few times before when I'd knocked off early enough and needed a night cap. It was close to home, after all. I wasn't surprised to find the last time I walked through the doors that my younger sister Addison worked here. I spent most of my time at the bakery either baking or managing the office, which left me little time for catching up or reaching out to Addison. She had no such interest in working at the bakery, and as all my time was spent there, I hardly saw her.

I picked my spot at the bar and sat down, then waited for the petite bartender in her all-black outfit to make her way over. Her lips turned upwards on one side at first, but when she recognised me the other side of her lips followed, and she waved her hello. She didn't even take my order, just placed a glass of white wine down in front of me. She knew what I liked. The bartender was my sister, Addison James. I was fifteen months older than Addison's nineteen years and portrayed the exact opposite demeanour to Addison's wild and free-spirited nature. I guess the choices we had made as sisters had shaped us.

Staring into the clear golden-yellow liquid in front of me I contemplated bringing the glass to my lips, but did it anyway. I didn't want to overthink things tonight. I was always overthinking, and tonight I needed to just go with the flow.

Addison attended to the customers waiting for drinks. For a Saturday night, the pub crowd was just starting to build now that the dinner rush was over. When there was a break in customers, Addison ran around the bar to hug me.

'I found the bakery on social media, but I can't seem to find you. How long has it been? I feel like I haven't seen you in forever.' My sister tilted her head as if she knew the answer but wasn't game enough to say it out loud.

'It's been too long.' I exhaled loudly. 'But you know how the bakery is. I don't have time for anything else and that includes a personal life.' The family business was busy, and Addison knew it.

Addison and I were supposed to have each other's backs and always stick together. We had promised our father we would always be there for each other. But when I started working full-time at the bakery after I finished high school, Addison found better things to do with her time, and our closeness started to slip away. Addison chose not to help me manage the factory or any of our three shop outlets. Instead, she decided to find work elsewhere, and when she turned eighteen, most of the work she found was bartending.

I was annoyed that my sister didn't help out with her own family's business. I could have used an extra pair of hands when I was short a staff member, but I couldn't change her mind. Even a stupid dare a year ago had torn our closeness apart with the burden left on my shoulders, not her carefree ones.

Our childish schoolyard dares, without the watchful eyes of our mother, had started to escalate of late. Our dares were no longer fun challenges to complete but had become impossible stressful tasks with dire consequences. I never should have dared Addison to be my apprentice while knowing full well she would have been repelled at the notion.

Tonight though, Addison just nodded her head and bit into her bottom lip, like she knew I had just done back-to-back double shifts to keep the business afloat. But she didn't say anything. Nobody except Addison really knew I didn't venture outside of the work bubble I had created for myself. I never stopped working. If I wasn't baking pastries or loaves of bread, then I buried myself in paperwork or social media for the business until I was burnt out from exhaustion.

But even Addison didn't know that the reason I worked so much was because I hadn't been able to sleep since that tragic night five years ago. On that fateful night, everything had spun out of control and smashed our once tight-knit family into pieces. My family hadn't been the same since.

'That new karaoke bar has opened, so I thought I might check it out tonight.' I changed the subject and told my sister about Jam like she was my best friend that I confided in every day, and not an outsider to my life who now knew very little about me.

Addison had rebelled against the strictness our grandparents had placed on us the day they insisted Mum, my sister and I move in with them five years ago. I, on the other hand, had followed my grandfather around like a lost puppy as I tried to navigate the changes happening in my life. My grandparents were old-school and saw the world differently, and that two country kids needed to be protected in a big city like Melbourne.

My father's parents kept a close eye on Addison and me because our mother was overridden with grief. She had shut the world out and fallen into a black hole. Addison found her own way to adapt and move forward, and I always envied her for that. Whereas I was like my mother, caught up in grief I didn't know how to handle. But instead of falling into a black hole, I was forced to put on a brave face and start over. I was a teenage kid who was expected to finish high school.

'My shift is over soon.'

I looked up when I realised Addison was talking to me, which pulled me from reminiscing. I knew that look on her face; it told me she had a plan up her sleeve.

'Let me come with you. We can hang out like old times.'

I nodded my head okay. Maybe she wanted to bridge the gap between us, maybe she missed me, maybe I missed her, and maybe I missed our closeness. I thought about my sister and me. Would it work? The two of us side by side at the bakery? Taking turns baking at the factory one week and managing our three shop outlets the other? I could try to convince her to come and work with me again. But if my sister were anything like me, I knew she wouldn't want to feel like I did, stuck on the hamster wheel. But would it feel like that if Addison gave working with me a try?

I stayed in the spot I had chosen as I drank my wine, then ate the bowl of hot chips that was placed in front of me and watched as two guys set up their guitars to play and sing later tonight. I observed patrons come and go from The Royal as I sipped my way through my first glass of wine and waited to see how this night would unfold. My sister, she was up to something, but I just couldn't put my finger on it.

I couldn't help myself, so pulled my phone from my purse and scrolled through my emails, making notes on my phone of the things I needed to do. Now that I was managing the bakery, it was up to me to make the family business current, and keep it successful.

My grandfather was old-fashioned and couldn't grasp that technology was changing. He turned his nose up at a computer, telling me I should be able to work out everything out in my head, from counting back change to customers to measurements for recipes.

By the time Grandpa James let me take over the reins, I was an expert, but I also knew how much easier a computer would make things. Balancing the books, cashing up and finding out how much money we made, even putting together a roster, could be done with the click of a few buttons.

Once I was up to speed with new computers and software for not only my office but the shop outlets as well, I then needed to work on our social media and how to have a bigger online presence. For the last five years, I had been just like Grandpa

James in that I didn't even own a mobile phone. But now any free moment I had I was glued to it, trying to navigate my way through its fanciness.

An hour later and three wines in, I put my phone away. I had gone cross-eyed looking at the screen. I'd heard a sound through the microphone and noticed the men had picked up their guitars and were about to start their first set. I admired the way they made standing behind a microphone look so easy.

When my sister tapped me on the shoulder, I gathered her shift was over. We made our way up the stairs to an apartment above the pub – Addison's current shelter arrangements. She changed out of her all-black work clothes and shook out her hair that was longer and a slightly lighter champagne colour than mine. Addison and I had inherited our father's facial features. If I stared in the mirror long enough, I could see his full lips, slim nose, and army-green eyes. But I would always be marginally taller and have a curvier figure to Addison's too-slim, tanned physique.

She found her clothes, and it was no surprise that her outfit was similar to mine: jeans, strappy flats and a low-cut V-neck singlet. Only her singlet was white and tighter than mine, and her necklace was a single pendant that sat just at the curve of her breasts. My singlet was loose and black, and my necklace was a white-gold Y-chain with a bar pendant that drew attention to the space between the fabric of my singlet and my breasts.

Running my fingers through my hair I contemplated a messy bun, but since I hardly ever wore my hair down, I combed my fingers through my soft waves and let my hair continue to fall down my back. I looked over at my sister; we could almost be twins with the way we looked tonight. Although our outfits were almost identical, Addison had chosen to ramp up her make-up by adding winged eyeliner to the already-bronzed eyelids she had worn for work.

We were out my sister's apartment twenty minutes later and on our way down the stairs of The Royal. We quickly shuffled through the cool April-evening Melbourne air past the Fitzroy Town Hall on our way to Brunswick Street where Jam was located. The new karaoke bar was only two blocks from The Royal. I could see how long the line was the closer we got to the front door. *Shit,* I thought to myself when I saw that tonight was the grand opening. *Maybe this is a bad idea.* I wasn't used to having this many people around me.

With a self-assured style that could only be my sister, Addison took my hand. We walked straight past everyone in the line, ignoring the comments being made, to stand in front of the bouncer at the entrance to Jam. The bouncer whistled once, then gave everyone in line a hard stare that made him look mean. The tick in his jaw only exacerbated his toughness. The line quietened down, and if it weren't for Addison's firm hold of my hand, I probably would have walked away.

'Marcus.' My sister leaned in to give the bulked-up bouncer a kiss on the cheek.

'Addison.' He wrapped her up in a hug.

I was only slightly jealous of their meaningful human connection, something I hadn't had in my life for a long time. There was no time for another human being with the hours I worked, let alone a relationship.

Once my sister and the bouncer untangled themselves, she stepped back and introduced me. 'Marcus, this is my sister Harley. Harley, this is Marcus.'

Marcus and I shook hands, and nothing more was said between the three of us. He instead reached for the door handle and stepped aside to open the door. 'You ladies have a good night,' he said as we walked past him.

We thanked him as we walked through the opened door and into the foyer. Beyond the entrance was more darkness, and I wondered if we were in the right place.

Not worried by the darkness, the ambience, the amount of people around us or the noise we could hear, Addison grabbed my hand again and led me straight to the bar to order a round of drinks. She ordered Chardonnay for me and a cherry bomb for herself, knowing I wouldn't change my drink now that I had started on wine.

I took in Jam's scene as I waited for my drink. The place was mysterious, and pockets of darkness surrounded us. There were no white lights to guide our way. The bar and the stage were aglow with a purple hue, which was the only light in this place.

As my eyes tried to adjust to the darkness, there was an uneasy vibe around me that I didn't like, and my skin crawled with a shiver. 'Maybe this wasn't such a good idea,' I said to myself as I decided whether or not I should stay.

My heartrate started to speed up to an uncomfortable level that made spots appear in my vision. The pit in my stomach that churned hot chips and wine around the same way a front-loader washing machine did, spasmed, then threatened to leave my mouth and make a mess on the floor in front of me. I fought for control of my body, but I was losing energy trying to keep my cool.

I knew it was too much to handle, and that I really should turn around and leave. I would be alright once I was outside in the cool Melbourne air and away from the stuffy and uncomfortable environment that had started to trigger a haywire response from my body. An experience I had only ever had once before and was a sure sign that I would more than likely black out.

My heart was running a race that my breathing couldn't keep up with. My world was spinning by too quickly, and I thought I would puke just from the uneasiness. The grip I had on my tightly controlled world was slipping, and I didn't know how to turn it around. If I didn't get a grip, I would slide right into the second blackout I'd had in five years.

My body didn't move, but my mind did. It spun around in circles, and I still couldn't breathe in enough air. I tried to take in a deep breath but choked on the stale air of alcohol around the bar, then spluttered on an exhale that now made me feel dizzy. I swayed, and it had nothing to do with the music I could hear or the number of drinks I had consumed.

How long had it been since I'd felt this way? I asked myself in hope that I could take my mind away from my spiral into the abyss and think clearly about the last time I had blacked out. I had only suffered one other blackout, and it had happened on one traumatic night five years ago. I tried as much as possible to avoid thinking about what had happened that night. All my thoughts and every single feeling I'd ever felt had been shut down, turned off and bottled up. I didn't want to experience another blackout, but I never knew how my body would react when it cracked from everything I'd bottled up. Just like tonight.

I reached out for purchase, and my palm landed on the bar. I tried once again for a deep breath, but the blackness crept in and started to take over. That was when I felt a hand on my hip. I turned instantly to face the person who had a hold of it, wanting to rage at them for begin so forward. But I hit a wall of muscle instead, and the rush of adrenaline that coursed through my body no longer had me on the verge of oblivion. I was thankful I hadn't blacked out yet as I knew my fight-or-flight instinct was confused and didn't know what to do. So it did nothing but block everything out and shut down every sense. My brain and body were stunned at the touch they felt on my hip, and I let go of the bar.

Sight, sound, smell, taste and touch had me frozen in a trance. With lips close to the shell of my ear, I heard a deep, husky voice say, 'Let it out, or I'll kiss those sweet lips of yours.' As the words reached my consciousness, I slowly exhaled.

'Breathe in and out. Let me have that breath of yours.' His voice was all but a whisper for my ears only.

I took in a few steady breaths and felt my heartrate return to its normal, stable rhythm. However, my senses had misfired in their reboot; they now orbited this man in front of me and nothing else. Everything else was still a blur.

I breathed in cedar, the aroma of the muscle-man that still had his hand on my hip, and I looked up to catch brown eyes take in my green ones. My hands moved from my sides to his pecs as I reached up and leaned in to ask, with my lips so close to his that I could taste the bourbon on them, 'Was I that far gone that I needed to be brought back with a kiss?'

My body stepped back to create space between us, not that there was space to give considering the amount of people around us. While I waited for this man to answer me, I took in his appearance as best I could in the purple hue that surrounded us. I tilted my head up to take in his clean-shaven face and hair that was short on the sides and at the back, but left longer on the top. With the perfect amount of tousle, his hair rivalled Zach Efron's.

His smile was delightful with his lips curving upward, and I saw the corners of his dark eyes crinkle. The man himself was gorgeous, making my knees buckle. His voice washed over me and made me feel a calmness I hadn't felt in a long time as he told me, 'I guess we will never know.'

I gave this stranger a smile that lit up my eyes as I whispered, 'Thank you,' into his ear.

In her true nonchalant sisterly fashion, Addison had missed my meltdown. I turned for my drink and didn't need to turn back to realise the wall of muscle had left. I no longer felt the heat from his palm on my hip. The level of unease in crowds that I was used to had returned, and there was no stable rhythm of my heart. Its pace was already quicker, and I already missed the calmness that the wall of muscle made me feel. Addison motioned for me to down my drink then she dragged me towards the stage for us to sing.

'Come on, this will be fun, just like old times,' Addison told me when she had a hold of my hand. 'When was the last time we sang together?'

I shrugged apathetically. We hadn't sung together since I'd dared her to be my apprentice twelve months ago. Before that, we had caught up a couple of times to try karaoke. But singing with Addison only reminded me of singing with my family. The last time we all sang together had ended in tragedy. So I didn't encourage myself to sing, not out loud anyway. Only in my head and when no one else was around me.

Addison teed up her song with the emcee. I had no idea what she had chosen until the music started to play. Temporarily unable to move, I let the melody wash over me the same way

I let every song I listened to these days wash over me, while I tried not to drown in all of the memories I had.

My sister had chosen the song that had played the night my whole world turned upside down. Maybe she didn't remember, or maybe her memories of that night were different to mine. I didn't know as we hadn't ever discussed the trauma of five years ago. But I couldn't let Addison down, so I reached for the microphone, stepped onto the stage and sang along to 'Flame Trees' by Cold Chisel.

I didn't even make it halfway through the song before the memories, both happy and sad, became too much. Our close-knit family had always sung together. My dad had been wild in his days before he settled down with my mum or, so I was told through bedtime stories. He had started his own cover band, and ever since Addison and I had been able to talk we had also been able to sing. I had even dragged Addison along to singing lessons as one of my dares, and in retaliation, Addison had found a talent competition and entered both of us into it.

Emotion coursed through my veins as my memories overwhelmed me, and with the wine I'd drunk, I felt my heart beating erratically. My body was shutting out the world around me, and tears were falling from my eyes. The blackout I felt encroaching only moments ago had returned.

Mum, Dad, Addison and I had sung that song together. Our last song. Our vocals had bounced around the car, just like every other road trip we'd made. We would sing all the way from Melbourne to Mulwala on the New South Wales border and back again. For many years, we had spent our holidays in Mulwala. Until Mum and Dad decided they'd wanted a change of pace and to live in that little country town for a few years. I felt the same now as I'd felt on our last road trip, when everything spun out of control.

But this time, I had come to rest against the floor. That night five years ago it had been a tree. Addison screamed the same as she'd done that night, but I couldn't calm her the same way as I had done back then. She was too far away for me to whisper any words to her.

In the haze of my blackout, I saw Marcus pull Addison from the stage and quieten her down. She would be okay. My eyes closed just like they did that night, once the screams had stopped and silence surrounded me. Then the darkness took over completely and pulled me under. I couldn't stop the screams inside my head even now, five years later. There was always ringing in my ears that got worse when I closed my eyes. I didn't normally close my eyes unless exhaustion wiped me out. Otherwise, the night my world smashed into a thousand little pieces would play on repeat in my mind.

Somewhere in the haze of darkness, a body rushed towards me. A familiar form from earlier in the night reached down to collect me from the stage floor. I knew only because of what I could smell. I breathed in the aroma of cedar as two strong arms cocooned me in safety, and I was carried away from Jam. All while 'I got you, I got you,' was chanted over and over as a forehead pressed into the side of my face.

I didn't know where we ended up, only that I had been laid down on a soft surface. I felt lips on my forehead and the bed dip underneath me. An arm wrapped around me and held me tightly, and the sleep I drifted into was blissful and the best I'd had in a long time.

Then next morning, I woke up to an empty room and wondered where I was. Not my house, that much I knew. I reflected on last night, how much was real and how much I'd dreamt, and how the hell I'd ended up in this bedroom that was as bare as my own. The bedsheets were ruffled as though someone had slept beside me. I looked down and saw that my clothes were still in place, but when I touched my chest, I found that my necklace was gone. The details of what had happened were a little hazy after a blackout, I'd realised after my first one. This second one seemed no different.

I sat up and found my purse on the table beside the bed then reached for my phone. Typical, my sister hadn't messaged me. Had she been too caught up in her own hysteria that she'd forgotten about me? Did Addison just not care anymore? Was being selfish her way of coping when things weren't always smooth sailing?

Standing up, I slung my purse over my shoulder as I stepped away from the bed. My legs wobbled as I made my way towards the apartment door. I could tell whoever had brought me here didn't spend much time here. Only the necessities filled this cold, lifeless apartment. My house was the same; I didn't see the point in making it homely when I spent a majority of my time working.

I didn't know where my mystery man was or what he'd planned. Maybe he thought I would sleep longer or that he would be back before I woke up. He hadn't left a note, but what did I expect? Reality beckoned and so did the family business. My night off was over. Now there was work to be done.

One

Five years later

Something wasn't right. That much I knew before I even opened my eyes. My head rested upon the softness of a pillow, but it wasn't my pillow. My shoulders, back and hips were flat against the mattress. Not completely rigid, but this wasn't how I would normally sleep; it was almost like I'd been placed this way.

One hand rested on my stomach, fingers flat against my skin; the other hand was curled on my bent leg. I moved my hands over the skin where they had been placed. No clothes, only underwear. There was a sheet and doona that covered my bare skin. I let my head fall, and my left ear touched the pillow. I wanted so badly to move, roll onto my side, get more comfortable and snuggle in, but I couldn't. Something just wouldn't let me.

I struggled and moved anyway, letting my body roll over onto its left side while pulling the doona over my nose. I immediately regretted it. My ears pounded to a bass line only I could hear, and with the dull ache in my forehead, it was almost too much to bear. I fought back wave after wave of nausea with deep breaths. In and out, in and out. 'You can do this,' I told myself. 'Just breathe. And. Don't. Throw. Up.'

Several moments passed by, and the pain in my head eased slightly. I wondered what I'd done to myself. I was always a little fuzzy after a blackout, or was it the alcohol I'd drunk? Maybe it was a combination of alcohol and exhaustion. But I had only blacked out twice because I stayed away from any little thing that would trigger one and continued to spend all my time at work.

That meant last night, after taking off from Melbourne out of the blue, I'd drowned out the stress of my life in bourbon and lemonade to the point I'd passed out. I had shoved all of my emotions off to the side and pushed down anything that made me uncomfortable until it was buried. Maybe my inability to deal with everything in life outside of my work had caught up with me, so I'd given in and let the other kind of blackness take over: a hangover.

My eyes slowly opened to a daylight-filled room. The windows were somewhere to my left and right. Although my vision was blurred and the doona obstructed my view of the space around me, I'd come to realise that none of this was mine and I had no idea how I'd ended up in this bed. *So stupid,* I berated myself.

I tried not to panic and to concentrate on my breathing instead. I fought off another bout of nausea and tried to think how I'd ended up here, but the fog of my hangover wouldn't let me. As my vision improved, I saw the pillows were untouched; I stretched out my hands and took note. The bed where I laid was empty. The other side of the bed was still made. I had slept alone.

But somewhere on the other side of the doona, out of my view, I sensed someone else. Cologne lingered in the air, a touch of cedar.

I wanted at that moment to bolt upright, then thought about the nausea and decided it was best that I lay still. I moved the doona away from my face to get a better view of where I was and knew there would be no easy escape. Not like the last time I woke up in an unfamiliar place. A memory from five years ago made this moment seem familiar. But my hangover wouldn't let me string the importance together.

This time, I wouldn't be able to sneak by the stranger that lay on the lounge opposite me. Was he asleep, or were his eyes just closed? I couldn't tell, and I couldn't risk a quiet exit. With the way I felt, I would be like a bull in an antique shop – plus it was anyone's guess as to where my stuff was, and that included my clothes. I laid in silence and watched him, my vision still a little fuzzy, but recognising he was fully clothed in black from top to toe. A uniform maybe? He looked like I felt, wrecked and uncomfortable, but he was tucked into the lounge, and I may as well have been naked.

While I watched the stranger on the lounge, I felt the nausea return. I breathed in and out but this time it wouldn't go away, and it didn't want to stay down. I struggled to move off the bed but the dizziness made it hard, and there was no way I would make it to the bathroom to hug the porcelain. Why did I have to drink until I passed out?

Before I could even muster the word 'bucket', out of nowhere, one was handed to me. I guess this stranger on the lounge wasn't asleep after all, his eyes had just been closed. As the bucket reached my grasp, vomit exploded from my stomach. Lucky for me, I didn't miss, and my mess sat at the bottom of the bucket. I leaned back into the bedhead and took a deep breath, then took a couple more.

As I passed the bucket over, my eyes travelled up the hand that had passed it to me, and I was able to get a closer look at who I shared this room with. Suddenly I remembered what I'd done last night.

I remembered the drinks I'd poured into myself. It had seemed like a good idea at the time as I tried to unwind and tell myself it was okay to disappear from my life in Melbourne for a little while. I hadn't consciously intended to end up at the only bar that was still open, Black's Bar and Grill, when I'd rolled into town. There was nothing left for me here in Mulwala, but I guess the universe had other plans for me, and it included this small country town I'd once called home.

'Oh my God,' I groaned, more to myself than to the stranger in the room. My memory was a little hazy from last night, but I was sure the man in front of me was one of the bartenders. It wasn't entirely his fault I felt the way I did this morning. I'd told him and the other bartender that I could handle my alcohol. But really, I should have known better.

'You're the cute bartender from last night,' I managed to state the obvious to his hand. I was a little red-faced he had now seen me spew the contents I'd told him I could handle last night.

'You need to take it easy.' His deep voice deadpanned as he let the cute bartender comment slide. Then he dropped a bottle of water onto the bed beside me before he turned to flush my mess in the bathroom.

'Because I threw up?' When I looked up, I saw him nod.

'Well, I'm fine,' I stated, although I wasn't sure who I wanted to convince, me or the man looking at me in concern.

'You passed out in the bar,' I was told as he leaned up against the door frame to the bathroom.

I could see him more clearly now that he was closer. His button-up shirt had the name of the bar, Black's Bar and Grill, embroidered in white over his left pec muscle. A tattoo played peek-a-boo with the short sleeve of his work shirt, and the sight of him made my heart flutter then skip a beat. The tattooed bicep on his right arm had me wishing he would come closer, so I could have a look at the rest of the tattoo that was hiding under his shirt. Of what I could see, his tattoo was the start of armour similar to what knights wore.

There was something about the way he stood there staring at me that seemed familiar. I just couldn't put my finger on it, not in the state that I was in. Was he checking me out the same way I was checking him out, trying to figure out if our paths had crossed before?

The man looking at me was tall and lean, well-groomed, with blemish-free skin. His features were dark, just like the clothes he wore. Had it been a couple of days since this man shaved or was this the normal amount of facial hair he wore?

'Where am I?' I was curious to know how I'd ended up in a bed. How had my night ended? In my inebriated state, had this man helped me stumble my way to wherever here was. Or had I really passed out when I'd spiralled out of control thinking about my life and adding fuel to the fire by the amount of alcohol I drank?

The bartender didn't need to know my life currently sucked, and that for the last five years every day had been Groundhog Day. Now I was tired and looking for a change. But I didn't want to be this woman who woke up in beds that weren't mine. I wanted something more from my life. Whether I wanted to believe it or not, my being here was a cry for help, and the man who leaned up against the door frame had seen me crying for help as I drank my way into my passed-out state.

'You're in the accommodation that's attached to the bar,' I was told by the man who didn't look very impressed.

Was he recalling last night like I was? 'And you bought me here?' I asked shyly, avoiding eye contact.

'What else was I meant to do with you?' His deep voice hardened, which made me look at him when he said, 'This may seem strange to you, but not many people pass out around here. We serve alcohol responsibly at Black's Bar and Grill, and most people who come to this bar know how to handle their liquor.'

I berated myself at how careless I'd been last night in my attempt to blow off steam. What would have happened if this weary-looking man hadn't rescued me? Would I still be slumped on my stool at the bar, sleeping off my hangover? I wanted to swear off drinking for the rest of my life considering how I felt this morning. But alcohol wasn't my problem. I was my own worst enemy, crying out for help and stuck in a Groundhog Day I didn't know how to get out of.

With one eyebrow raised, he continued to talk, unaware of the silent conversation I was having with myself. 'When no identification was found on you, I couldn't leave you passed out at the bar. It's not a good look for business. But I also couldn't send you home either, as I don't know where you live, so the hotel was the only option.'

I wasn't like most people, and last night proved I didn't handle my alcohol well. From the lecture I was in the middle of receiving, it seemed most people around here handled their alcohol responsibly. Or was that his job to make sure the patrons who came to this bar were sensible about their alcohol consumption? Did that mean he knew everyone in and around this town? The locals? And that I wasn't one of the regulars?

'And you stayed here with me? Why?' I didn't even know why I bothered to ask.

'It's not every day someone blacks out and a hotel room has to be offered up for a place to stay.' The bartender smirked at me, then let out a little chuckle that kicked my heartrate up a notch. 'There's this little thing you may have heard of, it's called a tab and ...'

'Oh my God! I didn't pay my tab?' I said with my face in my hands. *He jests, and I am such an idiot,* I thought as I scolded myself. He just wanted his money; why else would he be here? We were strangers. But why were notions of wanting to get to know him knocking on my consciousness?

And as if I hadn't spoken at all, the bartender continued. 'Yours was never closed out.'

'Oh!' I responded, removing my hands from my face and staring in his general direction. *How embarrassing.*

His chuckle was gone, and his poker face had returned. 'I also wanted to know you were okay.'

My green eyes were locked on his brown eyes, and I could see there was something on his mind, something he needed to get off his chest.

'There's just one thing I'd like to know,' he started. 'Why does one do what you did and pass out in a bar?'

I gulped from the water bottle. His question had caught me off guard. How did I explain all of this? What would I tell him? Would he even understand the dilemma I had gotten myself into?

There was a small hitch to his eyebrow, a slight change in expression as he waited for me to answer. He scratched the stubble of his beard just under his ear, then along his jaw. So cool, so collected, I almost drooled on myself.

'Lots of alcohol,' was the first thing that popped out of my mouth. 'I wanted to blow off steam,' I said more to myself than to the man sharing this space with me. 'And I guess I went a little too far.' That came out as a whisper.

This man didn't need to know how far I'd driven myself to blow off said steam, nor did he need to know about the latest dare, the one my sister had challenged me with: sing or lose everything I had worked hard for.

I knew Addison was pissed at me for the last dare I had challenged her with, when she'd refused my dare to be an apprentice and help at the bakery, I had stopped paying her, stopped topping up her wage out of mine. Addison's dare for me was revenge for cutting her off five years ago. I was surprised it had taken her this long to find a way to try and hurt me the same way I had hurt her. Was she that desperate for money?

'Wow, a little too far,' Mr Bartender said as he crossed his arms over his chest, his bicep muscles bulging against the short sleeves of his black shirt. Another drool-worthy moment. He raised his eyebrow again before he alleged, 'It must have been some steam you needed to blow off.'

'Give me a break,' I threw at him. I sure as hell needed one, and in return, I received a look of surprise bordering on annoyance. It could have meant anything, but I guess he was disgruntled, and just like that, silence filled the air around us.

This conversation is over, I thought, but I didn't say the words aloud. *Who are you to question my actions and lecture me? If only you knew about the last ten years of my life.*

How was I meant to do this? Talk about my life? Tell someone like this beautiful stranger that I didn't know how to confide why my life sucked so much. Or that I feared I would never escape Groundhog Day. That I woke up here in this hotel room this morning, but did that mean today would be different to every other day I have lived?

I didn't owe anyone anything, and what good would it do to spill the truth? I didn't know this man, and he didn't know me. As much as I wanted to believe that he was a stranger to me, I was once a part of this community. Had I already forgotten the people I'd left behind when the world crumbled underneath me? I'd never returned since that fateful night.

I knew I couldn't change what had happened back then, or what was happening now, but there would be no escaping or evading the dare that a revengeful Addison had thrown in my face. I would have to work out what I was going to do, not only now as I tried to leave, but with Addison's dare as well.

I threw the sheet and doona away from my legs. I wanted out of here, and I wanted out of here right now. I shifted to get out of bed, and the sudden movement to stand unsteadied me and brought on a bout of nausea that made me sit the fuck back down. Another round of nausea, I wouldn't be able to fight off.

'Bucket,' I managed to mumble just loud enough to be heard. My chance to leave was halted, and once again, as the bucket reached my grasp, I threw up.

He crouched down in front of me and rubbed tiny circles on my legs that hung over the edge of the bed. I hugged the bucket, and still lucky for me I didn't miss.

'I told you to take it easy.' The bartender had a smirk on his face.

Did he care? Was that a moment? My heart thought so. But it was over as soon as the bucket was taken away, and once again my mess was flushed.

I was baffled, or was that my hangover? He gave nothing away. His composure was completely unreadable. Stoic without fault.

'A pretty woman like you should take care of herself when she's out drinking. You never know who might take advantage of you. You're lucky I was working last night and was keeping my eye on you,' I was told sternly.

'Keeping an eye on me or stealing glances at me whenever you had the chance?' I let slip out of my mouth. Was my hungover brain flirting with this man?

He was silent. Not responding told me what I thought was true. He was checking me out. I threw the pillow next to me. It hit him mid-stomach, and in return I received another raised eyebrow. Arms closed around the pillow I had just thrown, but he didn't hold onto it; just like a hot potato, the pillow landed back on the bed.

'Oh, is that right?' I tried to hide my face, but I wasn't the only one grinning.

'It's okay to want to blow off steam, but not to the point you pass out on a stool at the bar. Alcohol isn't the answer to solving your problems.'

My whispered words hung between us. 'I know.'

I felt worse now than the first time I vomited. I laid back down to see if that made me feel better. I guess I would have to close my eyes and try to sleep off the consequence of my need to blow off steam. *Damn.* I cursed my stupid self, this hangover and passing out. My choices that had led me here to this moment weren't the best, and I would have to learn to make better choices in the future. Find another way to deal with my stress that didn't leave me vulnerable.

While I was giving myself a hard time about last night, I also cursed my life, my Groundhog Day, and the choices that both Addison and I had made that led her to dare me into singing in a public setting. Thoughts of singing with my sister in public again after I'd blacked out on a karaoke stage kicked the churning in my stomach into gear. I was thankful I was already lying down. What was I going to do with the dare Addison had given me?

The man in black covered up my almost-naked body and brushed my hair away from my face. His touch was gentle but didn't linger. This man didn't need to be this nice to me. He could have demanded I leave the moment I woke up, taken me to reception to pay for my tab and this room and sent me packing. But he didn't, and I wondered why. Did he see something he liked in my fragile state, under my smokescreen of make-up and shorter champagne-blonde hair? Or did he just like rescuing damsels showing signs of distress? I didn't know. I needed to be not in this condition to ask those questions.

As he turned to walk away, my body screamed, 'Don't leave'. My hand reached out to grab his arm as my mouth whispered, 'Stay with me.' If this man wasn't in a hurry for me to leave this hotel room, then I wasn't in a hurry for this man to leave me either. I wanted more sneaky glances across the bar and a conversation that didn't involve a lecture from him. But would I get what I wanted?

I watched as he climbed over me to sit on top of the doona and rest his head against the back of the bed. I snuggled in to get as comfortable as a hotel bed would let me. I outstretched my arm in front of me, my fingers stopping just short of his leg. His body was close to mine, and I felt his hand move to cover mine. Heat travelled through me that I had only felt once before. If my hangover hadn't fogged up my brain and clouded my memories maybe I would have remembered the last time I had felt this heat. My heart fluttered again and skipped another beat, and a moment later, I had fallen asleep.

Two

I woke to an empty hotel room, unsure of how long I had been out for. I slept a deep sleep that I never thought was possible again without blacking out from exhaustion first. I sat up slowly, did what I was told and took it easy. I felt better, the nausea had now passed, and my tummy rumbled. I was hungry now.

Reaching around for my bottle of water, I saw a note stuck to it that read: *Don't go anywhere. Take these. I have errands to run. Be back when I'm done*, with a smiley face in the bottom corner. I thought about the note and waking up alone, and a memory niggled in the back of my mind that left me wondering before it disappeared: Would things have been different five years ago if a note had told me to stay?

I swallowed the tablets, drank the rest of the water and silently looked around at the room I had stayed in. Although it was a typical hotel room, it was fancier than what I had ever stayed in before. Not that I had stayed in many, but this one certainly took the prize money, and for this little country town, it said a lot. The hotel room was spacious, and the bed I slept in was a queen. Two lounges faced the television at a right angle and the kitchenette was a modest straight line that included a round kitchen table. The bathroom from where I sat looked like the rest of the hotel room, modern.

I pushed back the bed covers and stood next to the bed. So far, so good. There was no dizziness, no blurred vision. Looking down, I saw I was still in my underwear. Moving around the bed and behind the sheer curtains, a sliding door led me out to a patio where I could sit and look out over the Murray River. I wanted to go out there but what I needed to do first was find my stuff.

I walked over to the bathroom. Nothing. Then I passed the lounge before heading to the kitchenette where I found my keys and phone on the kitchen table but no debit card. It must still be behind the bar. Pressing the home screen on my phone, I sighed when I noticed the messages and unanswered calls that I was just not ready to deal with. My family and the bakery would just have to wait.

In the twenty-five years that was my life, I had never done anything like this before. Taken off without telling anyone what I was doing or where I was going. But something had to give. I couldn't keep living out Groundhog Day for another five years. I could no longer hide behind my crazy working hours to cover up my inability to interact with the outside world. I needed a change.

My jeans and singlet hung over the chair in front of me. They smelled of last night: smoke and alcohol. Unfortunately, they were all I had for now. My boots and socks were tucked under the chair. In my haste to get out of Melbourne, I'd dismissed meeting my sister and her challenge to have me sing. Instead, I'd thrown an overnight bag together, got in my car, chose a playlist and headed north for a chance to change my life. Three hours later after the sun had gone down, I'd driven across the border into New South Wales to Mulwala, where I'd pulled into Black's Bar and Grill, which had shown a vacancy sign for The Diamond Hotel.

My overnight bag that held my change of clothes and toiletries was in my car, so I could go get it. But what I really wanted was to wash off some of last night's grunge. Grabbing my clothes, boots and phone, I headed to the bathroom for a shower.

Over the past five years, phone – once I'd worked through the fanciness of it all – had become my little obsession. My phone broke up the monotony of my life. I had started to crash less on the lounge in the office above the bakery factory, deciding that with the upgrade in technology I'd installed I could take paperwork home with me and pass out on the lounge at my house instead.

I had even found a couple of apps to install, one that let me listen to music and another I could download music from and keep on my phone. I'd built a collection of old and new favourites over the last five years and slowly rekindled my love for music. This love had been passed down to me by my father but had been taken away when my grandparents became my temporary guardians.

I now had an eclectic library of music from current songs to ones that were older than my twenty-five years across all the genres of music. I fell asleep most nights with one of my chosen playlists on repeat. I just hadn't quite found my voice to sing along out loud with the lyrics, but as I usually took advantage of my playlists to lull myself to sleep, I hadn't allowed myself much time to burst into song.

I scrolled through my phone for a playlist I wanted to listen to and hit play. The music started, and I found myself quietly singing along as I stood in front of the mirror. My voice was rough as one song led to the next, not properly warmed up as I hadn't sung more than one song in a row since the night everything changed.

I looked at my reflection and thought, *Fuck, what a mess! You look like shit.* My hair stuck out on its ends, my foundation had rubbed off, and my mascara and black eyeliner were in places they should never be. It was time I left last night behind me. I stood under the shower and let the water run over me from top to toe and rinse me clean.

I'd chosen my country playlist, and there were fifty of my favourite songs altogether. Music filled the bathroom, and I sang along to every song I'd collated. I used all the body cleansing samples this hotel had to offer to feel refreshed. I even found a toothbrush and toothpaste to scrub the fur from my feral teeth. I scrubbed my face in the hope that most of my makeup would come off and washed my hair more than once in the hope that would rid the smell from it. Lathering myself a couple of times with soap from the dispenser, I hoped that I would smell better than I did a few minutes ago.

Although nothing would make me feel like a princess more than fresh clothes and my own beauty products, for now I made do with what the hotel had to offer. As one song ended and another begun, my vocal cords loosened, and it felt good to get lost in the music I was singing. I belted out the words and my vocals echoed around me. I turned off the water, grabbed the towel and then got back into the only clothes I had.

'You're okay, you can do this,' I told myself, and as I turned to leave the bathroom, I realised I wasn't alone.

'Wow,' I heard as I walked out of the bathroom and into the view of the bartender, who looked a little surprised. That stopped me in my tracks as these were last night's clothes, and I had a towel around my head. This definitely wasn't my best look. I felt so far from my best that I almost felt ashamed, so maybe the wow was meant for my voice.

'You don't have to stop because of me.' He'd enjoyed what he'd just heard a little too much, so I reached over for my phone to turn off the music.

'I didn't hear you come in.' I could feel my cheeks blush and knew I must be red in the face. I was so embarrassed that this man had seen it all. First, I'd passed out, then vomited, and now he'd heard me sing. It had been a long time since anyone had heard my voice this intimately, where the words flowed freely from inside me and I didn't have to think about anything other than the music and lyrics. My voice never sounded like this when I sang karaoke.

'How do you feel?'

I was relieved he had changed the subject.

'Better.' I unwrapped the towel from my hair, squeezing it one more time over the dripping ends, then hung it up over the shower. Nothing would tame my unmanageable champagne-coloured mane without leave-in conditioner; it would go unruly curly now unless I wrapped it up in a bun. I was about to tie it back when the smell of food filled the space around me, so I left my hair down.

'I brought you food and drink. You must be hungry after last night, so I had the kitchen make you up something. Perks of the job,' he told me, as though he had the best job in the world.

'Great, thank you.' I moved closer to the table to look down at what he'd brought in. 'You really know the way to a woman's heart.'

He smiled at me and took a seat on the lounge, mobile phone in hand.

'This is good. Coffee and pancakes with jam, whipped cream and ice cream. What more could a woman ask for?' I devoured the pancakes and savoured the rich coffee.

My favourite. Pancakes. I looked over at him, but his eyes were glued to his phone. *I could almost kiss you right now*, I thought to myself, but there was something in the way he looked that made me hesitate. So I didn't stand up, walk over and kiss his lips. And how would he even react if I did? I stayed in my seat and all that I could make come out of my mouth was, 'Thanks.'

'You're welcome,' he replied, but he didn't look up this time. The beeps from his phone were the only sound in the room.

'What made you want to save this damsel in distress?' I asked once the pancakes were gone. My eyes didn't stray from my coffee cup; I was too shy to ask such a question and still meet his eyes.

'What made you want to pass out in a bar?' he asked in return.

There was a brief silence before I met his eyes, then I said. 'I asked you first.'

'Okay.' A grin toyed at the corners of his mouth, before full, upturned lips filled his handsome face. 'But you have to come a little closer if you want me to tell you.' He patted the lounge, so with my coffee in hand, I walked over to sit beside him.

He watched me get comfortable before he said, 'You were lucky we were having a quiet night last night and no one harassed you. It's not very often this bar has a problem with drinks being spiked, but it has happened. When you hadn't puked all over the bar, I brought you here.' He motioned with his head to the hotel room. 'If I hadn't brought you here, then you would be in the hospital.'

His eyes searched mine, like he knew something. But before I could ask what that was, he said, 'There's something about you that I can't put my finger on, but it's telling me that I shouldn't let you go just yet.'

Did he just admit he was attracted to the mess that I appeared to be? The thought made my breath hitch and my head spin a little bit.

'I know most of the people from around here. A few have come and gone, some returned, and others never looked back. I want to say that you're not local, but that doesn't seem right. Maybe you're one of the ones who left and now you've returned?' His gaze was soft on me, but my poker face didn't let him know he had hit the nail on the head. I was from around here, I just didn't live here anymore, but that wasn't my choice. Although showing up last night and sticking around today – that had been my choice.

Great. I wondered whether I should divulge myself. It was too late to keep my distance from this man. I was too close to him now.

'It was a dare.' The start of the truth was out. But the rest of the truth I wasn't quite ready to tell.

There was more silence as the bartender waited for me to continue. But before he had the chance to speak and give me the hurry up, I blurted out, 'My sister dared me to sing with her in front of an audience.'

'And?' he prompted, and I guess he wanted to know a few more details.

'I couldn't do it, the dare that is.' I couldn't look into his eyes when I explained. 'Just the thought of standing in front of a microphone next to my sister with a room full of people had my heart racing, and I panicked. So I got in my car and drove 270 kilometres to drink myself under the table.'

'But you can sing.'

I didn't need to be told what I already knew.

'I love those songs on your playlist, and I wish the bar would play more country music. But not all the songs on your playlist were country, were they?'

I shook my head and couldn't help but stare at him. The man next to me had noticed one of the songs wasn't a country song. Then I stupidly opened my mouth. 'There are two songs on that playlist that aren't country songs. You heard "Fast Car" by Tracy Chapman.'

'What's the other song on your playlist that isn't a country song?' he asked when the hotel room went quiet.

I thought my heart would race and that the memories I had of my parents would swamp me into darkness. I breathed in but didn't raise my head. Words left my mouth in a rush on a whisper because thinking about my parents these days made me emotional. 'My mum's favourite song, "Throw Your Arms Around Me" by Hunters & Collectors.'

It was the one song from that playlist that I didn't know if I could sing the lyrics. Not the same way my dad had to my mum. I was sure if I tried, I would black out and fall in a heap on the floor, just like the last time I'd tried to sing a song my family had sung together.

'Your voice is amazing, and I'm sure you could do anything you put your mind to.'

'Your vote of confidence is great,' I blustered, then I raised my head to face the man next to me. 'But I can't get up in front of a crowded room and sing with my sister like she's daring me to, nor do I have any interest in doing that again.'

'Why not?' he asked with a hint of curiousness in his tone.

'Because today is only the second time in a long time that I have sung more than one song out loud.' My words tumbled out as I tried not to break out into a sweat. Now was not the time to shake uncontrollably. 'But a dare is a dare, and if I don't want to take a back seat in everything I have worked hard to achieve, then I will have to prove to my sister, just to get her off my back, that I can still meet up with her and sing.'

'Wow, that's some dare and some serious sister rivalry you have going on.'

'Yeah, my sister somehow thinks I'm more talented as a singer than I am at my current job.'

'Your current job?'

I tried but failed to raise my eyebrow in the same fashion as the man I sat next to. I had to remember we didn't know each other.

'Bakery manager.' I said seriously, before I smirked. The man next to me showed off how easy it was to raise his eyebrow in question.

'How did a bakery manager decide to end up here to blow off steam?'

I knew my 270 kilometre comment hadn't gone unnoticed.

'I don't know, I just got in the car and drove.' But the look I got from him hardened, so I quickly continued with. 'I psyched out on my sister's dare and needed some time alone to process some things in my life. For years I have kept my head down, working hard and managing the bakery on my own. My family rely on me to keep the business afloat, but I don't know if I can do that anymore.'

'They don't know that you're here?' he asked.

I replied with a shake of my head. 'This is the last place they would look for me.'

He raised both eyebrows at me, and in this moment, I would have loved to know the thoughts that ran through his head. The guy next to me was a closed book. It was hard to read the contents if he didn't open up and let anyone in.

'Why?'

I stared at him in fascination, and he stared right back, his unreadable expression again on display. God only knew what he thought of me and the expression on my face.

We had started a staring contest, and I wondered if this was what it was like to let your guard down. I felt comfortable here in this bartender's company. Just before the silence turned awkward, I said, 'Because it was just too painful to come back here.' My words were more to myself as they had faded under the noise from his mobile phone. But as I watched his beautiful face, I realised he'd heard me. Something that, I didn't doubt, would be brought back up later.

Our conversation ended there. It was a bit hard to continue as the sound of his ring tone filled the hotel room.

'Do you need to get that?' I asked, and by the look on his face, his phone demanded all of his attention. I stood, collected my things from the kitchen table and moved towards the door.

While he was still drawn to his phone, I reached for the hotel room's door handle. It clicked as I opened it. But it closed as soon as it was opened. His hand had reached over me just above my shoulder and rested on the now-closed door.

'Not so fast.' His voice was like a caress.

I turned around, and all I could see was black. He hadn't moved away, but stood so close. My body tensed then relaxed into the wall of muscle around me. Neither one of us moved, so I took this moment to take in his aroma of coffee and cedar. He smelled so good my heart skipped a beat and my breath quickened.

I melted inside from how close he was to me. The last wall of muscle that had stood this close had smelled of bourbon and cedar. That man had curled his fingers over my hip and helped me catch my breath. He was the only one man who had ever stood close to me and made me feel calm. I wondered that if the bartender now reached for my hip while we stood this close, would I feel the same heat I'd felt that night five years ago? If I imagined this man without the beginnings of a beard and his hair a little longer, would they be the same man?

As if he could read my mind, he stepped back, and I leaned up against the door. My head tilted back as I looked into his brown eyes. 'You're busy. I should go.' I was breathless at how close we still were.

'Stay with me.' He said my whispered words back to me. His eyebrows knitted together when his forehead creased, but I still couldn't read the expression on his face.

I stared blankly at him. His hand was gone from the door.

'I'm sorry, please don't go.' His deep voice was like silk as it wrapped around me.

There was a fleeting silence. His expression hadn't changed, but he offered a brief explanation. 'Work is always busy, and I'm always needed. But today is my day off. I have plans, and it seems I am late for them.' His lips curled upwards in an irresistible smile, and I looked away as a flush heated my face.

There was a small lift of my lips as thoughts raced through my mind. *Did he just invite me to spend the rest of the day with him?*

His thumb slowly tilted my face for our eyes to meet, and the answer was right there in his eyes. 'Come with me,' his lips whispered, a mere inch from mine.

'Wait,' I exclaimed. *What was this?* I questioned myself. *You don't even know this man in black, but there is something about him that seemed familiar. Is it just that he makes me feel calm?* 'I don't even know you,' I said quietly, and I wondered if he'd heard me.

'I'm your cute bartender.' He had caught on that I'd called him cute earlier. 'But you can call me Zach.'

'Zach.' His name rolled off my lips, and I wondered how the mere mention of his name could make my body tingle.

Zach's lips twitched at the sound of his name. And in that moment, I was reminded of the boy I had once lived next door to. I hit pause. *Was this man that boy? He couldn't be.*

When I pressed my lips together, I hoped I didn't falter when I said, 'And you can call your drunk, passed-out damsel in distress Harley.'

Zach tried to keep a straight face but I saw the cheekiness of his lips as they curled further upwards. Then he stepped forward and, in my ear, he whispered, 'Can we go now? My friends are waiting for me.'

All I could manage was a nod of my head as I felt my body light on fire from his lips so close to my ear. I was caught up in the whirlwind this day was turning out to be. Neither Zach nor I confessed to the possibility of knowing each other. I didn't blame him. He had somewhere to be, and I wasn't quite ready to walk down memory lane just yet.

Three

Before I knew it, my hand was in his as Zach had led me away from The Diamond Hotel to a four-wheel drive parked outside the front doors of Black's Bar and Grill. The first thing that stole my attention was that the vehicle was just like him. Black. The paint, the tint, the wheels. All black. Even the number plate spelled BLK.

I wondered if the number plate was because of the truck's colour, or any reference to his name or the business we were standing outside of. Zach Black, Zach Black. I rolled his name over in my mind, closed my eyes and let the memories I had of a younger Zach come to mind. He had been a cool seventeen-year-old teenager I thought would never look twice at me. When my family had moved in next to his, it had been his last year of high school, and our sisters, being the same age, had become good friends. My interest in Zach had grown the same way his interest in me had grown slowly over that year.

But our relationship had been short lived. All we had done since the day I'd knocked on his door to collect my sister was talk in the quiet spot down the side of his house. I'd kissed Zach a few weeks later and that had now been almost ten years ago. It was the first kiss of many that I'd hoped we would share when I told him I would be back two weeks later at the end of the school holidays. But because life had thrown me the biggest curve ball, I'd never returned.

I knew there was a lot I needed to explain to the man who had just introduced himself as Zach if indeed he was my old next-door neighbour. Because if he was, then I was in so much trouble. I had kissed him and taken his heart with me when I walked away and never came back. I also hadn't told Zach how much I'd liked him. And after everything in my life changed, I'd never found a way to communicate with Zach. My chance to tell him how I felt had slipped away.

But I had to ask myself that even after all this time had passed, was I really ready to open old wounds? To be honest about the younger versions of ourselves and reveal the truth of everything that had happened since I'd been gone?

I was at the passenger door and wondered if I needed a step ladder just to get in, the truck was that far off the ground. But before I could grab the door handle, Zach was beside me to open the door and hold my hand to help me in.

I was shotgun in this beautiful truck and about to leave the safety of the hotel, where my car was still parked with my belongings inside, to head God only knew where. I should have insisted I follow him in my car, but that wasn't what was on my mind.

I was consumed by the man next to me. This was his world and I wanted to ask about the number plate, and about the easiness I felt between us. I wanted to know more, and I wondered if my suspicions about Zach were correct, but chickened out instead of asking him.

I was not ready for that conversation. I was still too vulnerable to ask questions that required me to give up information about myself. I had hidden myself behind working long hours at the bakery until I was exhausted. I had put on a brave face at fifteen years old and every day since when anyone asked me how I was, even though life as I knew it had crumbled around me. I had found a way to cope, and I'd never questioned if there was another way. Until now.

Zach turned the key and there was a soothing rumble, taking me away from thoughts about the past that had been ripped away from me and bringing me back to the present.

I was about to leave Black's Bar and Grill with this complete stranger, but deep down inside it didn't really feel that way. I watched the side profile of Zach's face as he manoeuvred his massive truck with ease. He made a right and a couple of left turns before he hit the speed limit. I turned my attention away from him and fumbled for my phone when I realised we were headed away from the main street of town.

The truck ride to our destination was silent, mostly because I spent it on my phone, reading the text messages I had received. Numerous messages and missed calls had blown up my phone. Mum, Addison and even Grandma James had all called a couple of times, and when I hadn't answered, they had texted me hoping I would reply.

There was only one voicemail message. 'Great,' I told myself. The only person who would leave me a message was Grandpa James. He didn't own a mobile phone, opting to use the landline from his house or the bakery. I held my phone to my ear and listened to what Grandpa had to say. His tone was irate as he demanded I return his call immediately.

I had never disappeared before. I was always reliable and had done exactly what had been asked of me, and everyone had always known exactly where to find me: at work. Were they concerned for my whereabouts or just worried I hadn't shown up for my shift at the bakery? I responded to everyone at the same time and set up a group text message thread to reply to Mia, my mother; Addison, my sister; and Grandma James who could pass on my message to Grandpa. I didn't doubt that Addison had dobbed me in and informed the rest of my family that I was MIA. I didn't know what to think of my sister anymore. All I knew was that she had been keeping tabs on me and hanging around the bakery more often since she had dared me to sing with her a month ago.

I typed out the message to inform everyone that I was, in fact, still very much alive and well and I would be on leave for the foreseeable future. Right now seemed like a perfect time for a much-needed break that most would call a holiday.

I knew my sister thought she could take the family business right out from underneath me. Even though she didn't have the same experience as I did and had never shown any interest in it before. Well, if she really wanted my job, she could deal with my absence and find out the hard way that I didn't spend all day in the office doing book work. I spent most of my days in the factory baking and making sure each of our shop outlets had plenty of bread and pastries to sell.

Would the bakery run smoothly without me? I got caught up wondering. It wasn't my usual style to go off the grid, and at some stage, I would need to resurface and face my family and the consequence of blowing off steam. But right now, I needed to process that today wasn't another Groundhog Day. While my fifteen-year-old self had had no idea her life was about to be turned upside down, it had taken me ten years to make my way back here. I could easily use the excuse that I had been stuck in Groundhog Day with an absent mother and strict grandparents for how the last ten years had turned out. But working was my coping mechanism. Where would I be now without it? How would life have turned out if I was less like me and more of a free spirit like Addison?

I had sworn I would never come back here, but last night I had driven straight into town. Right past where my life had spun out of control and smashed into pieces. But I wasn't the same girl who'd left here all those years ago, looking forward to returning home after the school holidays. I was older now and had taken a chance on myself when I put Melbourne in my rear-view mirror last night. I now needed a quiet place to think and some time on my own to sort out what I would do with my life. It was time for a change, and to do that I needed to reacquaint myself and make peace with this little country town.

The truck had slowed, and I sensed we had almost reached our destination. The tyres rolled off the end of the bitumen and onto dirt. I snapped my head up, wanting to know where I was. But I didn't know. In my ten-year absence, I was confident that even when I had lived here, I'd not been this far from the main street.

Before I tore my attention away from what I could see out the truck windows, I apologised. 'I'm sorry,' I said into the silence, still looking out the windscreen. 'I've just done to you what you did to me back in the hotel room, focusing on my phone too much.' With my eyes back on my phone, I continued just above a whisper, 'Guess my MIA status doesn't impress my family. I'm sorry, Zach.' I knew he had heard me when he placed his hand on top of mine.

His warm hand was so large it covered both my phone *and* my hand. He said, 'It won't work here, there's no reception.' Then he gently took my phone and keys from me and placed them into the centre console.

I wondered if Zach's comment was true about the reception out here being shit. Then again, maybe Zach didn't want me to worry about my family if I carried my phone around for the rest of the afternoon and evening.

'You won't need these here.'

I looked up at Zach and wondered where we were.

I thought I knew this town like the back of my hand ten years ago, so could it have changed that much? I continued to wonder as I turned to look out all the truck windows. I saw a homestead, a large garage and cars lined up like a supermarket carpark in a paddock adjacent to the house. Surely Zach didn't live with that many people? When I got out of his truck, what would I walk into on the other side of his front door?

When I couldn't contain my curiosity, I had to say, 'That's a lot of cars. Do you own all those or live with that many people?'

'I don't own all those cars.'

'You live with this many people?' It seemed like a silly question to ask, but I guess it was possible to live with a dozen people. The house looked big enough.

'They're people I know, but they don't live here.'

'You live here alone?' I wasn't looking out the windscreen anymore, I was looking straight at Zach. Gobsmacked at how peaceful and serene it was here, then I mused at how amazing the rest of the house including the backyard would be.

'Yes, babe, this is my house.' I was stunned by the view and by his words. He'd called me babe. It also felt like he knew how to make me come a little undone when his brown eyes rested on my green ones.

But what would I know. I was halfway into a brand-new day, though it definitely wasn't long enough to know with any kind of certainty how I should feel about anything and anyone in my life. I had avoided dealing with my thoughts and emotions for the longest time, but I knew I would have to deal with them sooner or later. I just didn't want that time to be this afternoon.

The house, his house, was beautiful. The front was wrapped in a veranda and two big bay windows faced us. It was modern and tucked away somewhere on the outskirts of town. Something I would like to have myself someday, a house just like this.

'Do you have neighbours?' There was too much curiosity to contain the questions.

'Just one.' Zach held up his finger. 'About half a kilometre that way.' He pointed in the direction of where the house was located. 'But I've never seen anyone there.'

'It's so beautiful out here.'

'What's beautiful is that it's quiet at the end of a long day or when I've worked all night.'

I nodded my head, but didn't say anything. This man worked long hours but still found time to have a life away from work. Something I wish I knew how to do. Maybe one day.

'Come on, let's go inside.'

That was when I heard the sounds of what could only be a good time coming from what was most likely Zach's backyard. From where I stood, all of sudden, all the cars and why people were here made sense. The laughter, the music, the occasional squeal. I had blindly followed Zach without a clue as to where we were going or what I was getting myself into.

Zach took a step towards his house, and while my arm had gone with him, my feet stayed planted, unable to move. My hand fell from his grasp to my side, and he turned to face me. While I wanted to go inside, I couldn't control my hesitation. My nerves had got the better of me, and that was never a good thing.

Zach's eyes pierced me, and I swallowed at the intensity of his gaze. He knew what I was about to say, and he patiently waited for me to speak.

'A party?'

He didn't answer, so I began to ramble. 'I'm not cut out for a party. I'm in last night's clothes, and they smell. I need a change of clothes and maybe a couple of shots of bourbon before I can even contemplate joining in with any festivities.'

By the time I'd finished I was breathless and a little dizzy. I wondered if I could do this in the state I had driven myself into and still walk into a party beside Zach. Right now was not the moment to be apprehensive or spiral out of control and shut down. I needed to pull it together or I would fall quickly through the looking glass and crumble into a heap on the ground in the foetal position.

Zach stepped closer to me, and I leaned back against the bull bar of his truck. For the second time today, his body was so close to mine. I didn't want to tense, but I did, and the word 'relax' rolled from Zach's lips and landed in my ear.

'You need to breathe for me. It's okay.' He breathed in through his nose and out through his mouth, and I copied his action automatically.

I cursed myself for the things my body did in his presence. I couldn't stop the heat that flushed from my face right down to my belly. But thinking how close Zach's body was to mine halted my battling thoughts and pulled me back from the edge of the looking glass. My galloping heart began to slow and stopped me falling off the edge.

Zach took my hand, and this time I followed, somehow a little more at ease. We entered the front door and headed through the lounge room, then passed his kitchen table towards his bedroom. Once inside, he closed the door. I guess he didn't want to be interrupted, and my body flushed with heat again.

The master bedroom was spacious and luxurious with a king bed and dark grey décor that suited this man dressed in all black. What I could see as I followed Zach through his house was the perfect bachelor pad. But was his life as perfect as it appeared to be? Or was he just like me, searching for what was missing?

I dragged myself away from my thoughts and watched as Zach approached his bed. There was something familiar about the bag in front of him.

'You brought my clothes here?' I was a little confused how my bag ended up here.

'You were pretty quiet last night at the bar, and I'm curious about you. I thought we could spend some time together,' he said as if it answered my question, then he turned towards his walk-in robe to search for his own clothes to wear.

He wanted to spend time with me. Did he want to get to know me? Did Zach have his suspicions the same as I did, that maybe he knew who I was, and like me, just didn't know how to bring up that conversation?

I sensed he could see that fifteen-year-old girl who wore pigtail braids and glasses every day that he'd lived next door to and had gone to the same high school with. Even though he was a couple of years older.

But Zach's demeanour neither confirmed nor denied a potential shared past, and his locked-down expression frustrated me. I wanted to know what went on inside his head, and I wanted him to be open with me. But I only kidded myself, nothing was that easy. If I wanted Zach to confide in me then I would have to reciprocate. We didn't have the kind of relationship where information passed easily between us. But if Zach wanted to spend time with me to get to know me, then I wanted to spend time with him to get to know him.

He had showered and changed from his all-black attire into dark blue jeans and a dark grey tee, while I had continued to stare at my bag of clothes. I was lost in childhood memories from a lifetime ago when my family was still whole. So much had happened in my absence from this town that I hadn't thought about any of it in a long time.

I looked up at Zach as he stood in front of me. The man looked good and smelled divine. His T-shirt was moulded to his muscled arms but didn't show off any more of his tattoo. I wanted to pout at not being able to see more of it, but Zach was ready to go and join the festivities, and I hadn't even changed yet.

Reaching into my bag, I grabbed the dark blue pair of jeans I'd packed, a fresh singlet and underwear. Then I pulled out my favourite Converse jumper, and the last thing out was my toiletry bag.

I kicked off my boots and peeled out of my socks. Zach didn't move from in front of me as I left my things on the floor. Although I was comfortable with how close he was to me, I wasn't at the stage where I was comfortable being naked with him. I hugged my clothes to my chest and picked up my toiletry bag then walked past him and headed towards his bathroom, closing the door behind me. If he wanted to see my nakedness, then he would have to wait until I was ready to share it.

I peeled off last night's clothes and left them in a pile on the bathroom floor. I would worry about them another time. Quickly changing into fresh underwear and pulling my singlet over my head, I stared at myself in the mirror. The shower at the hotel had done nothing for my panda eyes. I washed my face and used make-up remover for my eyes. I reapplied my moisturiser and took a second look in the mirror. I was almost myself again. My naked face would have to suffice against the unknown. Reaching into my toiletry bag for my deodorant and perfume, I sprayed both on my body and no longer could I smell smoke and alcohol.

I tugged on my jeans and took one last look at myself in the mirror, almost glimpsing a slither of the new me as the old me began to crumble. When I slid the bathroom door open, I found Zach had sat down on his bed to pull on socks and boots. As I moved closer to the bed, his eyes roamed my body and his lips turned into a grin at what he could see. Not once did he creep me out. I left my jumper on the bed, shook out the soft waves of my now-dry hair and fumbled in my bag for clean socks to cover my feet before I sat down to shove them back into my boots. Only when I was ready did I allow my eyes to land on Zach.

'You look incredible,' Zach whispered as we stood up together. I thought the same thing, but was too shy to voice words like that, so I simply gave him a half-smile at his kind words. 'Come on, babe. I'll show you around.'

And for the second time today, Zach had called me babe. He hadn't called me Harley, and I tried not to think of the reason why he hadn't said my name. I wanted to relax, enjoy myself and try to be as free-spirited as Addison. I didn't want thoughts of how good Zach looked or memories from when I lived here floating inside my brain. But they rattled around regardless and wouldn't let go.

Four

I searched for the courage I had constantly struggled to find but that my sister always radiated in spades. Following in Zach's wake as he left his bedroom, I snapped out of the place that had me deep in thought. Zach led me through his house, past his lounge and kitchen, but what I saw was only half of his home. I guess I would see the other half of his home another time. We stepped through the open glass doors in his kitchen onto the biggest veranda I had ever seen to find people who had gathered around Zach's backyard waiting for him to arrive.

The veranda ran the length of the back of the house to a pool at one end and a barbeque entertainment area at the other. All Zach had to do was step out of the shadow of his eaves and into the sunlight of the afternoon for everyone to know he was here.

People from all around his backyard swarmed towards him and with my hand in his he greeted his guests. I tried to remember when he'd taken hold of my hand again, but everyone that greeted Zach greeted me too. I felt my head spin. This was a lot to take in. Zach knew so many people. It must be nice to have that many friends.

I marvelled at how he knew all these people. Had he gone to high school with them or had he met them since? Did he work with them, or for them? Were they old neighbours or people he met online? My memories of the time I spent with a boy named Zach were only of private moments. Zach had been popular in high school, there were many people in his orbit, but I had not hung out with him and his high school friends.

Zach's friends disappeared as quickly as they appeared. I seemed as familiar to them as they did to me. They shook his hand and moved back to where they came from and were ready to kick this party up another level now that the man of the house was here. When everyone had said their hellos, we moved further into the backyard and over to a hut that had been fitted out as a bar.

It was all set up for today's party. There was alcohol everywhere and plenty of mixers to go with whatever you wanted to drink. The bar was fully powered with lights and a fridge in one corner. There was plenty of room to make drinks and a variety of plastic cups to hold your liquor. I guess this bartender didn't want glass spread across his backyard.

The outside of the bar was lined with stools, and the benchtop was smooth, level and covered in bar mats. This bar could almost be a replica of the one I'd seen at Black's Bar and Grill last night. Could Zach be more than just a bartender?

'A shot of bourbon as promised,' Zach said as he handed me a shot glass.

'Ooh, top-shelf,' I replied, and the amber liquid was gone a moment later, along with that thought of him.

'I only serve the best, thank you very much.' Zach and I shared a smile before I remembered my manners.

'Thank you,' I said and gave the shot glass back, not ready to jump headfirst into another night full of alcohol.

'Will you please relax?' Zach put his hand on my neck, and his thumb rubbed the skin under my ear.

For me that was always easier said than done. But I felt my body warm up from his touch. My whole body tingled, even my core. That sensation was new. I liked it and the effect Zach was having on me.

'Zees, my man,' someone yelled into the bar.

Zach turned around to the deep voice, and his touch was gone.

'About time you got here, bro.'

'Michaels, my man, the day is young, and we have all night.' They both chuckled at each other and clasped hands together, then slapped each other on the back.

They could almost be twins. Both looked the same from their tall figures to their hair colour, from their tattoos just peeking out to their taste in clothes. I couldn't help but feel like I had missed something, but not to worry, I guessed all would be revealed.

'I want to thank you for getting this set up without me today. Work was a little crazy last night and I needed to make sure everything was good this morning. That's why I'm late.'

'It's all good. Any time, man.'

The blush crept higher on my chest, and I was glad no one was paying any attention to me. I was the reason Zach was late to the party. I had caused the craziness last night that he had felt the need to make sure was okay this morning.

'Hi, I'm Brock.' The man talking to Zach turned in my direction.

'I'm Harley,' I said, directing my attention to Zach's friend and hoping when I stepped forward to shake his hand the colour on my chest was gone.

As Brock closed his hand around mine, he took the opportunity to talk to me. 'It's nice to meet you, Harley. I've known Zach a long time. How do you know him?'

'The bar,' was all I managed to croak out, my blush not quite gone.

I was an outsider looking in as the two friends communicated without speaking. They exchanged glances and raised eyebrows that didn't go unnoticed on me. Had Brock just called Zach on his bullshit about why he was late? I sensed Brock was curious as to why I was here.

They were interrupted by a pretty little blonde woman. She had run up to Zach and launched herself into his arms, planting her lips on his. I wanted to question the men on what their silent conversation was all about, but my head spun as I stood next to Brock.

I wasn't sure if it was from my hangover, the bourbon I just drank or that I felt out of place here, or if this sudden emotion I felt was jealously and not just because of the pretty blonde who had her legs wrapped around the man of the moment.

'Zach Hunter…' The blonde said as she peeled her lips from his, but she was cut off. His index finger was on her lips before she could say the last bit, which I assumed was his surname. I wondered why he didn't want it said out loud; then again, maybe he hated it.

'Happy Birthday!' I saw blondie whisper into his ear, and I guess I had all the information of what the rest of today was all about.

Zach placed blondie back on solid ground and without a sideward glance, reached for my hand and pulled me under his shoulder. I had all of his attention now. I relaxed into him, leaning into his side.

'Hi, I'm Shea,' the petite blonde said to me with an ear-to-ear grin.

'Harley,' I said back to her, and I put my hand out between us for her to shake.

'Nice to meet you,' she said as she took my hand.

'You too.'

Shea then tugged my hand and pulled me away from Zach's shoulder and into her hug.

'Don't worry about me,' she whispered to me. 'I won't step on your toes. Zach and I go way back.'

The ear-to-ear grin still on her face set me at ease. I tried to remember, as I pulled away from her, if she had been around before I left. I couldn't remember, though.

'You'll have to excuse Shea here.' Zach's eyes were locked on mine. 'It's the same every year, and this year makes it ten.'

That answered my question. Shea had started her birthday kisses after I'd left.

'You haven't stepped on anyone's toes, Shea,' I said to her, but my eyes were still on Zach and his unreadable expression.

He hadn't given anything away, and I couldn't read the look on his face let alone his body language to tell how he felt. Was there something between us? What fool would think that there was anything? I was just the damsel in distress who Zach had invited to come along today, then told me he wanted to spend time with me, when he could have sent me on my way. 'Argh,' I silently said to my damn ruminating thoughts. When would I ever learn to just be in the moment!

Shea waved goodbye and turned on her heel, then she was off with Brock on her tail, and Zach and I were alone again.

Zach turned to me, and before I knew it, he had lifted me up by the waist and placed me on the bench that was meant to make drinks. He poured another shot, and this time, he poured two. Zach stood close enough that he was between my legs, and before he passed my drink over, I cupped his face with both my hands and pulled his ear to my lips and whispered. 'Happy birthday, babe.' I wanted to kiss him, but I didn't. I wasn't sure what reaction my kiss would get.

But I did wonder if I had the same effect on him as he had on me when he whispered in my ear. He tensed and took a step back, and I had my answer. Only his hand with my drink in it was within my reach. I took it, brought the glass to my lips, and tipped it up.

I jumped off from where I sat, and moved to pass Zach to the other side of the bar into the afternoon sun. Soaking it up, I tried to remember the last time I'd let the sun cover me in its warmth. It had been so long I couldn't remember. Melbourne never had whether like this. It was early April and the weather was still warm here. I closed my eyes, tipped my head back and let the sunshine envelop me.

Zach, not one to be left behind, quickly reached me, spun me around and pulled me back into him. His hand reached for my shoulder and rubbed small circles on the base of my neck, I opened my eyes as his free hand tilted my chin up until our eyes were locked.

'Zach,' I said breathlessly, barely able to hold onto my resolve around this man. My hands though had moved of their own accord to his chest. His body felt so good under my palms, like they had somehow been there before, but I wasn't sure. My mind could have just been playing tricks on me. What I wanted to know was why Zach had invited me here. 'Why am I here? What is this?' I asked as my desire to know got the better of me.

What I really wanted to ask was, 'Why do you want to spend time with me?' But I didn't have the nerve to.

'Between us?' He'd answered with another question.

I nodded my head, and Zach dropped his fingers from my chin.

'I want to spend some time with you.' He had already told me that. Maybe just like me, Zach didn't have all the answers yet.

'Okay.' There were no other words I could think of to say. There were only so many questions I was brave enough to ask that pushed me outside of my comfort zone, and I was already 270 kilometres out of the comfort zone I had built for myself in Melbourne. Now that I was here in Zach's company, it was the most time I'd spent with someone that wasn't myself or a staff member at the bakery.

Zach's 'okay' to me was my hand in his while his lips pressed against my knuckles. His lips felt blissful against my skin, and it was the only gesture apart from our joined hands that let me know he was prepared to show me any emotion. Zach, the boy I had lived next door to, had also kissed my fingertips during our brief time together. What I felt now was the same as back then, and I was starting to see why Zach wanted to spend time with me.

Five

I wanted something more, not only from Zach, but myself as well. I wanted the answers to all my questions, but it was futile. This wasn't the time for a conversation of that magnitude. I wasn't that bold, and it wasn't fair to hog all of Zach's attention. This was a party, and everyone was here to have a good time. Myself included. Time to shake off the nerves, the doubts and enjoy Zach's company.

'Food's ready,' someone yelled into the afternoon air. I moved away from Zach's presence and immediately felt his loss of heat, but he didn't let go of my hand.

'Come on,' Zach said his smile ear to ear. 'Let's grab some food.' And the conversation about us was over, just like that.

I was lost in thought about this man in front of me and couldn't deny we needed to talk, but now was not the time.

Instinctively Zach squeezed my hand, and no longer was I deep in thought about his lips on my knuckles.

'Babe.'

He hadn't called me Harley all day. Maybe he just liked to call me 'babe', but my eyebrows drew together anyway at why he would do that. What did he know and wasn't telling me? I didn't want to make a scene, so I let Zach lead me, hand in hand, back to his huge veranda.

Zach's friends had set up his veranda with two tables, one to sit at and the other with party food, nibbles, salads, bread, condiments, cutlery. Another friend stood by the barbeque and cooked the meat.

We grabbed plates and food then moved down the table's length towards the barbeque where I could see steaks, sausages, chops, rissoles, onions and thinly sliced potato, all cooked on the barbeque hotplate.

Zach led me away from the tables and over to an undercover area with an outdoor table and chairs that were big enough to hold ten people with bench seats all around the three sides. We were the first to sit at the table, but Brock and Shea and a few of Zach's other friends were quick to join us.

The conversation started as soon as everyone sat down, and around mouthfuls of food, questions were asked and answered. I nibbled away at my food and listened to the conversation around me.

'The fire is ready to go,' said a blonde-haired man to Zach.

He nodded his appreciation and said, 'Light it up,' and the blonde man was gone to attend the fire pit.

'Are the festivities like this every year?' I asked no one in particular. I felt only slightly out of place here as a stranger to Zach's friends. I didn't want it to be that I was a city girl and didn't know what happened around here anymore. But the choice not to be a country girl hadn't been mine. That choice had been taken away from me the night my life had changed over a decade ago.

'Every year for the last ten years, hey Zach,' Brock replied. 'Your seventeenth was the start of it all. Although the last six years have shown that the party gets bigger every year.'

'So I take it you've lived here for the last six years.' I turned my attention to Zach as he nodded with a shit-eating grin plastered to his face.

'And because I don't have any neighbours, we can make as much noise as we want, and when we've had enough, the guys roll out their swags or tents and crash.' Then he leaned into me and whispered, 'I get to crash inside in my own bed though.'

'Princess!' I smirked. 'Can't even rough it for one night?'

'Hey, there have been some nights early on when I didn't make it to bed and passed out on the grass,' Zach told me, like he was offended I'd called him a princess.

'Your home, of what I've seen already, is gorgeous.' I changed the topic of conversation. It was homely and beautifully peaceful, but I didn't say that for fear I might get too comfortable and attach myself right here in this little town. If I ever did learn what it was like to relax, then it would be nice to have a quiet place to land just like Zach's. A woman could dream, couldn't she?

'That's not even the best bit?' Zach moved closer to entwine his fingers with mine. His other hand had found my waist. He knew I was lost in thought.

'The best bit is not that your property is gorgeous?' I raised my eyebrow at him. Not just for the question I had asked but for our closeness and our entwined fingers.

'The best bit is that this bad-boy piece of land backs on to the river, one hundred metres down the path on the other side of the bar.'

'Guess it doesn't get much better than that.' My eyes looked down towards the bar, and there was an overgrown path that could barely be seen next to it.

Zach leaned over my shoulder and whispered to me. 'Now that you're here, it's perfect.' I felt giddy and didn't dare turn to face him. He was already so close, and I didn't want this moment to be where he kissed me.

I felt my face flush as I asked, 'Why?' But my question remained unanswered as we were interrupted. Zach definitely knew more about me than he let on. *Oh, boy.*

'Will there be music tonight, Zach?' Another friend who had just joined us asked. He stood behind his chair in jeans and a flannelette shirt that covered a white tee-shirt.

'Tonight will be no different to any other year,' Shea said in defence of Zach. 'Why would you even ask?'

'He brought a woman this year.' The friend who had just joined us said in response, and it made me look up, first to where the voice came from, then to Zach who looked back at me. He still had a hold of my hand.

'Sit down and eat, Adam.' Zach looked Adam in the eye, shook his head then turned his attention back to me. 'A little later, everyone will let loose and sing a few tunes, and Brock will play his guitar. Do you feel up for a little a sing-along?'

'Sure,' I nodded. How hard could it be to join in with this sing-along? Earlier today had been the second time I had sung out loud in a long time, the first being last night on my way here. But how would I go singing with other people around me?

Would I be okay? Or would it be too much and I'd end up on the floor the same as I had five years ago?

That thought left me feeling a little uneasy, but I had to try, and it wouldn't hurt for me to loosen up and not be so uptight about singing. I could sing along to a few songs with Zach and his friends. I could pretend I was singing along in my car like I did last night on my way here or in the hotel room earlier singing along to the playlist I had chosen. 'As long as you don't ask me to sing a solo, I should be okay to join in.'

Zach shook his head again and laughed. The light-hearted sound calmed me and made me think I could do this, sing, and not get emotional and fall apart. The confidence Zach had was something I could only dream of. 'One day,' I told myself. He let go of my hand and waist, and out of the corner of my eye I could see his was observing me.

The conversation continued around the table as we ate our food. My sausage and onions, rissoles and potato chips were gone, and I had moved on to my salads. I looked over to see Zach's plate was empty. He had eaten his massive steak and sides like he did it every weekend.

'That's impressive,' I said to Zach about his steak.

'I didn't get to eat today. I've survived solely on coffee and bourbon, so yeah, nothing to it.'

Way to go, look what you did. You stole the man's attention so much he didn't even have time to eat. I shook my head at myself and Zach's feat. 'Your friends have done a great job with your party, the food especially.'

Zach nodded. 'They're the best. They set it all up without me. Now how about another drink?' Today was Zach's birthday, and it was supposed to be all about him. He could have spent the morning making everything here perfect, but he had chosen to spend the time with me.

'Yes. But,' I leaned up close to whisper in Zach's ear, 'I would like to get my jumper.'

Zach put my plate on his, and we both stood at the same time. He dumped our plates, then took hold of my hand.

'I know where I left my jumper, but you haven't let go of my hand since we got here. What's that all about? I can't go anywhere as my car is still at the bar.' I said to him once we were out of earshot of Zach's partygoers.

Zach was silent. I had hit a nerve. *Good*, I told myself. My arousal was sky-high, and I had only spent the day with this man. As Zach lead me through his home to the master bedroom, his face twitched. I passed him, grabbed my jumper from the bed and pulled it on.

I moved towards the bathroom and closed the door, taking my time as I needed a minute to myself, but it wasn't so I could think. I needed some space. I was hoping the sexual tension between us would ease but when I opened the door, it was still there. It had been a long time since I let myself feel anything for anyone. Zach was unveiling all that I had buried over the last ten years, and I didn't know how I was going to deal that, let alone the desire he stirred in me.

'I'm sorry, I just needed a minute. Being here is a lot for me. I'm not usually this social.' I stood at the threshold between the master bedroom and bathroom.

Zach pulled me away from the bathroom door and closer to his body. It was all I got a chance to say before he kissed my forehead, another sensation that felt far too familiar. But when I tried searching for that particular memory, I couldn't place it. Zach's arms rested on my shoulders, and I couldn't help but put my arms around his waist and my face against his chest to enjoy his cosy embrace.

'Harley.' It was the first time he had used my name all day. 'There, I've said it, I've said your first name.' It was almost like he had been given an electric shock. 'Woman, there is something about you I can't put my finger on. I don't know what it is that you do to me, but I haven't felt like this in an awfully long time. There's only one person that has ever made me feel this way before…'

Zach's words died on his lips as though he was lost in a memory from another time. Were his memories from the past just as painful as mine?

Oh boy, okay. It wasn't just me who felt this way, a tad unsure of our instant connection.

There was an attraction, and the more time I spent with Zach, the more I felt it. As sure as the shiver in my bones, I knew Zach felt the same heat that flared inside of me. It had been a long time since I had relaxed into anyone close to me. I'd leant into Zach earlier this evening without thinking it was the same way I had leant into Zach all those years ago when we would meet down the side of his house.

I moved my head away from his chest and said, 'You, birthday boy, can't hide out all night in your bedroom or your friends will send out a search and rescue team.' Taking charge this time, I turned Zach around and pushed him out of his bedroom and back towards his party. We walked in silence, and it wasn't long before my hand found his as he led the way across the lawn to his backyard bar.

We stood inside the bar and once again I was lifted up on the bench to the same spot as before. Zach poured two drinks, one for him and one for me, and without a word stood between my legs. I let my knees rub against his hips as he handed me a shot of bourbon.

'Cheers,' I said as our shot glasses clinked together, and we both downed the amber liquid at the same time.

'Thanks,' Zach smirked at me. 'I'm glad I dragged you along today.'

'I don't think you gave me much choice.' I scrunched my face up at him. 'Thank you for last night, this morning and for dragging me along today. Your party tonight has been wonderful. I've had a great time.'

'What other plans did you have for today?' Zach questioned.

I probably would have slept all day and driven back to my unhappy existence. But Zach didn't need to know that. 'Point taken,' I replied, relieved that he had taken me to his party.

The bourbon had loosened us both up, and Zach's outer shell was softer now. Maybe mine was too and I didn't need to worry about the sing-along that was about to take place around the fire.

Zach leaned in, and his lips touched my ear. 'It's time.' My heart fluttered and my body buzzed all over as he pulled me off the bar bench to lead me out into the middle of his backyard.

Six

The last remnants of the day left a pink hue to the sky. I looked up to see the sun had almost set. The evening air had turned cool. It wouldn't be long now, and the days would become shorter – a sure sign winter was on its way. The party tonight offered warmth by way of a fire, which was in full throttle. As I looked around me, the backyard had a glow to it that took my breath away. It was so pretty here, and right on cue, someone turned on the party lights. They lit up Zach's whole backyard from his veranda to the bar, and I thought to myself, *This moment couldn't be any more beautiful.* I squeezed Zach's hand, but he already knew how pretty it was here. After all, this was his house.

There was a strum of a guitar, so I guessed it was time for that sing-along. I turned around to see Brock at full height with his guitar up in the air, as only rock stars did. Zach's guests started to gather around the fire pit and took their seats.

Brock strummed a couple more cords on his guitar, and I could see he wanted Zach to join him. No way was I able to go over and join the others without more alcohol. I stepped away from him and moved back towards the bar. I reached for the bottle of bourbon when his hand landed on mine.

'Zach!' I said, and he responded with a murmur. I could feel his front pressed up against my back. 'I need alcohol to do this. My mouth will dry up otherwise. It's been a while since I've done this, sat down with someone playing the guitar. I don't want to embarrass myself in front of your friends, so I need this.' My dad would often sit in our backyard and play his guitar and wait for Addison and me to join him and sing along.

'Harley,' Zach said as he turned me around. 'I believe in you. You've got this. I'll be right next to you, and I'll even hold your hand if you want me to, okay, babe.'

'Okay.' Zach words were a boost of confidence I needed to get me through singing in front of others again.

Zach took the bottle from my hand and went in search of cups and a mixer. When he found what he was after, he grabbed my hand and led me over to where Brock was. Brock had seated himself on one side of the bench with Shea on one side of him and Adam on the other. I followed Zach to the only space left on the bench and we sat down. Everyone talked around us as we all waited for Brock to start.

Zach poured my drink while Brock strummed his guitar again. He started to play the intro to a familiar tune and then he started to sing. Of course, everyone knew the song and sang along while I looked around at everyone in awe, thinking to myself how cool this was. They had all done this before and took their cue to sing their parts. Even Zach was surprised by the compilation that had been put together for his birthday, all Aussie artists. His friends really did know how to go all out.

The first few songs were sung with only Brock on guitar. He warmed up Zach's birthday party crowd with songs from Noiseworks, Crowded House and AC/DC. Shea leaned into whisper in his ear. I wasn't sure what it was with those two, but Brock reluctantly handed over his guitar. Shea grinned from ear to ear, happy she had gotten what she wanted. She knew how to wrap the boys around her finger. Shea tightened the strings of Brocks guitar to the sound she wanted. Then she said, 'Are we ready to 'Kick It Up', ladies?'

I wondered what the hell Shea was up to. Then she started to play the guitar and all the ladies that had come tonight joined in to sing The McClymont's song 'Kick it Up'. I was glad I knew this song, and before I put too much thought into it, I sang right along with everyone else.

Shea gave up the guitar at the end of her song. Brock was happy to have his beloved guitar back. To my surprise, after everyone had relaxed into the warmth of the fire and the music that was being played, I saw Zach had reached around behind him to pick up a guitar.

'You play?' I asked once he had made himself comfortable with the guitar on his knee.

With only a nod of Zach's head, he started to strum.

There was too much curiosity inside me now. I needed to know, so I asked, 'Don't tell me you sing too?'

There were no words from Zach and there was no containing his grin on his way-too-handsome face.

Oh my, was there anything he couldn't do? Next he would insist we should sing a duet.

Zach strummed his guitar into the silence of the night. He was only a few chords into the song he'd chosen to play, and before he'd even sung the first line, I recognised the song as 'Working Class Man' by Jimmy Barnes.

The words out of Zach's mouth were perfect. He really knew how to work a crowd. I soaked in everything around me. I was overwhelmed but amazed at how easy it was for everyone to relax, sit by the fire and sing without any worry. I wished it were that easy for me, but it wasn't. I didn't want to feel the emotions in the music I heard or the lyrics I would sing, and then fall apart when it got to be too much. That was why over the last ten years I had never sung more than one song at a time. But last night and today, when the music surrounded me, it felt good to sing along. In the past it had been easier to shut the emotion of music out of my life. The same as I had shut out the night my life had changed.

But I couldn't do that tonight. I couldn't shut out the music. I had to tell myself I would be okay. That I could sing and nothing bad would happen. That nothing would spin out of control tonight.

Zach looked at me, taking in my body language. I tried to cover my awkwardness by singing along, I'm not sure if it convinced Zach, but he continued with the song. Of course, everyone here helped as they sang right along with Zach.

My face was impassive, and my body felt numb. Not only could Zach sing, but his voice was like velvet, the perfect mix of smooth and husky. The words Zach sang surrounded me and made me shiver from the inside out. He just sang the words, and he didn't even know how much I loved this song.

In my mind, there was no one else around, and it was just me that Zach sang to, and only me. I opened my mouth to sing right along with him, and in my daydream, we sang in perfect harmony. But I heard the other voices around me and remembered where I was. I sang the words along with everyone else, and Zach held my stare as I sang with him. Did he really think I wouldn't join in and sing like everyone else?

I reached down for my bourbon and took a sip, and as the song ended, I heard someone say, 'What song would you like to hear, Harley?' It was Brock who had asked me this.

I peeled my eyes away from my drink then turned to Brock and asked, 'So, the theme is Aussie artists?'

Brock didn't speak, only nodded his head. I needed to pick a song, and it wasn't up for discussion. I had been put on the spot, and by the grin on Brock's face, he was enjoying this moment. But I knew how to think on my feet. Working at the bakery had taught me that, even though this was the first time I had been to one of Zach's birthday parties and left with no choice but to pick a song by an Aussie artist. I told myself I could do this and not make a fool of myself.

Okay, I said to myself than to anyone else. *Don't take your time or think things over, just say the first thing that comes to mind.* '"Dumb Things" by Paul Kelly,' I said out loud.

There was a smirk now on Brock's face that let me know he knew the song. 'Good choice,' he told me before he moved his eyes to Zach and asked. 'You got this, Zach?'

'You gonna back me up?' Zach mocked back.

'Is Harley going to start us off?' The banter between Zach and Brock came naturally. I cursed the two of them under my breath as everyone turned their heads to look between Brock, Zach and me.

'Wow!' I said silently to myself, mostly at their banter. Way to make myself the centre of attention.

Everyone's eyes were on me, and I felt like I had no choice but to do this. I shot the rest of my drink, and as best I could, took a deep breath. I breathed in and let it out and tried not to be nervous. There was no walk to the stage to pick up the microphone, there was no screen in front of me to read the lyrics and there was no instrumental backing tape coming through the speakers. Instead, it was just my voice, the lyrics that I hoped I remembered and the men and their guitars.

There was a time I could easily do this, when my biggest fans were watching me. Be in the spotlight, put on a show and sing my heart out. But it had been ten years since my biggest fans had seen me sing. I thought I could sing without them and had even tried a couple of times over the years with karaoke.

But nothing had felt like it did right now. I was being put on the spot, and the number of people sitting around Zach's fire were the same number of people I would sing to at karaoke. This should be a walk in the park for me as long as I didn't black out.

I turned to Zach, who squeezed my hand for encouragement and nodded. The start of the song was played on both men's guitars, and when it was my time, to sing, the words that came out were the first few lines of Paul Kelly's 'Dumb Things'. I had sung them solo; they had come out raspy from not warming up properly, but I didn't care. I had heard my dad in those four lines that I'd sung. His voice had always been raspy when he sang, and I'd loved it.

To my relief, by the time I got to the fifth line Zach joined me as I sang, and by the time we got to the end of the first verse, everyone belted out the best part of the song: its title. Everyone knew this song and when we got to the second verse, we all sang the words through to the end. My voice had been drowned out by everyone else's, but I was happy everyone had joined in with me.

'Damn, woman! You really can sing.' Brock was as impressed by my vocals as much as Zach was. Their kind words were nice to hear.

'Your voice gives me shivers,' Shea said as she smiled at me. 'You would sound great at the bar, the one Zach works at. You should sing next time there's an event on.' She sounded confident that I could do that, but I wasn't so sure.

I didn't answer Shea. What was I supposed to say to her? While I had proven to everyone here that I could sing, it didn't mean I could get up in front of a bar full of people and be in the spotlight. Tonight felt the same as when I would sing with my family. I was comfortable with myself and my voice. But I was a long way from any kind of performing again.

'What song would you pick for your man to sing?' Someone asked, but I was not sure which of Zach's friends had spoken to me.

'My man, I'm not so sure about that.' I was caught off guard by the question. 'Maybe something country.' I turned to Zach, and his eyes pierced me. Maybe he didn't know any country music. Maybe I could school him, but that wouldn't be tonight. 'But if he's not up for something country, there is one song,' I said, 'that I would like to hear.' I leaned over and whispered into Zach's ear, '"Bow River," and not the Cold Chisel version either. I want a laid-back version like Troy Cassar-Daley.'

I busied myself with another drink while I let my whispered words hang in Zach's ear. As I brought my cup to my lips to soothe my parched throat, Zach's jaw tensed. I guess he hadn't quite gotten used to me whispering in his ear. His expression hadn't changed, though. Was he always this cool under pressure? When I saw Zach's fingers tune his guitar, I knew he was about to comply and sing the song I had chosen.

Zach sang the first verse acapella, and I couldn't take my eyes off him. The intensity of his return gaze was what I got for putting him on the spot. Then Zach's fingers moved along the guitar, and I heard the acoustic rhythm of the song. I melted in my seat. Zach's eyes hadn't left mine. He serenaded me, and once again I felt like it was just the two of us. As he built the song up, everyone joined in, including me and Brock with his guitar. When Zach got to the last verse of the song, my favourite part, he was singing again solo. Until I joined him to finish off the song.

I reached for Zach's hand and mouthed a thank you, then turned my head to look out into the night. There was a dark figure moving towards the fire pit. I felt my heart start to race, and I panicked. What I saw look ethereal. Was my mind playing tricks on me? It couldn't be my dad coming to watch me sing?

Someone had turned up late to the party, or was that someone uninvited? I didn't know, he was just a figure in the darkness to me. When the light crossed over the man walking towards us, I saw his face. That man was not my dad, or ethereal, or even someone I wanted to know. What I couldn't understand was why the mean son of a bitch was here.

This was too much. Last night and today had been too much. Too different to what I would normally do. I didn't know how to cope with all of this. I hadn't learnt how to deal with life when it became too much. That's why my body had tensed, and I felt the darkness wash over me. My hand that rested on Zach's leg tightened, and I thought maybe he had put his guitar down in time. God, I hope he caught me. I had no control now. It went all black, and all I heard were whispers of, 'I got you, I got you.'

Seven

'No, no, no.' My eyes opened then I closed them just as quickly. Something wasn't right; this was too strange to be comfortable. It had happened again. I wasn't sure where I was this time or who I was even laying next to.

'You're okay, babe, I got you.' That familiar voice. I opened my eyes to his touch on my face. Zach was propped up on his side next to me as I laid flat on my back. The words Zach said niggled at my brain as it tried to trigger a memory but didn't quite get there; it was too much for me to handle right now.

'Not again,' I groaned out loud, and Zach's eyes were on mine. He looked pained, and I knew my freak-out didn't help. That was when I felt Zach roll me into him and put his arms around me. I now faced him. He moved me closer to him, and this was the closest we had ever been. I liked it; I felt safe like this.

'Babe,' Zach's voice calmed me. I was here in his bed, his king bed. He'd caught me, and I felt a little better in his arms. 'You're okay.'

I stayed locked in his arms far longer than two people who had just met should be allowed to, but neither of us pulled away. I stayed there long enough for my heartrate to slow down.

I finally pulled back from his embrace and asked, 'Your party?' My hands were on Zach's chest, but I didn't want to look up.

'We wrapped it up when you blacked out,' Zach told me, and I was horrified that I had ended his party.

'Why?' I wasn't completely sure I wanted to hear his answer. The dark figure I saw and the light across his face, why would he be here?

'An uninvited guest showed up,' Zach said as he touched my face, caressed my cheek, and pushed my hair from my face. 'Brock, Adam, and a few others had to drag him off the property.'

'Who?' My voice was small, and when there was no answer, I asked again, a little louder this time. 'Who was your uninvited guest, Zach?'

'Why does it matter, Harley?' Zach lifted my chin up so our eyes could meet.

'Zach, please?' I knew he wasn't happy I pushed this.

'This person who showed up, is he the reason you blacked out?' Zach asked me like it was the most important question in the world that needed to be answered.

'Yes. No.' There were some things you just didn't beat around the bush about. But it was clear I was making a mess of this. 'It's complicated.' More so by my inability to handle my emotions.

For ten years I had stayed in my lane and not ventured out of it to cope with what I had lost. But I had ventured out of my lane two nights ago and now I was struggling to cope with breaking Groundhog Day.

Before I could work out what to say, Zach had asked me another question. 'What does that mean, Harley?'

I didn't think, I just blurted out. 'It means driving 270-kilometres the night before, waking up in the hotel room yesterday and then the lead-up to singing around your fire last night was too much for me. I don't do those things. I don't know why I thought I could. I work until I'm completely exhausted and avoid any little trigger; otherwise, like last night, I black out. And when I wake up, I'm in a haze trying to piece together what happened.'

'I shouldn't have insisted you come with me yesterday,' Zach whispered between us. 'I'm sorry.'

Was the pain I could still see on Zach's face a reflection of what was on my face. I wasn't very good at handling moments like this and when my hand travelled up between us, I didn't stop until it reached Zach's jaw. There, my fingers caressed the stubble that was the making of his beard.

'I was glad you did,' I whispered back, then with as much confidence as I could muster, I said, 'I was fine until I saw a dark figure coming towards us. I had already started to freak out and when the light shone across his face it was already too late as the darkness was closing in.'

'Harley, the guy who showed up was Connor Black.' Zach watched me closely. His brown eyes boring into my green ones.

'Connor Black,' I repeated, and all of a sudden, I was in a hurry. To get out of bed. Out of this house and out of my own way. I moved to get up, but before I even pushed the doona away, there was a hand around my wrist. 'Zach.' My heartrate was out of control again, and now I was breathless. I squeezed my eyes closed; I didn't want to lose control again.

'You know him?' Zach's grip on my wrist had eased.

I had lost my voice, and all I could do was nod my head. I knew Connor Black was a mean son of a bitch, and if Zach had told me his name, then Zach knew him too. That thought made me shake all over again. Did both men share the same last name? If they did, it could only mean they were related.

'Breathe.' The word travelled from Zach to me. 'Just breathe, babe.' His mouth was right next to my ear. I pushed away from Zach's chest and rested there flat on my back breathing in and out. As 'babe' left Zach's lips, I was almost calm.

'Zach, do you know Connor too?' It was crazy how one person knew how to calm me, while the another turned my irritation up to eleven and had every hair on my body standing on end. As much as I tried most of the time not to let my frustration get to that level or the better of me, some people just didn't know when to quit.

Like me, Zach nodded his head. Unlike me, he was quite capable of voicing his answer. 'Connor and I work in the same industry. He's also my brother. We don't socialise together very often because I don't like the way my brother does business. I had no idea he would be here last night.'

'I'm sorry, I have to go.' I paused. 'I can't be a burden to you; I'll drain you until there is nothing left.'

'Harley,' Zach said. 'Please stay.' There was something in his voice that didn't want to let me go. 'Tell me how you know Connor?'

Why did he want to know how I knew Connor? I knew the man from the envelope he'd handed over after he saw me sing karaoke. An envelope I imagined that invited me to sing at his bar permanently. Then just above a whisper I asked. 'Why do you want to know?'

'I want to know, Harley.' Zach was firm. 'What has got you so worked up over my brother?'

'If you want to know then I need coffee. Then I'll tell you this story.'

Zach stood up. He was shirtless, and I got to lie here and stare at him in his boxer briefs.

The view made me blush. The man was lean all over. His muscles were impeccable, and his skin was perfectly tanned. I had to stop the drool before it left my mouth. I enjoyed the sight now I could see more of Zach's tattoo, on his chest and upper arm, which was hidden last night by his tee-shirt. There were intricate details of Zach's tattoo that I couldn't make out from where he stood. Of what I could see I wondered why he felt the need to tattoo armour over his heart. Zach had caught me staring and his eyes flashed with desire as mine roamed his naked skin.

'Okay, two coffees it is.' Zach was about to leave his room to make coffee.

'Wait!' I sat up, and Zach stopped and faced me. 'Are we here alone?' I was curious to know what happened to his partygoers last night.

He turned as he reached his bedroom door and moved back towards his bed. Standing over me, he brushed the hair from my face and tucked it behind my ear. 'We are alone. There's no one in the house but you and me.' And just like that, he was gone.

Zach was back moments later, as promised, with two coffees. He sat down next to me and leaned back into the bed. I hadn't moved from my spot against the bedhead.

'Connor Black?' Zach questioned as he took a sip of his coffee.

'Connor Black,' I replied as I wrapped my fingers around the cup and took a sip. Coffee hit my tongue, filled my nostrils. The man knew how to make a good brew.

'How do you know him?' I sensed a little impatience from Zach, but to him, I guess this was important.

'I wish I didn't.' There was a pause for a moment. 'I met him one night about twelve months ago at a bar called The Groove. I had signed up to receive notifications about all the karaoke events going on around Fitzroy. The Groove had started up karaoke and I thought I would check it out. I went for a drink, sang a song and that's when Connor approached me.'

Zach didn't interrupt me, but I sensed him tense at the mention of The Groove and reminded myself to ask him about it later. There was more than one elephant in this room, and one elephant at a time they would be dealt with. In this moment, that elephant was Connor Black.

So, for now, I continued with, 'Connor approached me, introduced himself, told me he'd seen these videos of my vocals. When he showed me, I realised the videos were from this karaoke bar called Little Beats. Someone must have recorded my performances. I didn't even know about the videos.' I had sung at Little Beats twice in the last three years. Since I'd fallen on the floor in a heap singing karaoke with my sister five years ago, it had taken me two years, but I wanted to know if I could still sing. After I'd tried it a couple of times, I wanted to see if I could do it again. That's how I wound up at The Groove.

Zach's hand that didn't hold his coffee reached out to grab my free hand, and at the mention of Little Beats he tensed again, letting go of my hand. Why did I get the feeling that Zach knew more than he was letting on about these two bars? Would I get the answer I wanted if I asked what I was curious about?

'You know those bars?' I voiced casually, pausing my recollection of the night Connor had approached me.

'I do.' Whatever Zach knew about those two bars, he wasn't about to share what he knew with me.

'How do you know them?' I don't know why I asked, but those bars seemed important to Zach. Maybe I wanted this man to share with me the same as I was sharing with him.

'Like Connor, I'm also a businessman.' There was something about this dreamy man next to me that he held back. Maybe it was a secret. I didn't like it, but it was what it was. And I wasn't going to drive myself round the bend trying to figure it out. I had enough on my plate trying to figure myself out.

If Zach didn't want to enlighten me about the bars, then there was more to my story about Connor so I continued. 'My sister and I would catch up every once in a while, usually when work wasn't too hectic, and we would find a karaoke bar, let down our hair, have a couple of drinks, get up and sing together, and we would alternate who would pick the songs. But we haven't sung together in the last five years.'

Singing with Addison brought back memories of when we sang together without a care in the world. After our first competition when we were younger, Addison and I would put on performances for our parents then beg them to let us enter other talent competitions to see how far we could go with our vocals. I loved hearing about my dad on the road travelling around and singing his songs in his cover band, the Ethan James Band. The adventures Dad had told Addison and me had started out as bedtime stories, but he'd loved sharing his wild days and his singing with us. And what my dad adored the most was that his daughters loved singing and music as much as he did.

I hadn't sung with my sister since the night I had collapsed on stage. I'd avoided singing with Addison since that day. But I didn't say that, instead I said, 'I blacked out a few years ago and up until yesterday I thought music was a trigger to my blackouts. On three occasions over the last few years, I wanted to see if I could do it by myself without my sister, sing without my world falling apart around me. I did it and now there's video proof. But I know my sister, she won't be satisfied seeing the videos. No, she would want to see that with her own two eyes.'

I stopped to take a couple of breaths and drink more of my coffee. I turned to see where Zach's attention was, and it was on me. The colour in his face drained when I continued. 'Connor approached me one night, with his cocky demeanour and smug look on his face, thinking he was about to get what he wanted. He handed over his business card and an envelope, gave me his award-winning smile and told me to give him a call. I knew I had to get out of The Groove as quickly as I could. The Groove, just like Connor, gave off a vibe I just didn't like.'

'What did Connor want?' Zach still pierced me with his eyes.

'If I had to hazard a guess then I would say he was offering me a job. I don't know, I tore the envelope in half and threw it in the bin along with his business card.'

'And you haven't seen Connor since?'

I moved my head from side to side. 'Zach, I looked Connor up. He is one ruthless man, and there are a lot of opinions in the world of social media. Connor always gets what he wants, and he won't stop until he gets it.' I turned away from Zach's stare. 'I don't want any of what Connor has to offer. I don't want to sing for a living or even record an album. I want to sing for me, for fun, like last night and not because I have to, to make ends meet. I don't want that pressure. I can't handle it, and last night proved that. But Connor, just like my sister, doesn't know about my struggles.'

By the time I'd finished, my hands shook, and I was thankful my coffee was all gone. Zach's hand covered mine again, and I stared into his brown eyes. It was like there was a protective force field around me, and I felt safe.

'Everything will be alright,' Zach told me, but I wasn't convinced.

'You don't understand, Zach.' I looked away from him. 'I never turned Connor down on whatever it was that he was offering. He's probably still chasing an answer, especially if he thinks I can make him a ton of money.'

'Hey!' I dared to look up at Zach. 'It will be okay.' He moved the hand that was in his to his lips and kissed it. 'I won't let Connor get too close to you.'

Silence filled the space around us, and my hand was still pressed against Zach's lips. Then I heard him say, 'Come on, let me make you breakfast.' Zach moved off the bed, and this time he moved towards his walk-in robe for a tee-shirt that had a picture of a motorcycle on it.

I was about to leave the comfort of his king bed when I realised what I was dressed in. My underwear.

'You undressed me?' It was twice now I had woken up in only my underwear.

'You managed that all by yourself,' Zach told me as a matter of fact. 'Last night and the night before.'

Oh my God. It had been years since I had undressed myself without remembering. After spending all my free time with Grandpa at the bakery and with the exhaustion I'd descended into, I also fell into the pattern on undressing in bed under the covers. And now I was doing it again.

'Here.' When I looked up at Zach, he was handing over what looked like a folded-up piece of material.

'Where did you get this from?' I pressed as I got out of bed, slipping the long black tee-shirt over my head that had Babe written across the front.

'I bought it for you yesterday, Harley.' My insides did a happy dance at the use of my name. 'And that tee-shirt dress is perfect for you,' he told me.

I raised my eyebrow at him, and before I could speak, Zach continued with, 'I wasn't sure what was in your overnight bag, but now you have pyjamas.'

'Okay.' I was only a little freaked out at how close I felt to Zach already.

I took a step away from the bed and followed him into the kitchen.

'Another coffee?'

I wasn't ashamed to admit I needed more than one coffee in the morning to get going. I needed the extra kick especially when I worked myself to exhaustion. 'Sure,' I said as I moved over to the glass doors in the kitchen.

'Eggs and bacon or pancakes?' Zach asked, and I wondered if the two options he had offered were the only two he knew how to cook for breakfast.

'Eggs and bacon please,' I replied as I turned to face him.

'I was sure you'd want pancakes,' Zach told me.

After yesterday's brunch, I wasn't surprised. 'They are my favourite,' I informed Zach, 'but I feel like eggs and bacon to-day.'

'Eggs and bacon it is.' He handed over my coffee.

'Babe, you really blew everyone away last night. You were unbelievable. Everyone was like, wow. They were surprised by your song choice, but your voice really impressed them.'

'It felt good to sing along with everyone,' I told Zach. 'Shea surprised me with her song, and she did the ladies proud. Brock, though, really gave me no choice but to belt out the intro to Paul Kelly's "Dumb Things".'

'Even I was surprised by Shea; she comes up with something new every year. But I'm sorry about Brock,' Zach said on behalf of his friend.

'It's fine. I'm grateful that both of you didn't make me sing the whole song acapella.' There was a shyness inside me that I didn't want Zach to see, and I told myself to watch out for Shea and her mischief. Zach was the essence of cool, calm, col-lected and confident. A natural at everything, whereas I was the polar opposite since I had blacked out and buried myself in work.

'You did great.' Zach stated of my ability to wow his friends. 'How do you like your eggs?'

'Poached.' I took a seat at the breakfast bar and watched Zach move around his kitchen with ease. Not once in my presence had he wavered; he was perfectly confident, and I was only slightly jealous.

To be that confident, to be able to handle my emotions and to not be exhausted all the time would make me extremely happy. But I wanted back the one thing that was missing in my life: One day, music would wash over me, and I wouldn't feel so crippled by it.

'Hey?' Zach sought my attention. 'Earth to Harley, your brekky is ready.'

I looked up and I realised I had zoned out. 'I'm sorry.' I wished I was confident just like Zach. We ate our breakfast in companionable silence, and then with my coffee cup in hand I moved back to the glass doors behind Zach. 'It's beautiful here,' I said to myself and opened the door to go outside.

Eight

'I wouldn't go out there.' But it was too late; I was outside on the veranda. I was about to ask him why when on its way towards me the meanest looking dog I had ever seen.

I stood still, coffee cup in hand, staring down at the dog and cursing myself. 'Holy shit. Holy shit. Holy shit'. The Staffordshire bull terrier that had appeared out of nowhere came to a complete stop in front of me.

I breathed a sigh of relief as the black dog with a white tummy panted at my feet, turning my head while the rest of me stayed still just in case I was about to be dog meat. I saw Zach standing behind me in disbelief. The look on his face made me want to turn around and kiss him, but I didn't move, just turned my attention back to the dog.

'She doesn't like a lot of people, that's why you didn't see her last night. But I've never seen her drop at anyone's feet.'

'What's her name?'

'Abby.' Zach now stood beside me.

'Can I pat her?' I asked as I handed over my coffee cup.

'I'm sure she'll let you. She seems to like you.'

I reached down and scratched behind Abby's ear. The way she moved her head to look at me, I knew I had hit the right spot.

'Hi, Abby.' I crouched down to introduce myself. 'My name is Harley. It's very nice to meet you, and I appreciate that I am not your next meal.'

The dog panted and lifted her paw onto my knee, and Zach laughed.

'Really.' I turned to look at Zach. 'I thought I was about to become dog meat.'

'At least you didn't black out,' Zach said to me with a shit-eating grin on his face that bordered another laugh. 'That would be twice in twelve hours that I would have had to catch you.'

I stopped mid-scratch, and Abby barked once at the loss of contact as I stood and turned to Zach, slapping his chest. 'It's not funny.' But I tried really hard not to crack my lips into a smile or laugh.

'Come on, babe. I just want to see you scrunch your face up a me.' Zach grabbed my hand and entwined our fingers. 'Same as last night. Come on, you know you want to.'

'Why?' I fought to keep the emotions away from my face.

'Because you're beautiful.' Zach took hold of the hand that rested on his chest and moved both of my hands behind him until we stood toe to toe. Somehow my coffee cup had landed on the kitchen windowsill.

I looked up at Zach as he looked down at me. I was about to protest his comment when I felt warmth on my lips. Zach's lips were on mine. Like a zap of electricity, I stepped back, not yet ready for his affection. I was a mess of sentiments I hadn't dealt with in ten years. Standing a foot back from Zach I wondered if it was possible to feel this way after only twenty-four hours with someone. Like. Lust. Love. The heady emotions tumbled over me, but I had really fallen for the comfortableness that Zach emitted.

'I'm sorry.' This wasn't exactly how I thought this moment would go, a kiss from Zach. But I had to expect the unexpected from now on. My life wasn't going to be Groundhog Day anymore. As for Zach and his lips pressed into mine, what was he thinking? I wasn't a sleeping beauty; I didn't need a reawakening. Then again, maybe I did. Maybe I was naïve and maybe Zach knew more than he was prepared to share with me. But I didn't want this to be how Zach kissed me, not without opening up to me first. Because the boy I'd known, he'd talked to me, he'd let his guard down, he'd held my hand and kissed my fingers all the while I'd leant into him.

Back then, we'd met as often as we could. Always in the same spot, down the side of his house. It had taken me weeks to work up the courage to kiss the boy I'd lived next door to. Our first kiss was a goodbye kiss, and I'd given Zach the promise of more when I'd pushed him up against the side of his house with my hands on his chest, pressing my lips to his. I remember the moment I stepped away, and how quick Zach was to spin me around and pin me to the same spot to kiss me more passionately. It was a kiss I had never forgotten.

Zach and I would talk most afternoons when I went to collect Addison from the house next to ours. Addison and Lex, Zach's sister, were in the same year and after we'd moved in next door, they had become best friends. I'd met Zach one afternoon when I'd knocked on his door wanting Addison to come home. From that day, Zach and I gradually became friends.

Those afternoons were the only time we'd spent together, but I hadn't cared. I'd had all of Zach's attention and he'd had all of mine. I had never crushed on a boy or even liked a boy before Zach, and I hadn't even known if what I felt then had been the beginnings of love.

Did I even know what love was? After all I had been through? My world crumbling around me, while I suppressed anything in my life that was a reminder of that fateful night. Living every day the same and not knowing how to move on.

With tears in my eyes as I remembered how that kiss felt and the events that had happened after, I turned away from Zach and in a quiet voice, said. 'I just don't know what this is between you and me.'

Then I started to ramble. 'We locked eyes over my bourbon and lemonade two nights ago, then you rescued me from the bar and made sure I was okay the next morning – before you dragged me along to a party that was actually your birthday. As for your lips when they land on my skin, there's a connection between you and me that I don't know how to explain.'

Zach still stood in the spot where I left him. Was he also lost in memories of another time? Had he even heard anything I had rambled on about? Was he stunned that I pulled away from his kiss? Had I left him speechless? I didn't know what to make of his balled fists, the look on his face or his deflated posture. I moved backward away from him as he shook his head in disbelief, or was that for me not to move another inch. I wasn't sure, so I stopped and stared at him. I could see the pain, his face contorted, and I'd done that.

I wanted so badly to say something, but the words wouldn't come. Had I said something wrong? Done something wrong? I needed to move. I took a deep breath and turned. Putting one foot in front of the other. I walked down the steps of the veranda and across the lawn with Abby at my feet.

I wiped at the wetness in my eyes. I was not used to confronting how I felt. Abby nudged my fingers, and I reached down to scratch her head. 'What's up, girl?' I said quietly.

'Hey!'

I heard this yelled behind me, and I wondered if it was for the dog or for me, but I couldn't stop. I didn't look back; I needed to walk off these feelings I didn't know how to process. What I had bottled up over the last ten years now had stress lines and the beginnings of cracks. The pressure was working its way outwards. There had to be a way to let go of whatever had worked its way up to the surface before my breathing became too ragged and my heart raced out of control.

'Harley, please wait.'

I stopped but didn't turn around to look at Zach.

'Here, put these on.' A pair of thongs landed near my feet, and I slipped into them as Zach spoke. 'Will there ever be a day where you won't surprise me?'

He asked the question, but I wasn't meant to answer.

'I hope not,' Zach continued. 'I don't know what this is between us, but I would like to. I'd like to spend some time with you and see where this goes.'

'Okay,' I told him with a small smile, happy that he'd opened up to me in the tiniest of ways.

'Good, it's settled then. Now do you want to see the best part of this property?' The grin on Zach's face was ginormous.

I nodded my head, and a jubilant Zach led the way with my hand in his through the rest of his backyard and down a little track just behind his bar. He whistled for Abby to follow, and we walked the one hundred metres down to a little piece of cleared beach that led to the river. Abby ran right past us and straight into the water. That dog was crazy. The water must be anything but warm.

'This is paradise,' I told Zach. 'But your dog is nuts, that water must be freezing.'

'She's a little crazy,' he admitted of his dog. 'But you should try the water.'

I walked towards the water, about to try it, when I was picked up and ceremoniously dropped into it.

'Zach!' I screeched more than screamed, surprised first by how cold it was and then by how quickly I warmed up under the water. I stayed here for a few minutes and watched him as he watched me. Thoughts of Zach filled my head, like how he would feel stretched out on top of me. That man was something, and I suddenly wished he was already mine.

I stepped out of the water completely drenched, making a beeline for Zach. Jumping on him, I covered him in my wet clothes. He caught me, and I wrapped my legs around him.

Minutes passed with my legs wrapped around his waist. The parts of me that touched him felt delightful, felt like I belonged right there in his arms. I wanted to resist the urge to kiss him, but I couldn't. There was a need in me that wanted to know if the zap of electricity would always be there. As I moved my lips closer to his, I was one breath away when Zach spun us around away from the river to dump me into the sand.

Air escaped my lungs as he pressed his body on top of mine, but my legs weren't wrapped around him anymore. I was flat against the sand, and his lips were close to my ear when I heard, 'Harley, you feel so good. I want to taste you, all of you.' I knew he meant the feel of my body against his, and while his body felt so damn good against mine, I knew this wasn't the right time or place for intimacy. It had been some time since I'd been intimate with a man.

But did I want to resist? I was trapped under Zach and on top of the sand, yet while he felt good against me, the sand didn't. Even though I didn't want to stay here forever, I did want this moment to last a little longer.

I felt the brush of Zach's lips on my skin and his hardness press against my pubic bone. Then his lips were at my ear again when he said, 'I'm going to make the first move, Harley, make no mistake. And when I do, you'll feel so good, and it will be for keeps.'

I felt tingles run through my body and hit my sex as his words registered in my brain. My panties were wet and not just from the river. Then as if it never happened, the tingles disappeared as Zach's body was gone from mine. My body was unhappy at the loss of his touch, but he didn't notice. He just took hold of my hands and pulled me up off the sand. As soon as I was steady on my feet, he let go of my hands, turned towards the house and walked away.

Maybe Zach thought I was one step behind him, even though we were both lost in thought. Would he look over his shoulder to notice I wasn't there? I didn't blame him for being lost in thought: first he'd kissed me then I pulled away, and then when I wanted to kiss him, he'd dumped me in the sand. Had I confused Zach by not knowing what I wanted?

I willed my legs to move, but they didn't. I stood there shaking, a little from the cold water all over my body and a little from the loss of body contact. In my mind, I replayed the words he'd whispered to me, and the feeling of our chemistry. There was positively something between us, something familiar with a dash of the unknown. I hoped that my haste to get away from Melbourne didn't make me regret my snap decision to blow off steam in this little country town on the Murray River.

I shook what sand I could get off me, but I was wet so not much came off. Only a shower would get it all. I tried not to think about what had just happened between my legs and the wetness that had pooled there when Zach had laid his body over mine and pressed against me. But a rush of excitement flowed through my veins, and I almost felt giddy. My connection with Zach was something that had never happened before, and now I wanted more. My body wanted more.

Sex wasn't new to me. I had lost my virginity and even tried a few one-night stands, but had only been going through the motions. I didn't feel anything compared to how Zach had just made me feel. After I'd blacked out that night on stage five years ago, I shut down completely to focus on work. Sex was the last thing I'd thought about or had time for.

I made my way back from the river through the backyard and up to the house to see Zach at his kitchen door. Abby was by his side, my coffee cup in his hand. He'd waited for me. I stripped out of my sandy clothes and wiped what sand I could off my body with my tee-shirt as I reached the veranda, thankful I was still dressed in my underwear.

I gave the tee-shirt a shake and threw it over my shoulder. As I walked up to the kitchen door, I felt Zach's eyes on me, on the parts of me that were naked. Did he like what he saw? My curvy pasty-white body. His eyes lingered on my body but then moved back to my face. As stoic as Zach was at times, and as much as I wanted to believe he gave nothing away, when my eyes snagged Zach's, I saw the arousal in them from our moment on the sand.

Nine

'What are your plans for today?' I threw at Zach, but what I really wanted to know as I stood at the edge of the kitchen was what his plans were for me today.

'Work,' he replied over his shoulder as he crossed the threshold into his bedroom.

'Do you work every day?' I asked as I followed him to the same threshold, curious to know more about the man in front of me.

'Just the days that end in Y,' Zach told me in a serious tone, and I wanted to laugh, I really did, but I didn't. I couldn't help the smile though that played across my lips. He didn't want to give anything away. I wasn't sure why there was so much mystery with this man.

'Actually, I need to go in to work today.' Zach turned around, faced me and stepped closer, then took my hand and pulled me into his bedroom. When I was close enough, his other hand reached for my face and cupped my cheek. Then his hand slid down my skin to rub circles at the base of my neck. In a whisper close to my ear Zach said, 'Because you haven't paid me yet.'

There was nothing to say. Zach was right. I hadn't paid him.

Zach's hands moved up to my face, both thumbs brushing my cheekbones, and I felt my whole body shiver. Then his touch was gone as he disappeared into the shower. I melted every time Zach was close to me, and I wondered if it would always feel this good, whatever this was. But I told myself not to get my hopes up and not to fall too hard. This may only last as long as I was here, and if that was the case, I may not be ready to leave just yet.

I knew we still needed to talk and that I needed to explain more than a few things. Then Zach appeared beside me, hair wet and wrapped in a towel. He had showered already, and I questioned how long I had spaced out for. Everything I wanted to know about Zach, I was sure he wanted to know about me.

'I'll leave you to shower,' Zach told me and just like a gentleman, he intended to leave me alone. 'There's a towel on the sink for you.'

'But…' It was all I got to say. I wanted to protest, but I didn't really know what to say. I guess Zach really did need a minute to himself.

My head told me this might be where I take my bags and go back to Melbourne. My heart, though, beat away as if it knew nothing but what it had done for the last ten years, yearn for a future that would never be with my parents and my sister or the boy I'd lived next door to.

I spun myself around to grab my bag and wondered how I would tell Zach who I was and that he had more than one piece of my heart. And had for a long time. When I reached for my bag in search of clothes, a brown paper bag at the end of the bed caught my eye. I debated whether to look inside but couldn't help myself. I reached inside the bag to find a pretty watermelon-coloured maxi dress. I pulled it out to find there was underwear hidden under the dress.

'This man can buy me clothes anytime,' I told myself, especially if they looked as good as this dress. I was curious as to when Zach had had time to buy me clothes, both the tee-shirt dress I had worn down to the river and now this watermelon maxi dress. But I had gone back to sleep in the hotel room and had woken up alone to a note that had told me not to go anywhere. Was that plenty of time for Zach to purchase me clothes?

I didn't know why he had bought me new clothes when the clothes from my car were right next to the bed. The gesture was sweet, and it let me know he cared. I pulled my denim jacket from my bag and laid the maxi dress out on the bed then took the underwear with me into the bathroom.

I showered, maybe not as quickly as Zach, but this was not the time to take things slowly either. I rinsed the sand from my skin, and with the help of my own toiletries, I lathered beauty products from top to toe and rinsed off. I washed my hair with Zach's shampoo and conditioner, the one thing I'd forgotten in my rush to get out of town.

When all the sand was gone from my hair and skin, I turned off the shower and dried off. I rushed through my beauty routine and admitted my beauty products made me feel like a princess again. Slipping into my underwear, I then got dressed before standing in front of the bathroom mirror.

The dress was pretty and comfortable, and I confessed to myself it did look damn good on me. I applied make-up that was softer than I had previously worn, and I felt the most comfortable in my own skin than I had in a very long time. My hair I tied into a messy bun. Now I was ready.

I opened the bedroom door to see Zach seated on his lounge, phone in hand. He hadn't heard the bedroom door open, and for the shortest of moments, I got to check him out. He was dressed in light blue jeans, boots and a black tee-shirt. Zach looked good, and his armour tattoo (that I hoped I would one day be able to trace my fingertips along) played peek-a-boo at the edge of his tee-shirt. Zach hadn't shaved since I'd been here, and I had to admit facial hair looked good on him.

He looked perfect, surrounded by everything that was his, while I stood in the middle of his lounge wanting the level of comfort he had. I moved forward slowly towards him, and he must have sensed my presence as his eyes landed on mine.

'Wow!' I heard, and there was no music today. I wasn't singing. So, the 'wow' wasn't for my voice. It must be for me and the way I looked.

'You blow me away with how beautiful you are.' Zach's face lit up, and his eyes sparked with both warmth and desire.

It wasn't just his closeness that could make me come undone, now his words were having the same effect. My heated stare caught Zach's own as he told me again how beautiful I was. This time, I didn't move or look away from him.

'Harley.' Zach had come around behind me and wrapped his arms around me. He took hold of my hands and pulled my back to his chest. His skin was warm against mine, and I felt my skin spark from our contact. The rush that coursed through me was immediate. When my body relaxed into his, the spark travelled over my skin, through my veins and left me with sensations I hadn't experienced before. No way near as intensely, anyway. Was this what true desire felt like?

I felt Zach's stubble brush down my neck and along my shoulder. I shivered at how he felt on my skin and breathlessly said, 'This dress…' My words were just above a whisper.

'Is absolutely gorgeous,' Zach finished. 'And it looks good on you. I knew you would be more comfortable if you had clean clothes.'

Zach was right. I appreciated the clean clothes. 'Thank you,' I told him. 'For this dress. For this weekend. I'm grateful you didn't leave me passed out in the bar.'

'You're welcome.' Zach's lips were against my ear, and I melted again from the inside out. His voice, his touch, turned me into a puddle of goo.

'Are you ready?' Zach was still behind me. 'I need to go into the bar.'

'Right. I need to pay you.' I was still lost in Zach's touch. The sparks from our contact had made its way to my pussy. Wet heat pooled between my legs the same as at the river. This time, I was left with an ache. A longing for his touch. My body, starved of attention over the years, craved more of what Zach could give me. Leaving me to think that only Zach could soothe my ache. This intense desire was something I had never felt before with any of my other partners, but was something I definitely wanted more of.

'Babe,' he said into my ear. 'You and I have a date at the bar, but it isn't so you can pay me. Though I will return your card when we get there.' He turned me around, and I felt my mouth form that perfect O when he said, 'There's a band up from

Melbourne to play today's Sunday session, and I need to go in to make sure everything is okay.'

I followed Zach through the house and out the front door, where I was surprised by the sight of my car that was parked next to his truck.

'Zach?' My eyes darted between my grey Impreza hatchback and the man next to me, before I threw my one raised eyebrow at him in question. 'How did my car get here?'

'Harley, I had your car brought out here. I couldn't very well leave it parked at the bar. Anything could have happened to it.'

My insides did a happy dance. I guess this meant I got to stay here a little longer.

'Come on.' He took my hand and led me towards his truck.

Once we were buckled in, Zach passed over my phone and keys. He reached for my hand to kiss my fingertips before he turned the key to his truck and his engine started to rumble. The sound soothed me. He pulled away from the spot next to my car and drove towards town and the bar.

The ride back to the bar was part dirt road, part bitumen. I paid attention to my surroundings this time. We weren't that far out of town, I realised as Zach drove towards Melbourne Road, the main street of Mulwala. Zach turned right at the roundabout and headed towards Black's Bar and Grill, where it sat on the bend on the Murray River. It had only felt longer when Zach had brought me to his house because I'd had other things on my mind.

As he drove down Bayly Street, we were first surrounded by bush as we travelled along the dirt road. Once we hit the bitumen, the bush started to disappear and was replaced by houses on one side and the high school on the other. When Zach turned onto Melbourne Road, we passed houses and the caravan park that backed onto the river on one side. The other side was a combination of necessities this country town had to offer, like food, money and clothes along with a couple of motels and the mini-golf course. Peering through the windows of Zach's truck, I found myself realising I wanted my own piece of paradise just like Zach's piece of paradise.

'Hey, are you okay?' Zach reached for my hand. He must have sensed me thinking.

'Sure.' I didn't want to tell him the truth. Some truths were just too hard to admit too.

'Harley?' But damn it, this man made it tough to stay silent.

'I'm fine, Zach, really.' How did I explain to this man what I had only just realised. There was a moment's silence between us before I continued, because I knew he wouldn't let anything between us go. 'I don't want to go back.' There went the spanner into the works. Then I added. 'To my family, to my life in Melbourne, not the bar.'

Zach breathed out a sigh of relief. 'Harley.'

'I'm not on the run, Zach…'

'Harley.' The sharpness in his voice made me turn my head and look at him. 'It's okay, you don't have to go back to your family or the city.'

'I want to stay here.' My voice was barely audible. Now that I had spent some time here, I wanted what Zach had. A balance between work and life.

Zach stared at me for a moment. I thought he'd heard what I'd said but I wasn't so sure. Then he said, 'We'll work it out, if you don't want to go back.' His lips curled up on his handsome face, and it made me think he wanted me to stay. If only it were that simple.

Ten

Zach parked his truck, and the rumble of the engine stopped. He turned to me, his eyes giving me the once over, and I shivered as he took me in. Maybe he was happy I wanted to stay. His lips danced upward, and I came a little undone; the happiness on his face was infectious, and I couldn't help my own grin.

'Come on, Harley, if we hurry, we can sneak in unnoticed and have lunch together.' We rushed towards the front entrance.

I was right behind him as he pulled me through the front doors, but as soon as we reached the concierge desk, a male voice called out Zach's name. Damn the person who had called out his name about to take my time with him away.

But Zach was a wanted man, and with an apologetic look on his face, he said, 'Sorry, babe, duty calls.' Then he was gone, and I was left to my own devices.

'Great, I guess the grand tour is out,' I mumbled to myself, only slightly jaded I had been left alone at the entrance to Black's Bar and Grill.

'Andy won't be long,' someone said from behind me, and I turned around to face the voice.

'I'm sorry?' I said to the brunette behind the desk. I was the only one here, I was the only one she could be talking to.

'Andy is on his way up, and he won't be long.'

'Okay,' I had no idea who Andy was.

'Ms James?' I heard from behind me. I turned around at the sound of my name. At the stranger calling me 'Ms James'. They would only know my surname if they were holding my debit card in their hand. Did that mean Zach had seen my debit card and the surname on it? 'Ms James?' The deep male voice said again. 'My name is Andy.'

He was dressed in all black with the Black's Bar and Grill logo on the shirt, and the name tag confirmed the man was who he said he was.

'Harley,' I told Andy. 'You can call me Harley, please.'

'Harley, right, well, I'm head of security here at Black's Bar and Grill and Mr Black…' Okay, now wasn't the time to be surprised about the connection between the man and the bar. Zach had after all told me he was a businessman.

'You mean Zach?'

Andy gave me a quizzical look at the question I asked. Andy wasn't to know how complicated things were between Zach and me.

'Yes, Mr Black…' Andy repeated, which confirmed the suspicion I'd had all along.

'Oh my God!' I exclaimed then shut my mouth. No one wanted to stare at a goldfish with an opened mouth. I took a deep breath and a moment to process. Did all of Black's Bar and Grill belong to Zach? Or did he co-own the business? Either way, Zach had done alright for himself.

'Mr Black,' the man in front of me had said three times now, 'would like me to give you the grand tour of his business as he is otherwise occupied.'

'Wow,' I told myself. I was a little astounded. Zach was more than the bartender he portrayed to be behind the bar the night I'd passed out. But I wasn't really surprised because we didn't know each other and we both had secrets. I nodded my head in response to Andy, and the grand tour was underway.

The entry to Black's Bar and Grill had a long concierge desk to direct customers to their destinations. Everyone who came here had to walk through the same doors I just did, the same doors I'd walked through two nights ago.

'Ms James.'

I gave Andy a hard stare and a quick shake of my head.

'Sorry, Harley, this building has three levels and is split into six rooms. And if you will follow me?'

I followed Andy through automatic doors to the rooftop beer garden called The Graphite Bar.

'The beer garden, I believe you are familiar with,' Andy said to me.

I nodded. This was where I'd drunk myself under the table, or bar, which would be more appropriate. The Graphite Bar had a hut that served alcohol, a stage big enough for acoustic music and plenty of seats for a relaxed crowd.

'I also believe you are familiar with The Diamond Hotel.' Andy walked to the far end of the beer garden that overlooked the hotel. I followed and peered over the edge at the fifteen-room hotel. The hotel met the bar at a right angle; both overlooked lush green grass and the river.

Opposite The Graphite Bar, on the other side of the concierge desk, Andy directed me towards what sounded like a lot of loud noises. But as we moved closer, I could see the roadies about to set up the band for their gig this afternoon.

'This is The Carbon Bar, and all our headliners from the Melbourne play here,' Andy informed me. 'Occasionally, Zach hosts one of his events in there too.'

I peeked in through the double glass doors that others would rush through later today to see the band from the Melbourne. The stage, big enough to hold a full band, was set to the left-hand side of the rooftop opposite a long, slim bar. I kept my eyes peeled for Zach, but he was nowhere to be seen.

Andy led me down a set of stairs behind the concierge desk to Pepper Grill.

'This is the restaurant, Harley,' Andy pointed out to me.

Even though I could see the sign overhead that told me where we were, and the restaurant-style tables and chairs through the clear glass windows, I didn't think Andy would lead me inside, but he did.

I followed him, through the empty restaurant to the kitchen.

'This,' Andy extended his arm out and waved it around for effect, 'is Pepper's state-of- the-art kitchen.'

I was impressed by the clean lines and stainless steel. There was a comfortableness that I could cook in if ever I was able to let loose in here. The workers carried on with their shift, oblivious that Andy and I were even there.

We left the kitchen and restaurant and walked across the hall to the Midnight Wine Bar. As we walked through the doors to the bar, I noticed that there was a relaxed feel here. Comfortable seats and low lighting gave off a romantic atmosphere. I almost stopped Andy to ask if we could put our feet up and enjoy a glass of wine, but something told me he wanted this tour over with. And to add to my disappointment, there was no one behind the bar to serve me my wine.

There was one more level to see and two more rooms left. We moved down the stairs to the bottom level of Zach's business. Walking straight past a hallway on our right that seemed private, my curiosity piqued when Andy didn't mention it. As we walked past on our way to the nightclub, I wondered if that was where Zach's office was. Something I told myself I would explore later.

Onyx Nightclub was in front of me and the Charcoal Lounge behind me. Andy moved towards the nightclub entrance, and I followed. The nightclub was one big empty room with a DJ booth at the far end and a stage big enough for acoustic sessions beside it. There were three pool tables opposite the stage with bars on the other two sides, and in the middle was one large dance floor. Intrigued by the unknown, I wondered how often the nightclub was open.

The Charcoal Lounge was the last room to view, and it wasn't open to the public. It was a function room for hire, and beyond the glass bi-fold doors was a deck that overlooked the Murray River, with a private bar that led out to a large green grass paddock for outside entertainment.

'This concludes your tour, Harley. Now if you will excuse me, I have other matters to attend to.' I could sense Andy's relief. 'Before I go, Graphite is the only business open at the moment while we set up the band from Melbourne. You are welcome to move around Black's Bar and Grill as you please, but it would be preferable if you stay here in the lounge.'

'No problem.'

But Andy continued as if I hadn't spoken. 'The kitchen staff have been instructed to prepare some food for you and bring it down shortly, oh and before I forget, Mr Black has requested me to give you back your debit card.' Andy handed over my card, but I didn't dare ask if my tab had been paid.

'Thank you for the tour,' I told Andy before he slipped out of the function room door and back the way we came.

I turned around and took in the Charcoal Lounge. There was a large oval wooden table with twelve seats, lounges to relax on, and a simple straight-line kitchen to prepare food and drinks. This lounge was private and very quiet. Everything in this room was black, the chairs, the lounge, even the kitchenette and the appliances. Only the oval table was made of pine and contrasted the room perfectly. Even with all the dark colours in this room, it didn't feel heavy with light shining through all the panes of glass.

It was now mid-afternoon, and I stood in front of the glass doors and stared outside at the sun as it shined off the river. I was so lost in thought that I didn't even hear the kitchen staff when the food was brought in.

It hadn't escaped me throughout the entire tour how modern each room was and how everything centred on the colour black. The names of the rooms and the colours in each room were all different shades of black. No two rooms were the same style, and no two rooms had the same atmosphere. I wondered if it was Zach's choice to brand himself that way or not.

As I turned away from the glass doors, I saw the kitchen staff had left the food they were instructed to bring down on the table: a chicken and salad wrap and a bowl of fruit salad. I didn't think I would be hungry after the breakfast that Zach had made, but I couldn't pass up delicious-looking food.

I sat down at the oval table and rested my mobile phone in front of me. There had been no more messages from my sister, my mother or my grandparents, and for that, I was relieved. I ate the chicken wrap and picked away at the fruit salad, wondering how long I would be here. I wanted to go in search of Zach, but knew he was busy.

And then as if he knew he was in my thoughts, my phone buzzed silently with a text message.

Z: Hey, babe.

H: Mr Cute Bartender or should I say Mr Black?

Z: Ms James is better than Ms Bakery Manager.

H: So formal. I guess there's a lot we don't know about each other.

Did he roll my full name off his tongue, through his lips? Did he like what he heard as he said my name? Could he believe after ten years that I was back in his orbit again?

I had already rolled the name Zach Black around in my head. But I was yet to push his full name through my lips. As I said his name out loud it was if Zach was standing behind me whispering in my ear. That sensation ran through me now, and I couldn't deny how much I liked it.

Z: I know your name, got your number. I know there's more to the woman who passed out in my bar, and I'd like you to share it with me.

H: What do I get in return for sharing with you?

Z: Anything you want? I'm an open book?

H: Open book, huh? Do I even want to know how you got my number?

Z: No.

Okay, I told myself, but I wasn't overly surprised he had my number; there had been plenty of times he'd easily had access. I had never bothered putting a lock on my phone before. But that was about to change. I scrolled through my settings and set a pin.

I saved his name to his number and let Zach Black roll off my tongue a couple more times. I was happy to be right where I was.

Z: How was the tour?

H: The one I thought you would take me on?

Z: Harley.

H: Okay. Black's Bar and Grill is incredible. You have done a great job with everything.

Z: Thank you. How was lunch?

H: Good, but it would have been even better if you were here.

Z: I'm sorry, babe.

H: It's no big deal. How long are we here today?

The question I asked received no response and I wasn't even surprised. Once the fruit salad was gone, I decided to go in search of something to drink. I texted Zach as he still hadn't replied.

H: I take it your non-response means I'm here for a while. Well, if that's the case, I'm off to find something to drink. The beer garden looks good.

Eleven

I washed my dishes in the kitchenette sink of the Charcoal Lounge and left them to dry. Then I went in search for what was down the hallway Andy and I passed. There were three doors, and all of them were locked. No surprises there. None of the doors had names on them, so I was left wondering what was behind each door. Behind one door had to be Zach's office, the other two at my best guess would have to be a cashier's room and the security room.

Once I had entertained my curiosity, I climbed the two flights of stairs to the beer garden. Walking through the glass doors and over to the bar to order a drink, I handed over my card to pay, but the bartender shook his head.

'It's on the house,' I was informed. He was dressed in the same uniform as Andy from security and Zach from the morning I'd awoken in the hotel room.

'Thank you.' I nodded my appreciation.

I took my drink from the bar and wandered through the crowd. It had started to build for the band from Melbourne that would entertain on this afternoon's Sunday session. I found a spot at the edge of the beer garden that overlooked the river. The late afternoon sun washed over me and danced over the water, and the view from here was magical. I took a seat amongst the crowd, sipped my wine and got lost in my phone as I let the background music surround me.

'Harley James?' I heard from not too far away.

I looked up from my phone at the mention of my name. When I turned my head in the direction of the voice, I raised my eyebrow in question.

The woman who now stood in front of me said, 'Zach texted me. He said you would be here in the bar and that I couldn't miss you in your watermelon maxi dress.'

It took me a few seconds before the connection clicked. She was tall and lean with dark features that resembled the appearance of her older brother. It was Lex Black.

'He sent you to check up on me?'

There was a companionable silence between us, but her smirk and raised eyebrow said she knew more than she let on.

'How long has it been, Harley?'

It was a reference to my absence from this town, my disappearance from the face of this earth.

'Ten years, Lex.' I reached out, and she wrapped me up in her embrace.

'It's good to see you.'

'It's good to see you too.' I reached for my almost empty glass of wine.

Lex signalled the bartender for more drinks, then she pulled the chair out next to me and we both sat down. A moment later, drinks were placed in front of both Lex and me.

'What brings you to town?' Zach's younger sister asked as she sipped her wine. Her name was Alex Black, but everyone called her Lex. Lex was the same age as Addison, twenty-four. Fifteen months younger than me. We'd lived next door to each other for about twelve months while we waited for my Dad to unravel his grand plans. Zach was older than me, but I hadn't known about his even older brother Connor back then. I'd never met him, all I'd known from Zach was that Connor had already left for Melbourne.

'I just wanted to blow off steam,' I admitted to the youngest Black sibling as I brought my glass to my lips and drank my wine.

'And you chose here, of all the places you could have gone?'

I watched as Lex barely contained her scoff. She had a carefree attitude the same as Addison.

'Uh huh,' was the best answer I was prepared to give. Of all the things I needed to say and explain, Lex wasn't the person I wanted to have that conversation with.

'Must have been some steam?' There was a questioning look on her face, and I wondered if being able to raise a single eyebrow was a Black family trait. Who did they learn their signature move from because both Zach and Lex raised their brow in exactly the same way?

'It's complicated.' It was a two-word answer that only spelled trouble but it was all I was willing to explain to Zach's sister.

'Uh huh,' was the response Lex gave.

Was it written on my face that there was more to say? As much as I tried to be as stoic as Zach, I wasn't sure if I was pulling it off. Either way, Lex didn't push for more information.

'You know, your brother said the same thing,' I smirked. 'About the steam.'

'You and Zach, huh? He always did have a soft spot for you since the first time you knocked on our door.' She told me like it was a secret and I needed to know it. 'You know he wouldn't let anyone answer the door when you knocked? Zach insisted from the first day you came to get Addison.' Lex laughed as she walked down her own memory lane. 'Addison and I always tried to spy on you two. But all you did was talk and hold hands. Addison and I were like, hurry up and kiss.'

I shook my head in disbelief that my sister and her next-door neighbour best friend had spied on Zach and me. But Lex just nodded her head.

'So,' I pursed my lips together. 'Is Black's Bar and Grill a family business?' My eyebrow shot up in question and I wondered how easily I had deflected from talking about Zach and I spending time together back then.

'It's all Zach's,' she said matter-of-factly.

I was impressed. I really had no idea who Zach Black had turned out to be.

'Yeah. Zach decided to stay here while the rest of the family moved to Melbourne. He's worked hard to build Black's Bar and Grill up to what it is today.'

Lex and I finished our wines before she hugged me goodbye and slipped into the crowd that had built up around the bar.

I collected my phone and empty glass and made my way back to the bar for another wine when I was stopped by someone who stood a little too close.

'Well, well, well, if it isn't Harley James.' The voice that said those words made my skin crawl. I already knew by the bad vibes that Connor Black was behind me.

Connor's hand landed on my shoulder with a hard grip, which I was sure would leave a bruise, and I was thankful my phone and wine glass were in my other hand. He pulled my shoulder back, and I had no option but to turn around. I was now face to face with the eldest Black sibling.

I wanted to stand my ground and tell him to fuck off, but I didn't even get a chance to open my mouth. Zach now stood right behind Connor.

'Let her go, Connor.' His voice had an edge to it. I had grown to love the timbre of it.

'Stay out of this, Zach. This is between Harley and me.' Connor's voice was no match for Zach's, but his hand hadn't left my shoulder.

'I said let her go, Connor.'

'You ghosted me, Harley. What the fuck?' Connor continued talking to me, ignoring Zach.

Before I could open my mouth, Zach was talking again. 'Let her go and get the fuck out. You're not welcome here.' Zach's voice still held its edge but was so calm. His manner, however, screamed, 'I will hurt you in a heartbeat.'

Connor made no move to relieve the pressure on my shoulder. I stared at Zach and tried not to wince at the pain I felt. I could see his eyes communicate with me to wait a moment longer. Then Zach moved aside, and security stepped up to pull Connor towards the exit.

'Harley.'

Two strong masculine arms wrapped around me and I realised Zach had pulled me against his chest in one swift motion. I hadn't blacked out, but something else was happening to me and didn't know what was going on. 'Let's get out of here.' His voice was a soft caress in my ear that I melted into.

I moved my hands to his chest. 'Zach, I'd like to stay for a while longer if your brother is gone and not allowed back in. I'd love to have a few drinks and a dance.'

'Okay, Harley.' Zach kissed the shell of my ear. 'Come on, let's go.' There was a look on his face, and I knew he wasn't completely unhappy that my body would be close to his on the dance floor.

Zach grabbed my hand, entwined our fingers and pulled me away from the beer garden, past the long reception desk and into the Carbon Bar. Once we were through the glass doors, I saw how many people had shown up for this afternoon's show.

There were people everywhere waiting either for a drink or for the band to start their show. The Carbon Bar wasn't quiet as there was a DJ next to the main stage, and his music filled the late afternoon air. Zach walked us straight up to the bar, leaned over the edge for the attention of a bartender and ordered our drinks. I wouldn't have been surprised if the amber liquid in the bottom of Zach's glass was bourbon, and by the way he swallowed it straight, it made me think there was some tension that he needed to burn off.

Zach leaned back to leave his glass on the bar. There was no way I would drink my wine that quickly. I took a slow sip as Zach pulled me away from the bar and into a space just for the two of us as we faced the stage. I stood next to him, and it didn't take long for his arm to wrap around my shoulder and for me to be stuck to his side and tucked under his arm.

Now it was time to dance. Not once in the whole time we were together were we interrupted. Everyone knew Zach was off duty, both the customers and his staff. Zach and I sang, danced and drank through two of the band's three sets before I was pulled out the front doors and into his truck.

'Sorry, babe,' Zach said to me once he started the engine. 'It's been a long day and I'm tired as fuck, so we need to go home.'

I turned and took in the man next to me as he reversed out of his car park, and I smiled. 'We didn't have to stay as long as we did.'

'You had a good time?' Zach asked and smiled back at me. He shifted his truck into drive, and we were on our way back to his house.

'I had a great time,' I told him, then I told myself that it was okay to close my eyes for a minute.

Twelve

'Harley,' Zach whispered, gently waking me. 'I have to go into work for a few hours, I'll be back later.'

'Hmm,' I murmured when Zach kissed my forehead goodbye, not registering anything he had told me.

I woke up more than a little confused. I must have fallen asleep in the truck. I guess Zach hadn't been the only one who was tired as fuck. I breathed in – his scent was all around me – and I knew exactly where I was, but I was unsure how I got here.

Undressed and in Zach's bed, and I hadn't stirred once. I didn't know it was possible for me to relax that much. The part of the bed where Zach had slept was now empty as he'd gone to work, so I rolled over to it, catching the hint of bourbon and cedar as I stretched out.

Then I remembered Zach's warm lips on my forehead. He had whispered he was going into work. I was relieved he'd let me stay here and hadn't dragged me out of bed to go with him. After last night, I could do with a little me time. The same way Zach could do with a little alone time.

Zach could have put me in one of the spare rooms he had in his house, but he didn't, and that made me feel warm and fuzzy from my skin through to my bones. He'd laid me down right next to him, and I was only a little freaked out at how comfortable I felt right now. I wasn't used to this level of comfort, but I could get used to it and wake up here every morning right next to him and be the happiest woman in the world.

I got up, went through the motions, made the bed, showered and stared at my shoulder in the mirror before I dressed in comfortable clothes. There was no bruise, just a dull ache. I wished I could have found my words last night to tell Connor I wasn't interested in any business he thought he had with me before I told him to fuck off. But the memory of Zach as he'd stood right behind Connor last night made my heart skip a beat.

I would never want to piss Zach off intentionally, which Connor must have done by the way Zach spoke to him. Zach had stood up for me against his own brother, so I must not be the only one who thought Connor was an arsehole. We both had our reasons, and we had both come to the same conclusion about Connor. I guess both of us had dealt with a bad experience when it came to him.

I dragged my thoughts away from last night and focused on the here and now. I moved to the kitchen with the need to scratch an itch only a baker knew how to soothe. A job I thought I would enjoy as I'd worked alongside my grandfather, the best in the business. Only because I'd wanted to follow in my father's footsteps, to carry on the family tradition and be well compensated. But in the last five years, it had turned into my family relying on me to singlehandedly keep the business afloat. I didn't want to do that anymore. If I had learnt anything from being here and not at work, it was that there was more to life. Now more than ever I needed a balance. I know my Groundhog Day started ten years ago and I'd been going along with it because that was my way of coping with the upheaval in my life. But there had to be a better way to live and a better way to cope with everything that came my way.

It had been three days since I'd left and three days since I had been under the pump to perform, to be perfect, to bake my little heart out and then, at the end of the day, balance the books. With a bit of time away from the pressure, I felt I could bake at a casual pace, and a smile spread on my face.

I found a small radio in this relaxing kitchen and turned it on. The station played a mixture of country and pop. I smiled to myself at what I heard, it was good stuff, and I let the rhythm from the speakers fill the kitchen. I made scrambled eggs for breakfast as I danced around in search of ingredients to make a few of my favourite easy recipes: bread, muffins and pastry for apple pie.

Once breakfast was eaten, I went in search of something to make for dinner. I found a chest freezer full of goodies in the laundry. I reached for mince in the hope there was enough food in the pantry to make spaghetti. I was surprised to find the pantry was well stocked with everything I needed, and I wondered how much this man let loose and cooked for himself.

I spent the first part of the day engrossed in baked goods. Secretly, I hoped that Zach would walk in at any moment and smell what I could smell right now. The bread was first on my list to be made, as it took the longest amount of time. It needed to be given time to rise.

Next was the pastry that would be the base for my apple pie. I threw all the dry ingredients into a bowl and stirred like crazy until it resembled what I wanted it to look like. I added egg and water then worked the mixture into a dough and before too long, it was a mound wrapped up in the fridge.

My bread had risen to perfection, and it was time to get it ready to bake. I kneaded the dough and let it stand again. While I waited for my bread dough, I made muffins, and banana muffins were my favourite. They were quick and easy, and with the over-ripe bananas on the kitchen bench, I couldn't let them go to waste or pass up the opportunity to make this favourite.

Once the muffins were golden on top, the bread was ready to be placed in the oven. While the muffins cooled on their rack and I waited for my bread, I got to work on my spaghetti sauce. I fried the mince, cut the onion, and added the garlic, the tomatoes, the tin soup and a few secret ingredients that would make the taste pop.

By the time I had the spaghetti sauce brought down to a simmer, the bread was ready to come out of the oven. I turned it out on to the wire rack alongside the muffins to cool and got to work on the apples for my pie. They needed to be cut thinly and evenly for my recipe to work, and as my pastry wasn't quite ready, I placed the apples in the fridge for later.

I cleaned up the mess I'd made in the kitchen while I sang along to the radio. 'Now what's a girl to do?' I asked myself. No way did I want to stay inside all day.

With my goodies baked and my spaghetti sauce on the stove, no word from Zach and an afternoon to kill, I went in search of something to do. I could sit down and teach myself to play the guitar I'd found at the other end of Zach's house, or I could go for a swim in the pool in his backyard or sunbake on the lounge by the pool to try and tan my pasty-white skin.

I could choose a book from the study and curl up on the lounge or I could relax on the sand down by the river, but I didn't do any of that. I decided to go for a walk instead. It would clear my head. I knew the exercise and fresh air would do me good.

I stepped out of the glass kitchen doors to find it was a beautiful sunny day, and Abby was curled in a ball with the sun on her. She looked up as I slid the door closed, curiosity on her cute little face.

'I'm off to explore,' I told the canine next to me. 'Want to go for a walk?' She got to her feet and turned in a circle a couple of times. I guessed that meant yes.

Abby and I walked through the backyard and down to a stretch of river that was sandy and clear of bush and scrub where access to the water was easy. We walked along the sandy edge of the river in one direction for as long as we could before we had no other choice but to turn around.

Walking back the way we came, past the path leading to Zach's backyard, we continued for as long as we could until there was another choice to be made: Go back the way we came to Zach's house or continue up a path away from the river that led into the unknown. I turned and took in the view around me, and as I wasn't ready to go back just yet, I chose the unknown.

It was a dirt track that Abby and I walked up. The bush got thicker around us as we walked away from the river. Abby and I continued up the path until we reached a cleared piece of land just like Zach's, and I thought to myself that this must be the neighbour he'd told me about.

I stopped at the end of the dirt track and looked around at what seemed to be the next-door neighbour's yard. I glanced towards the house and wondered if I was about to trespass and if someone was about to warn me off with an axe in tow. It seemed too quiet here, so somehow, I didn't think so.

I moved away from the cover of the thick scrub and stepped further into the yard and closer to the bungalow. The place looked abandoned, like it had been built, and then nothing else had happened. It didn't even look like anyone had moved in.

Now the little bungalow had started to fall apart. *Such a shame,* I thought to myself. This place could be someone's piece of paradise. Or at least the piece of paradise I now seemed to be in search of. 'Was that really what I wanted?' I asked my-self. I didn't even know, but I wanted to find out.

Thirteen

'What are you doing here?' Zach asked me as he came to a stop beside me. There was worry in his voice, a genuine concern about my wellbeing.

When I found my voice, I rambled like I often did in Zach's presence. 'Abby and I went for a walk, and we ended up here. I was curious about your neighbour, this house is abandoned, then all these thoughts about my life passed through my head.'

All of a sudden, a memory from ten years ago rushed through my mind and I was right back there in the car as it spun around. I was still spinning even though the car wasn't moving. Back then, my vision had blurred as the impact shook my body, and I'd willed for the screams to stop. But everything had gone black.

My face was now wet with tears. That night my whole life had changed from carefree and happy to just moving through the motions. Would I always struggle with my emotions and racing heart? Would I ever get a handle on the sentimental mess that I was? Then I felt Zach pull me closer to him. 'I got you, I got you,' Zach said softly on repeat.

I had heard these words before, long before today and Zach's party. His hands cupped my shoulders, and my hands fisted Zach's tee-shirt when he lightly caressed my neck with his thumbs. I closed my eyes and let his touch distract me, my heartrate had slowed, and the rest of my body was almost calm as I tried to reach for the first time I had heard those words.

'You've said those words to me before.'

'Yeah, babe, I've said them to you before.' Zach embraced me a little tighter. I felt relief wash over me and relaxed into Zach's arms. 'At my party.'

I wasn't talking about his party. 'I got you, I got you,' played on a loop in my head. Those words were familiar to me. But a haziness surrounded some of the finer details of my memories. I had heard them somewhere before but I couldn't place where.

Zach kissed my forehead, then moved his arms under my legs and picked me up. He carried me down a path that wasn't beside the river but led back towards his house, with Abby right by his side. It was only when she saw the veranda that she took off to her favourite spot in the sun. Zach, though, didn't let me go. When we reached his backyard, he walked up the steps of his veranda through the glass doors into the kitchen. Only when we reached his king bed did he let me go and lay me down. I rolled onto my side and closed my eyes. I felt the bed dip beside me, and Zach's hand brushed the hair from my face.

'I'm going to run you a bath while I get dinner ready,' Zach told me as he stroked my cheekbone with his thumb.

'But I already made…' I only got to say some of the words I needed to say.

'Harley,' Zach interrupted, and the movement of his hand on my shoulder forced me to roll over and look at him. 'I know you made more than dinner, my house smells delicious, but I need to cook the pasta and heat up the sauce.' Zach then kissed my forehead before he left to run my bath while I rolled back over to my side.

It wasn't long before Zach was back to pick me up from the bed and carry me towards his bath. He stood over the bathtub with me in his arms and lowered me down fully clothed until I was entirely submerged in water, and it wasn't warm and bubbly like I thought this bath would be. The water was cold. Cold like the river water I was dumped into, but this water wasn't straight from the river, and it wasn't about to warm up.

'Zach,' I yelped and splashed water everywhere as I tried like hell to get out of the bath, but Zach kept me down with his hand on my chest. 'What the hell?' I screeched, then I shivered, the water had seeped through my clothes to my skin. I was cold and started to feel my body shut down, the shakes were bad, and my heartrate was too slow. It never beat this slowly.

'Trust me, Harley, it's for your own good,' Zach told me, and I was in half a mind to believe he was right.

I laid back, rested my head on the back of the bath and breathed. In through my nose and out through my mouth. And I did it again. And again. My body still shook from the cold water, then turned numb, but my mind was completely calm, and it felt good, like I should always feel this good. I never knew calm could feel so good.

Zach's eyes never left me, and now that my body had gone limp, he reached down to pull the plug. I watched as the water rushed out the drain and away from my body. Out the corner of my eye I could see Zach reach for the towels. All I wanted to do was peel out of these wet clothes and into something dry.

'So cold,' I managed to stammer through chattering teeth.

'I know.' Zach threw a towel over my legs. 'Can you lean forward?'

I looked up at him and shrugged.

'I need to wrap the towel around you.' He held the towel in his hands ready to wrap it around me.

I reached out, my hand landing on his forearm, and I pulled myself forward enough for the towel to land on my shoulders and fall down my back. Then Zach picked me up and carried me back to his bedroom and into his ensuite.

'You need to get out of these wet clothes, babe.' Zach placed me on the closed lidded toilet. 'I'll find you some clothes to wear.'

I peeled out of the wet tee-shirt and singlet, placed them on top of the towels. I stripped off my leggings and waited for Zach. He stood in the doorway with everything I needed in his hands. As he stared at me, there was something in his eyes that said he didn't see a cold naked mess, but rather something else. Zach dropped clothes into my lap, and I noticed they weren't my clothes.

'Zach?' His lips kissed my forehead and his hands landed on my biceps.

'Harley,' Zach whispered as he lifted my chin up so our eyes could meet.

'What the hell?' I wanted to be more than angry at Zach for his bath stunt, as normal people didn't have cold baths. But I couldn't be angry when I felt this calm. The calmest I'd felt in a long time.

I believed that Zach was only trying to help with whatever was going on with me, and I wondered where he would get an idea to use cold water as a calming mechanism. No one had ever helped me before with the many things I didn't know how to handle. Had Zach seen something no one in my family had picked up on?

'Come on, let's get you fed.' Zach tucked me under his underarm and we moved into the kitchen.

I sat on the stool at his breakfast bar, and he draped a blanket over my shoulders. I glanced into the kitchen and saw that my bread was sliced, my sauce was on to be heated up, the pasta was cooked, and I smiled to myself when I noticed a muffin was gone.

But what had got my attention was that my pastry wasn't a mound of dough in the fridge anymore. It had been rolled out into the glass dish I'd found earlier, and the apples I'd sliced had been layered over the pastry. There was even a little twist to this apple pie as there was no top layer of pastry. A sprinkle of cinnamon covered the apples and now it just needed to be cooked.

Zach dished up the spaghetti and we both sat down at his kitchen table. We ate in silence, and it wasn't until I finished that I started to feel better, a little warmer and not so washed out. And that was when I saw Zach's knuckles, an angry bruise and red broken skin. He had been in a fight, and I could only hazard a guess as to who the other person was, after the thunderous look on Zach's face last night. There was no doubt in my mind that he had paid Connor a visit.

'Did you seek Connor out?' I didn't want to be the one that drove a bigger wedge between the two Black brothers.

'I see you feel better.' Zach stated. His eyes stayed on his dinner while I stared at his sore hand.

'Zach?' I tried for calm in my voice but didn't quite get there. Zach had stuck up for me last night at Black's Bar and Grill, so why had he sought out Connor today?

'Connor's an arsehole, Harley. He won't bother you again.' Zach looked at his bruised knuckles.

Did Zach's bruised knuckles mean that he didn't like the way Connor had touched me? Or did he have other issues with his brother?

'What did you do, Zach?' I know Zach said he wouldn't let Connor get too close to me, but I didn't know Zach would hurt Connor. But having read online how mean Connor was, karma was catching up to him.

'Nothing Connor didn't deserve.'

No doubt, Zach gave Connor what he had coming to him. Not that I felt at all that sorry for him. I couldn't help but stare at Zach a little shocked. 'Please tell me what you did to your brother?'

'Connor has a black eye.' Zach still wouldn't meet my eyes. 'I gave Connor a touch up because, even though I asked him to take his hand off you, he didn't. No one gets to touch you without your permission. And we also have some other issues you don't know about.'

'Wow!' I stated, a little flabbergasted. 'I don't know what to say to that. I'm not used to someone in my corner, fighting my battles.'

Suddenly bone weary, I stepped back from the kitchen table and walked towards Zach's bedroom, stripping out of the clothes I wore except for the singlet. After turning down the doona, I got inside his king size bed and as soon as my head hit the pillow, I was asleep. These last couple of days had shown me that I could fall asleep before exhaustion took over. I wanted to fall asleep like this every night, not just while I was here at Zach's house.

Fourteen

When I woke the next morning, Zach had left for work. I decided it was time I stood up for me, stopped hiding myself away at work and made a decision about what I wanted. I knew that to do this, I needed to go back to Melbourne and talk things over with my family. I made breakfast, toast and coffee, then cleaned up the mess.

There were still dishes from last night that hadn't been washed. The apple pie had been forgotten about after the words Zach and I had shared. I turned the oven on and waited for it to heat up. I didn't want the apple pie to go to waste, so I cooked it, cut it up and then I would freeze it. If Zach was smart enough, he would figure out it was in the freezer.

All the mess I'd made was now packed away. The spaghetti, pasta and sauce were in containers now ready to be frozen. I bundled the muffins and slices of bread two at a time and found just enough room in the kitchen freezer to stow these goodies away. The oven beeped, the apple pie was ready, and I took it out to let it cool.

I wandered aimlessly around Zach's house, picking up the items that had moved out of place and putting them back. Zach's house would once again be the bachelor pad he had styled it to be. I would no longer be here, and there would be no trace I had ever been here.

I packed my bag and made Zach's bed with fresh sheets so my scent would no longer linger. The ones I'd slept on were washed and dried. New towels hung from the bathroom rails, and the old ones were washed, dried and put away. The house was immaculate, and that was my cue to leave before I could fall anymore in love with this house or the man who lived here. If my heart had a say whether to go or stay, it would choose the latter hands down. But I couldn't rely on my heart. I needed to use my head.

It was late afternoon when I put my bags in my car and for the first time since I'd arrived, got behind the wheel of my own car. It felt bizarre not to have Zach right beside me, but I needed to go and sort out my life. Was I ready for a change? Was I ready to let someone else in? As much as I wanted to stay here and as far away from Melbourne as I could, I didn't want to wear out my welcome as Zach's house guest. He had been a perfect gentleman and nothing but kind since my arrival. In return, I had often been an emotional mess and not exactly forthcoming about who I was.

I started my car, letting the engine warm after it had sat idle for the last couple of days. The sound of the engine wasn't loud enough to calm me the same way Zach's truck did, and I wondered if I was right to just leave and not face Zach with my goodbye.

Last night played on my mind as I pulled away from Zach's front veranda. He had stood up for me against his own brother. I wasn't used to having someone fight my battles. While I wanted to be angry at him for what he'd done, I was angrier at myself for not being able to fight my own battles. I braked and put my car in park. I pulled my phone from my bag and sent a text. I needed to reach out to Zach and tell him about my decision to go back to Melbourne.

H: I'm heading back to Melbourne. It's time I faced my family. Thank you for your hospitality and for showing me a great time.

With my phone back in my handbag I didn't wait for a reply. I turned my car around and followed the road back into town the same as Zach had done two days ago. Only there was no need to stop at Black's Bar and Grill today. Once I hit the black-top, I continued until I reached Melbourne Road, the main street of town. Bayly Street marked the centre of this country town, where there were several shops, two pubs and another hotel, the primary school, the service station, and supermarket. But I didn't need to turn left today for any of those. I turned right and passed what I had seen before when Zach had driven me to his establishment. There was no traffic to hold me up as I made my way over the bridge that crossed the river and out of town, down roads that turned left and right and would eventually lead me to cruise-control speed.

'Oh crap,' I swore to myself. He'd read my text. I knew that was Zach's black dot in the distance of my rear-view mirror. 'Guess that goodbye is about to happen.'

I knew this road like the back of my hand as the number of times I had travelled this stretch of road with Mum, Dad and Addison were too many to count on one hand. There was a rest stop not too far ahead. It made no sense to start a car chase when we only needed to say goodbye.

Memories of that night from ten years ago played on my mind. I didn't want my car to spin out of control, the same way our family car had spun out of control with my dad driving. My body couldn't take that sequence of events again, the shift to the left then the right as the car moved in a continuous circle, the screams and cries before I blacked out. I planned to pull over off the road and wait.

The black dot grew larger the closer it got, and just when I thought Zach was about to drive right past, he stopped in front of me with a scream of his tyres and spray of gravel. The massive black truck had barely stopped its motion forward before Zach had gotten out of it.

He stomped towards me, his jaw set to show all the hard lines of his face. The man didn't look to happy. Was he pissed I was leaving? When he read my text, did he still want to say goodbye face to face?

I debated as to whether I got out of my car or not. The vibe he sent told me he was more than pissed. I didn't hesitate then to move. I was out of my car and about to lean back against it, as naturally as one could.

'Zach?' I said just loud enough to reach his ears. His jaw eased slightly at the sound of his name. But anger radiated off him, so I waited to see what he would do.

He stood in front of me, said nothing and did the last thing I expected him to do. He stood close enough to lean into me and push me back into the door of my car and kiss me. And boy did he kiss me.

Zach kissed me in a way no other man had ever kissed me. His anger had dissolved into desire, and I instantly felt light-headed. His lips were pure softness and fit perfectly against mine, while his two hands reached up and cupped the sides of my face. Zach's body dominated mine, and I was wedged between him and my car. There was nowhere to go this time as the volt of electricity coursed through my veins. Zach took my moan as sign to move his tongue inside my mouth, and if he hadn't already had a hold of my face, my head would have fallen back against my car.

I took hold of the bottom of Zach's shirt and kissed him back. Our lips moved, our tongues danced and by the time Zach pulled away, my legs felt like jelly. If every kiss was as blissful as this, then he could kiss me anytime.

'Please don't disappear on me again.' There was a desperation in Zach's voice I had never heard before. This was not farewell, that was not a goodbye kiss.

'I have a life to sort out, and the sooner the better.' The words tasted as bitter as they sounded.

'I got your text. You don't have to do this alone, Harley, let me help you.'

Did I really want to pass up this opportunity to spend more time with Zach?

'I can't let you walk out on your job or your friends just to help me.' I stated matter-of-factly. But would it be so bad if I let Zach in?

'Harley, do you remember what I told you?' Zach asked me. His hands had moved down my body to take a hold of my hands.

'Like I could ever forget.' I locked eyes with the man who was again dressed in his all-black uniform. There was a silence between us as he waited for me to recall his words. 'I'm going to make the first move, Harley, make no mistake.' That was what he'd said. 'And when I do, you'll feel good, and it'll be for keeps.'

'I just kissed you,' Zach's husky voice informed me, his lips were so close to my ear that my legs felt like jelly again. 'Get your bags and get in the truck, babe. I'll take you to Melbourne.'

But Zach wasn't quite ready to move away from me just yet. His body still dominated mine, then he pulled me towards him and kissed me again, his beautiful warm lips against mine for the shortest of moments.

'Come on,' he said as pulled back from my mouth. 'Let's go.' This time he moved away from my body, and I took a full breath in as I willed my limbs away from their jelly-like state.

'What about my car?' I still hadn't moved from the driver's side door and that was when I saw Shea step out of Zach's truck and walk towards us.

There were two bags on the back seat of my car, so I reached in and grabbed them. When I turned around away from the door, Zach pushed it closed behind me.

'Hey,' I said to Shea, who was now in front of me.

'Hey,' she said back, giving me a quick hug around my bags. 'Take care, Harley. I'll see you soon.'

We both smiled and I knew, somehow, she was right. I knew I would see her soon.

'Take Harley's car back to my house, then get Brock to come and pick you up. Can you tell him I'm out of town for a couple of days as he'll need to watch the bar and feed Abby.' The instructions Zach gave Shea sounded like he had done this before, but he owned his own business, so he gave orders all day long. This was nothing new to him.

Zach kissed her cheek. I gave her my keys and a moment later she was gone in the opposite direction to what we would travel. I watched as my car disappeared into the distance.

Fifteen

Zach took my overnight bag in one hand as I shouldered my handbag. As my hand dropped to my side, Zach's other hand took a hold of my free hand. We moved towards the rumble of his truck, a sound I had grown to love. Zach dropped my bag onto the back seat then helped me into the passenger seat. He manoeuvred us out onto the road that would lead us to the freeway, and we continued south towards Melbourne and closer to what I needed to sort out in my life.

'It'll be okay.' Zach reached for my hand, his fingers curling around mine, before he brought them to his lips to kiss.

'I know you think that, but I still have to confront my family.' The very thought made my pulse quicken, and I didn't know if I could do this.

'We can do that together. I know I overstepped with Connor, and I'm sorry.' To hear Zach apologise said something about the way he felt about me, and I liked it.

'Together.' I shook my head in disbelief. 'We don't know each other, not really, and you don't know anything about the mess I'm in.' It was too late to take back those words. 'Oh my God. That came out mean.'

Zach squeezed my hand for my attention. 'You're right.'

I turned my head to face him. His eyes caught mine before he turned his attention back to the road. 'I don't know anything about the mess you're in. But I know who you are, Harley.'

'You do?' I asked still looking at the side of Zach's face.

Zach nodded.

'How?' I whispered. 'How do you know?'

'When I saw you seated at my bar that first night you rolled into town, I thought maybe I recognised you. Then I couldn't help but wonder why I felt a connection to you, and you seemed oddly familiar. When you passed out, I didn't want to let you out of my sight, and taking you to my birthday party meant I could spend some more time with you, talk to you and get to know you.' Zach stopped for a breath, then he smirked before he continued. 'When I was told a debit card was left behind, I was thrown for a loop when hearing the name on the card. Then all I could think of was the girl who lived next door with pigtail braids and red-framed glasses and sang with her sister and Dad every chance she got.'

So Zach had been suspicious from the moment I drank myself under the bar. 'You never said anything.'

'I was trying to wrap my head around seeing you again after all these years. You disappeared, and I told myself if I ever saw you again, I would be cautious. But after spending the last couple of days together, holding your hand and seeing your tattoo, I didn't want to be cautious anymore.' Silence filled the cab of Zach's truck, then he said, 'I don't want to let go of your hand.'

I gasped at Zach's whispered words. I liked that he didn't want to let go of my hand. I wanted to hold him as close to me as he was willing to hold me close to him.

'Zach.' It was all that came out as what else was there to say. I was not surprised Zach had seen my tattoo just above my left hip. I had stripped out of my 'Babe' tee-shirt after being covered in sand from our walk down to the river.

'You inspired me, Harley, every time we talked down the side of my house. I remembered the day I gave you my dragonfly sketch, it was the day after one flew right past us. That sketch was my first and from that day I started carrying a sketch book around with me. I would sketch the little things around me. When the land for Black's Bar and Grill came up for redevelopment, I started sketching how I wanted the bar to look.'

'That's amazing, Zach.' It was wonderful to hear that Zach had continued to sketch long after I had disappeared and had turned those sketches into inspiration for his bar. What he had done in the years I had been absent impressed me. It would be nice to be as successful as Zach and be as proud of what he'd achieved since high school. If there was one thing I knew now that I didn't know before I drove myself here was that a few things in my life were going to change.

'You have my dragonfly sketch tattooed on your hip.' Zach's words filled the cab of his truck, a hint of curiousness in his voice. Maybe Zach thought his old next-door neighbour didn't have enough courage to get a tattoo. Maybe he just wanted to know the story behind my reason for getting a tattoo in the first place.

I reminisced of a simpler time with my sister. 'Addison found your sketch amongst my things when I moved into my own place. She said I should get it tattooed on me and never have to worry about ever losing your sketch. Addison even dared me, but I knew she was just pushing me to try something new.'.

'It's beautiful,' Zach said of his sketch on my hip.

'You like it? I made the tattooist copy your dragonfly exactly as you drew it, then she inked it on my skin.' What Zach thought of my tattoo meant a lot to me.

'I love the way the tail curves with your hip, babe.' Zach still had hold of my hand. A warmness that I hadn't felt in ten years rushed through me, and I wasn't ashamed to admit that I liked it.

I took a deep breath and pushed my words out softly. 'You'll forever be a part of me.'

Zach turned his trademark raised eyebrow towards me and smirked. He liked that there was a piece of him on my skin. He gently squeezed my fingers then brought them up to his lips to kiss my fingertips again. I wasn't used to being this vulnerable in conversation or with my emotions, then I remembered Zach's lips on mine and I felt the electricity run through me again. I no longer wanted to feel vulnerable.

I wanted that spark from our kiss earlier, the feel of electricity in my veins to never fade, and I wanted to hold onto the warm and heady feeling I got when Zach was close to me. But was I bold enough to admit to Zach that I wanted to explore where this was going between the two of us? Give ourselves a chance to explore the relationship we never got to start ten years ago? I wanted to feel the rollercoaster ride of emotions I had yet to experience in my life but only wanted to with the man who sat next to me in this truck.

'When did you realise I was your old neighbour?' Zach asked as I took back my hand. I didn't care that I was letting my guard down reminiscing with Zach. All that mattered was that he was right beside me.

'Your number plate and the colour of your truck made me curious. From the moment you got in your truck, before we had left Black's Bar and Grill to head to your party, I was imagining you without a beard and longer hair. And if there was a possibility that you were Zach Black, my next-door neighbour from way back when. But it wasn't until I heard Andy say Mr Black a few times that the penny dropped.'

I explained this, all the while taking in the man in the driver's seat. He was so handsome, even though all I could see was the side of his face.

'Ah, Andy!' Zach said, like he knew Andy would give him a hard time whenever he could.

'So proper.' I laughed a little at the man who was Zach's head of security and apparently liked to keep Zach on his toes.

Then I heard Zach say, 'What happened, Harley? I remember you were off to Melbourne for two weeks, but you never came back. I never forgot that kiss goodbye, our only kiss.'

Zach's words took me back to what happened that night long after the kiss we shared.

All of a sudden, I felt a little uneasy, I hadn't spoken about what had happened to anyone, and now Zach wanted to know about that night. Could I do this? I had to do this. My heart sped up and I felt a little dizzy. 'No way,' I told myself. 'You will not have a meltdown here. Take a fucking deep breath.'

'Harley, you disappeared, like off the face of the earth ten years ago. There was a massive gap where I didn't get to see you, the girl next door, and share more of your kisses. We are stuck in my truck for the next couple of hours.' There was side-eye and a cheeky half-grin on his too-adorable face to be able to resist filling Zach in. 'Time to spill, don't you think?'

I kind of did owe Zach that much.

I took a couple more of deep breaths. 'I… I…' I stumbled over my words, 'I have never talked to anyone about what happened ten years ago. My grandparents became mine and Addison's temporary guardians. They gave us a routine that my mother couldn't, and what happened was never discussed at the dinner table. Even Addison and I didn't talk about it.' And no one had ever asked what I knew about that night.

'Harley, you don't have to if you don't want to.'

I loved that Zach didn't push for an explanation as to why I'd disappeared. But it was time I spoke up and talked to someone about what I had been holding in, pushing down, bottling up. I needed to ease the cracks that had begun to show.

'It's been a long time. I think it's time to get it off my chest.' I never realised until now how tightly I'd held on to that night. It was time to let it out and let it go.

'Okay, Harley.'

Silence filled the cab of Zach's truck. I took this moment to gather my thoughts while Zach waited patiently for me to speak.

'I can't tell you how many times we made this trip as a family, and that trip ten years ago was meant to be like every other time. Down to check on my grandparents, make sure everything at our bakery business was okay and be back before the end of the holidays.' I stared out the window as I recalled what had happened over those holidays all those years ago.

'My dad was driving. We were on our way home from Melbourne. We all knew how long the trip was so we settled into the music from the playlist on my dad's phone, and we would sing along. Sometimes together, sometimes on our own. We sounded great, and we were happy. Our road trips made me fall in love with music, and my dad was always encouraging Addison and me to sing, especially if we wanted to continue singing lessons and entering competitions. I loved to sing, but I'd always hoped my dad would teach me guitar. He said he would but we never found any time to play.' I stopped for a breath. This next bit was hard, and Zach felt my hesitation. He reached over for my hand to wrap his fingers around mine. I loved how easily he read me; he knew exactly what gesture made everything feel okay.

'I don't know what happened that night. We'd had a good run, no interruptions, and then all of a sudden our car was out of control. It spun around so many times, I lost count. The screams were so loud and my heartbeat so fast, I thought it would explode.

'Our car finally stopped against a tree on the driver's side, and that's when the screams stopped. Dad's head rested on the driver's side window, and both Mum and Addison were unconscious. I managed to pull Dad's phone from the centre console and called triple zero. I tried really hard to stay conscious, but at the sound of the sirens, it was too much. The shock and my injuries took over, and I blacked out.'

There were tears in my eyes now, and Zach squeezed my hand and kissed my palm. My heartrate was wild, but with every breath in and slow breath out, I managed to get my heartbeat and how I was feeling under control.

'Harley.' Zach whispered my name into the silence as I paused, but I hadn't finished yet. There was so much more to explain.

'That was the first time I ever blacked out, and after that night, whenever my heart raced out of control, I would black out. I have blacked out twice since that night. Most of the time I'm too exhausted for my heart to beat that fast, which is why I've thrown myself into work since then.' My words had tumbled out in a sob as tears fell down my face.

'I woke up a couple of days later in the hospital. Mum and Addison were okay, just minor injuries, but my dad didn't make it. He had hit his head too hard. I couldn't fall asleep after that night; it became too hard. Hearing the screams in my dreams were the worst. They played on repeat every time I closed my eyes. I avoided sleeping then, and turned myself into an insomniac. The only time I ever rested was when the exhaustion was so bad I passed out, most of the time it was in the office of the bakery.'

'Fuck, Harley.' I heard Zach say, the frustration evident in his voice. Then he gently asked, 'No one in your family ever talked about the accident or your insomnia?' Zach's eyebrow shot up as he looked my way.

I shook my head in Zach's direction, and he took his foot off the accelerator and brought his truck to a stop on the side of the freeway. He took my face in his hands, and my eyes closed as Zach kissed my lips. He held his lips to mine, and I let whatever this was that we shared calm me, soothe the pain I had in my heart from everything I had lost. I wanted to treasure this moment forever, but there was still more to explain.

'Why?' escaped through Zach's lips before I had a chance to continue. His concern was evident in the one word he spoke.

'I don't know why no one talks about my dad. It's like that topic is off-limits. As for my insomnia, no one knew about it except for my grandfather. Physically, Mum, Addison and I were okay, just minor injuries. I was fifteen, and Addison was almost fourteen. But my grandparents saw us as children rather than teenagers. They are old fashioned, and we had a strict routine to stick to. And my dad wasn't mentioned again. My mum never left her bedroom, looking back maybe she didn't know how to cope. I remember she slept a lot of the time and was highly medicated. I didn't make many friends at my new high school, and I wasn't close to any of them to confide in why Mum, Addison and I were living with my grandparents. No one but my family knew about what happened to my dad, and I guess it was too painful to talk about him.'

I opened my eyes to Zach's forehead against mine. I took his face in my hands and just like the few times he had shown me tenderness, I kissed his forehead. Talking about that night with Zach and explaining my disappearance ten years ago soothed a part of me I didn't know needed to be alleviated.

'Babe, I'm so sorry about your dad. It sounds like you have been through hell.' Zach wiped my tears away from my cheeks with his thumbs. 'I remember for as long as you lived next door to us that your dad would cook a barbeque on Sundays, then he would play his guitar while you and Addison would try and pick which song he was playing and sing along with him. I would watch from my bedroom window and try to guess the song. Sometimes I wanted to yell out the answer, but I didn't want to interrupt your family time.'

Mum, Dad, Addison and I would make such a racket I was surprised the whole town couldn't hear us. Zach's memory of my dad made me miss how wonderful a man he really was. 'Everything changed after that, Zach, and not always for the better.' The words I told Zach were the truth. I didn't get to see Zach again, so yeah, not always for the better.

Zach kissed me again gently and returned his focus to the road. He put his truck into drive, and we were on our away again. After a few moments of silence, I felt comfortable enough to continue to recall what had happened next.

'The day we left the hospital, my dad's parents picked us up and took us to their house. I don't know if living with my grandparents was meant to be temporary or not, but we never left. I don't know if Mum accepted my grandparents' offer to help or if they just took over caring for all of us. By the time we had settled in at my grandparents', my mum had shut out the outside world. I guess she didn't want the reminders of my dad around her. My grandparents organised everything for Addison and me, our clothes, our bedrooms, even the high school we would attend. Addison and I didn't even get a say. We were too young to make our own decisions, apparently. One day led to the next and city life became normal, and I knew Mum, Addison and I would never move back here. Maybe Mum thought it would be too painful for all of us.'

'The day the movers packed up your house was the worst day. I knew you wouldn't be back, and it made me wonder if we would ever cross paths again,' Zach admitted.

I was shocked. I never knew someone came to pack up our house and store it away. I know it made sense to pack up the things in the house we'd rented and let someone else live in it. But Addison and I were never asked if we wanted any of our things. No matter how many times I'd brought up wanting my things, my grandparents had always said no. I'd always wondered if my mum even knew that our house had been packed up and stored away. Out of sight, out of mind, and never to worry about it again.

'No one showed up at my grandparents' house with our stuff, and to this day I don't know what happened to it.' My grandparents had a lot to explain, I had come to realise. I may have only been fifteen and grieving my dad, but I lost more than him back then. I lost my friends, my personal belongings, the comfort zone of a country town, spending time together as a family, and I also lost Zach and the time we could have spent together.

While my grandparents supported us for five years after the loss of my dad, it wasn't until I had started managing the bakery and Addison had finished high school that Mum, Addison and I moved out of our grandparents' house. Mum moved into her own house and slowly found her new normal without my dad. I moved into the house my grandparents gifted me when I became a manager of the bakery. Addison had had other ideas on what she wanted to do when she'd finished high school, so she was on her own.

'That must have been horrible to have to start over like that?'

'School and work, that's all it was.' There wasn't ever much time for anything else, unless I'd snuck away to be rebellious. The insomnia made that easy.

'Work?' Zach asked me, and I guess he didn't know that I'd worked my life away from my first night at the bakery.

'Yeah, just the days that end in Y.' I repeated the same words Zach had said to me. Wasn't that only yesterday?

'Very funny, Harley.' Zach's words filled the space around us.

'My grandpa found out about my insomnia and let me go with him at night to the bakery, and that's how I learned to bake. When his shift was over, we would sit in his office, and by that time most nights I was so exhausted I would fall asleep on the lounge while Grandpa did his paperwork.'

The nights my grandfather taught me to bake were my fondest memories. He was old-fashioned and set in his ways, from baking to paperwork and even how he treated Addison and me. He was a kind man, yet a strict one. Times had changed from when my father was a teenager, and my grandfather had no interest in moving with the times as technology changed. I'd had to wade through the changes in technology when I turned twenty and took over managing the bakery. It had taken five years, but the bakery, the shop outlets and me were now up to date with the latest technology.

'Harley, that's incredible.' Zach told me.

If only he knew. 'Grandpa set it up so that by the time I finished high school, I finished my apprenticeship too, and that's when I started to work alongside him. Three years later I took over as the manager of James Family Bakery. Grandpa told me when he retired that Addison would come and work at the bakery too. But day after day I would do a double shift. Bake, serve in the shop, then the paperwork needed to be done. Addison was supposed to help ease the pressure, but never once did she come to help. I was by myself the whole time.'

I knew Addison couldn't wait to finish high school and move out of our grandparents' house. She was always going to forge her own path and was never going to let anyone dampen her free spirit. What I didn't know was why she couldn't help around the bakery. Maybe Addison needed time away from the strictness of our grandparents to do her own thing, whereas I, on the other hand, needed the structure in my life to not fall apart.

'Until now.' Zach had remembered that there was a dare between Addison and me.

'Until now,' I repeated as I thought about why my sister had all of a sudden started showing her face around the bakery. 'Maybe Addison finally realised working at the bakery would be worth her while.' I knew I sounded bitter as I spat out my words. I was hurt that Addison thought she could show up after all these years and undermine everything I had worked hard to achieve with the family business.

'What do you mean?' Zach asked, and it was time to fill him in on what had led to this moment.

'Five years ago, I dared Addison to be my apprentice, and she refused. As a consequence, I stopped paying Addison, something I know she hasn't forgiven me for. But the money she was getting, I was paying out of my wage.' I'd never wanted Addison to miss out. She had been a bartender since turning eighteen and never stayed in the one place for too long. Addison was always going to blaze her own trail and do things her own way, and I always knew where she was from her texts. She would send me these to boast about what she had been up to. So, I'd topped up Addison's wage because she was a member of the James family too. I hadn't minded giving Addison money; I earned a good wage and had little expenses.

'But Addison suddenly showing up isn't the only reason my life is messy.'

'You found something?' Zach asked as he glanced at me.

'My grandpa is old fashioned, and it has taken me from the day I started managing the bakery until now to update the whole business. While there has always been money in the business accounts to grow the bakery and purchase the additional shops, I have never been able to get a loan for new equipment. In my search for a reason why, I found that Grandpa had only kept manual bookkeeping entries for all of the bakery paperwork. There are no digital records.' But what also bothered me was that I couldn't find any documents that told me Grandpa was still the owner of the James Family Bakery. Was my grandpa hiding something?

'But that's not all you found, is it?'

Zach watched as I shook my head. 'I found Grandpa's business terms, and they stated that at least one James family member must either work for or manage the business for it to stay in the family and continue to be handed to the next generation. If there's not a family member working for the business, then the bakery is to be sold.' I knew my grandpa wanted to keep the business he'd started in the family and was happy when I showed an interest in managing it, but the business terms I'd found seemed dated just like the rest of the bakery paperwork.

'And you found out all this three nights ago?' The man next to me sure knew how to use the power of deduction.

'Yes.'

'No wonder you needed to blow off steam.'

I guess how I'd ended up in the hotel room Zach owned wasn't a mystery anymore.

'Exactly.' It was the only word I could think of to say, and that word summed it all up.

'Harley, how does your sister's dare fit into all of this?'

I must remember the high level at which he paid attention. 'Addison needs a stable day job that will pay well.' The fact that my sister had only just realised the family business was a stable, well-paying job made me angry. Addison could have helped from the start. My sister still had a lot of growing up to do.

'What does that mean?' His question let me know he wanted to understand the mess I was in.

'It means my sister wants what I have. She wants my benefits, to pay herself a managerial wage and live in my house.' Also, according to the business terms I'd found, once a quarter there should be a payout of bakery profits. But in the last ten years of working at the bakery, I hadn't received any extra income.

'But why?' Zach asked.

'Because Addison's pregnant, and she wants more than her bartending wage to raise her baby on,' I blurted. It hurt that Addison had used her dare to rattle me and try and take what I had been working hard to achieve, keeping the family business running.

'Your sister's pregnant! That's a curveball I didn't see coming. What's the time frame for the dare?'

'I don't know,' I said as I turned to look out the passenger side window. I wanted this conversation to be over. But I could tell Zach wasn't going to let it go. 'I was meant to meet Addison three nights ago and when I texted to ask where she was, she gave me the address. When I looked up where my sister was, she was at a karaoke bar, one we had not been to before in Brunswick Street.' Had Addison been trying to get me to sing for her. I didn't know because I didn't meet her. 'It doesn't matter because instead of meeting with her, I packed a bag with a few days' worth of clothes and got in my car and wound up at your bar.'

'What do you mean it doesn't matter?'

'The dare, it doesn't matter, can we please just drop it?'

'No, Harley,' Zach snapped back. 'We can't just drop it. I want to know why you drove 270 kilometres to drink yourself under the table.'

Does anything ever get past this man?

'I didn't want to meet Addison for karaoke.' It felt good to say that. 'Things have been awkward between us since the night I blacked out on stage, and I don't know how to reconnect with her without our dares. I guess these last three days have proven I needed a break, to not be reminded every day that my family was counting on me to make sure the business continued to be successful.'

I paused momentarily before I admitted, 'None of it matters because I don't want it. Any of it. I don't want to go back to the way things were before. I want to make some changes.' The words, now that I had said them, were a weight off my shoulders. Some of the heaviness that surrounded me was suddenly lifted. Was there a way to bring my family closer together? Did it start with me and the changes I would make?

I couldn't run the James Family Bakery by myself anymore. Now that Addison was showing an interest in working maybe there was a way to also spark Mum's interest in working at the bakery as well. Had my mother not considered over the years working in the family business? She'd had several jobs since moving into her own place five years ago, but none were enough to keep her interested and happy. Was she missing the one thing we were all missing in our lives and never talked about? Her husband, and my dad?

When I looked back out the windscreen, I saw the city lights of Melbourne. We weren't far away now. I leaned my head against the passenger window and stared at the colours of the city lights as they lit up the darkness in the distance.

There was a silence that surrounded Zach and me. But it wasn't uncomfortable. Maybe this conversation was over, maybe it wasn't. But right now, there was nothing left to say.

When I stole a glance Zach's way, I knew he understood the need for a break. Maybe that was why he was here with me right now.

Sixteen

The view of Melbourne's city lights now surrounded us. The darkness was well-lit by bright streetlights. Zach had manoeuvred his truck off the Hume Freeway through the suburban streets of Melbourne, something that I thought was impossible, but he made it look so easy. He found High Street with ease and headed towards Fitzroy, and not once did he ask me for the address to my house. I had no idea where Zach was headed, but then he turned into Wellington Street. I should have known this man had his own apartment here in Melbourne, but had we always lived this close together? A few minutes later, Zach pulled into an underground carpark.

I turned to face him, and like always, he didn't give much away. I wanted to say something, but Zach beat me to it and broke the silence first.

'I know we are here to sort things out with your family, but Harley…' The way my name rolled off Zach's lips told me there was something he wanted from me. 'Tonight, I'm going to take you up those stairs, lay you down on my bed, trace my fingertips along your tattoo and kiss that dragonfly.' Zach turned his head towards me and caught my eyes.

I let out the breath I was holding as a shiver ran over my skin.

'Any objections?'

I was now too aroused to speak. My mind had gone into overdrive at the thought of Zach's hands on my body and what that would lead to. I shook my head, so Zach knew I had heard him and that I agreed to what he was about to do. Touch me. My full lips curved upwards as my body screamed with excitement.

Zach rounded his truck and pulled me from the passenger seat, like he was in a hurry to get somewhere. I grabbed my handbag as he grabbed my other bag, then I was tucked up against his shoulder as we walked to the stairs and up four flights.

Zach unlocked the door to an apartment that I assumed could only be his and let us both inside. It was cold and dark, but he didn't need warmth or any lights to lead the way.

After dropping my bags on the floor, Zach spun me around. I had no other choice but to walk backwards along the edge of the lounge. Before the lounge ended, Zach picked me up and carried me towards his bedroom. My legs were wrapped around his waist. Just inside the door, Zach let me go, and I slid down his body until my feet hit the ground. A rush of heat filled me.

'I never stopped thinking about you, even when you disappeared from our little town,' Zach's whispered words hung in the now-sexually charged tension between us. 'You were always going to be the woman I wanted in my life. I wanted to wait for you, but I couldn't find you.'

I put my finger to Zach's lips. He didn't need to explain why he hadn't waited for me or that he had slept with other women. I hadn't waited for Zach either and had had a few one-night stands. But all that mattered was that the two of us were together in this moment.

Our bodies were close as Zach continued to walk me backwards until my knees hit the edge of the bed. I fell, but Zach grabbed me and pulled me back towards him. He kissed me the same way he did up against my car, intense with the same bolt of electricity that made me reach out for purchase. My hands didn't fist in his tee-shirt this time, they went straight around his neck. His skin reacted to my touch, and I felt the hairs on the back of his neck stick up. Zach's hands lifted me off the ground and my legs automatically wrapped around his hips, and he didn't let me go this time.

He knelt on his bed and walked me back towards the pillows, his lips never leaving mine even as he laid me down gently. Zach's body covered mine, and I felt his weight press into me. There was nowhere else that I would rather be.

'Babe, you've got to help me with these clothes,' Zach murmured when he moved his lips away from mine.

I undid the button of my jeans and pushed them over my hips as Zach pulled off my boots then took the ends of my jeans to yank them off of me. I watched as he toed out of his work boots then he unbuckled, unbuttoned and unzipped his black pants and slid them over his hips to the floor.

Zach and I were a mirror image as we pulled our tee-shirts over our heads and all that was left were his black boxer briefs and my matching black lingerie. I unhooked my bra and watched as Zach removed his boxer briefs. I couldn't help but stare. My jaw dropped and eyes flared with lust. Zach took advantage of my momentary gaping. He reached forward and ripped off the last of my clothes.

Then Zach's body covered mine. We were skin to skin, and nothing had ever felt this incredible. Especially when he pressed his lips against my skin. I had always believed that sex could be magical, and now I knew what had been missing: the right person.

He reached past my head into a drawer beside his bed for what I could only assume was a condom. Zach peeled himself off me and, in his hand, I could see the foil packet. My eyes moved from his hand down to his long, hard cock that curved up towards his belly, and I had to take a deep breath.

'Zach.' It was just above a whisper. I felt silly, like I should be better at this and know what I was supposed to do. But I didn't.

'Harley, you have done this before?' Zach whispered back as he looked down at me.

He must think my life was sheltered. It wasn't, it had just been a while since I'd had sex. *But with none that have looked like that,* I thought, not taking my eyes off Zach.

'Look at you,' I panted. 'Every muscly inch of you is perfect.' My eyes moved down Zach's body to stare once again at his beautiful cock.

I wasn't a virgin, but I'd just never taken the time to enjoy my sexual partners. We'd done what we'd needed to do and didn't hang around after. My few one-night stands had always been sloppy, and the excitement and anticipation had always died by the time we'd gotten through the foreplay. But I didn't feel like that tonight. And all Zach had done was take off my clothes and lay his body down on top of me. My body was filled with electricity, and the anticipation had only just started to build.

'Babe, I'll go slow, I'll make you feel good,' Zach told me. He had rolled the condom on and now he moved closer on his forearms to my hip, first to trace his fingertips over my tattoo, then he kissed along the edge of my dragonfly. His fingers, then his lips danced across the rest of my skin. Zach's touch felt so good.

He moved up my body, his hands brushing the hair from my face as his lips grazed mine, then his lips moved along my jaw and down my neck. Zach continued his kiss his way down, his lips moving towards one nipple as his fingertips played with the other.

I had never felt anything like this before. A moan escaped from my lips as the wetness pooled outside of me. Zach moved to the other nipple to give it the same attention, and I could feel my arousal start to grow wild. My hips moved upward of their own accord and pressed into Zach's groin. There was a smile on his face as he realised just how sensitive my body was. I knew he would torture my flesh in just the right way.

Zach continued to kiss his way down my bare flesh, and I almost levitated off the bed when his lips touched my most sensitive area. The purest jolt of electricity ran through me, and Zach placed his hands on my hips to hold me against him. I didn't want to lay still while Zach pleasured my clit. I writhed under his hold and as his tongue moved up and down the length of my pussy, and my hips bucked against his face.

'Ahh. Oh my God,' fell from my lips over and over. I felt so good. Zach made me feel so good as he pleasured me higher and higher into a frenzy. I moaned his name and just when I felt my body start to shake, Zach slipped a finger inside me and my muscles clamped down on it with the strength of my orgasm.

Zach's face had moved away from my pussy, his lips glistening with my essence. Then he bent down to kiss my clit again as my body shuddered with wave after wave of pleasure, his finger still inside me, moving in and out.

'Ohhh,' escaped from my lips. The pleasure was almost unbearable, but there was still a rhythmic pace to the movement of Zach's finger. I didn't know it was possible to come again so quickly, but I writhed and shook again all over with my second climax.

Zach started to kiss me, first my clit, and that caused my back to arch. Then he continued his kisses up over my pubic bone to my belly button and all the way up to my breasts. He licked the tips of each of my nipples, then placed quick kisses up my neck to my chin to claim my mouth, where I could taste myself on his lips. Zach's finger was no longer inside me, and instead I felt the head of his cock brush against all the wetness he had just created.

Zach's lips were gone from mine and before he could speak, I moved my fingers and covered his mouth, then I whispered the words he wanted to hear. 'I want you, all of you, inside me. You make me feel so good.'

Zach wasted no time. His length thrust through my wetness and pushed deep inside me. My body arched and I groaned, delighting in the feel of him. My hands moved to Zach's hips so I could feel each thrust as he started to move inside me.

'Kiss me,' I told Zach, and he did as he continued to move in and out of me.

The movement of his mouth over mine made me heady with desire as lips, tongues and teeth came together as one. I felt the bliss take over. There was a pulsing ache in my lower body, and it built with each thrust that Zach made. My hips moved up as Zach's hips moved down. My lips left Zach's mouth and my head landed on the pillow as a string of 'Oh my Gods' left my mouth. I thought I was about to come, but I didn't know. I had never felt this sensation before when a man was inside me. The pleasure, the sensation inside, made me shake and my pussy muscles started to pulsate around him.

'Holy shit!' I heard, and I knew Zach could feel my sex muscles contract around his.

'Zach, oh my God,' I cried out with pleasure as he groaned and exploded inside me.

We both had been milked dry, and I didn't know about Zach, but I felt delicious. If this was how sex was meant to feel, I wanted it to be this magical every time.

Zach slowly eased himself from my body, then caged me in with his arms and legs.

'That was ...' Zach's voice trailed off as he tried to think of the right words to say.

My eyes never left his face, and when his eyes landed on mine, he said, 'You are so beautiful.'

No one had ever called me beautiful before, and not right after amazing sex. I was sated and happy. I knew in this moment that Zach would be the only man I would want for the rest of my life.

'Babe, I'll just take care of this.' Zach pointed to his condom. 'Then you and I need to sleep.'

He left the bed after a quick peck on my lips, and I manoeuvred my body under the covers. I snuggled in on my side and was about to close my eyes when the bed sank behind me, and he slid in next to me. He pulled me into him, my back against his chest, and with his arm around me, I took one deep breath and fell asleep.

Seventeen

I woke to feel the heaviness that had held me all night had gone. But his smell dominated the space. I stretched, not unhappy that Zach had let me sleep in. As I looked around, something at the back of my mind thought this room was familiar, like I had woken up here before. I knew I wasn't crazy. I knew there was a memory somewhere inside my head, I could feel it. I just couldn't remember, and I didn't know why. For some reason, the memory didn't come to me clearly. What I *did* remember was last night and what had happened. The corners of my mouth turned up as I thought about having had the best sex of my life with Zach Black, and I wanted him to be all mine for the rest of time.

The morning light poured through the gap of Zach's bedroom window. I pushed back the covers and sat up as I fully took in the room. It wasn't the same as Zach's other bedroom, and I could sense that Zach either didn't stay here often or hadn't stayed here in a very long time. This room was bare, with minimal furniture. It was a room to sleep in and nothing more. But now our clothes laid in piles on the floor, and the sight of our mess made the space felt lived in.

I moved off the bed, still naked from the night before, and walked around to find that there was one item that hung from the wall in this room. As I moved closer to see what it was, I gasped. I hadn't seen what hung from Zach's wall in five years, and as I reached out to run my finger along the edge of what was in front of me, I felt a warmth wrap around me.

'I was just about to wake you up,' Zach said, appearing behind me.

'Zach?' I questioned. I wanted him to tell me about the object I couldn't take my eyes off. But he didn't mention what hung on his wall.

'I bought breakfast,' Zach told me instead. 'Come and eat.' He stepped back, but I didn't move. I continued to stare straight ahead at the wall. I *had* been here before. My necklace hanging on the wall was my proof. How long had it been since I'd been here? Did I lose it that night I blacked out at Jam? Was this where my necklace had been this whole time? In Zach's apartment?

Zach had found my robe amongst my things and dropped it over my shoulders. He then spun me around, placed his hands on my hips and his lips on mine. His passionate kiss left me breathless.

'Babe?' Zach said against my lips as he moved his hands to take mine.

Zach manoeuvred me through his bedroom and into the kitchen to sit at his round kitchen table. He placed in front of me a paper bag and takeaway coffee.

'Earth to Harley. I bought breakfast,' Zach said to me again.

I didn't get to answer. I was too stunned as a flicker of a memory from five years ago clicked through my mind like an old school slide projector. Images quickly flashed one after the other. I didn't know why all of a sudden that memory chose now to come to the surface to remind me.

'I didn't know,' I blurted.

'Babe.' Zach lifted me up into his arms and carried me to his lounge where he sat me down on his lap. 'It's okay. You had blacked out and never got a good look at me.'

'I didn't know it was you at the bar that night at Jam.' My eyes locked with Zach's as I continued. 'I'd wanted a break, to check out the new bar, relax and sing karaoke with my sister like old times, maybe even have a little fun. I'd wanted some normality in my life.'

'Harley,' my name meant Zach wanted my attention. 'I didn't know it was you that night either. The place was so dark that it was impossible to know who anyone was. My brother is such an arsehole, and so many shady exchanges happened there. I just knew the woman I had spoken to earlier at the bar had collapsed on stage and that I had to get her out of there.'

Zach's thumb rubbed circles at the base of my neck. 'That next morning, I'd gone downstairs to get breakfast, coffee and a muffin, just like today, but when I came back, the woman, you, was gone.' Zach took a deep breath before he continued. 'I didn't know it was you, Harley, but I told myself that if I ever let a pretty woman out of my sight again, I would at least leave a note. So, when I left your hotel room and went up to the kitchen to get breakfast after you passed out in my bar, I left a note hoping you would stick around.'

I moved to straddle Zach. Taking my hands, I placed them on his face. My body absorbed what he had just told me, and I leaned forward and pressed my lips to his in a gentle kiss.

'You are all I want, all I've ever wanted, from the moment you had me pinned against the side of your house.' The words fell from my lips, but before Zach could speak or take things further, I put my finger to his lips. 'But I'm still such a mess, as you know from what I told you in your truck last night. My life, my family, my job, I can't do it anymore.' These were the most honest words I had admitted, and not just to myself, in a very long time.

My phone buzzed from somewhere behind me, and I wanted to get up and read the message that was there, but didn't. I already sensed it was my family. And that someone had called an intervention. There was no way anybody knew I was back in Melbourne. It was just a coincidence.

'You want to get that?' Zach asked as I shook my head. I didn't, but if I knew Zach at all, he wouldn't let this go.

Zach reached over the lounge for my handbag and pulled out my phone. He pushed the button that lit up the screen, the text message that was meant for me visible. However long the message was didn't matter, the gist of what was sent would be readable on the screen of my phone.

Zach sat back down next to me and handed over my phone. I glanced at the message and knew it was an intervention. A group message for Mum, Addison and me from the patriarch of this family, Grandpa James, written by Grandma. She was only acting on behalf of Grandpa because we all knew how old-fashioned he was and how he had no use for modern technology like mobile phones.

GJ: Harley, darling, it's not like you to take off and not let anyone know where you're going or for how long. This family needs to meet. Tomorrow at your house. 12 pm. Don't be late.

There were no responses. Responses weren't needed as everyone knew to attend. It had been a long time since the James family had sat down to a family meeting.

Eighteen

Silence filled Zach's apartment and surrounded me. But silence wasn't all that filled the air, there was a little tension mixed in. Unease radiated off me as the reality of the situation I was in sank through my skin now that I was back in Melbourne. How was I meant to handle this? How did I tell my family that how things had been were not how things were going to be? How did I fight for what I wanted and still be left standing? What was it that I wanted? After spending time with Zach, I knew it was some time away from the working at the bakery.

Zach broke the silence. 'So what's tomorrow all about?'

I shouldn't have been surprised that Zach wanted to know more.

'The business,' I told Zach, but that wasn't the whole truth and we both knew it.

'Harley?'

'Me,' I said quietly as I stood up from Zach's lap. I didn't want this to turn into an argument, so I told Zach in an even tone. 'Tomorrow will be about me. How I let everyone down because I disappeared for four days.'

'Huh? Even though you needed a break. It's not the end of the world. I'm sure your family will make allowances.'

It didn't matter that I had single-handedly managed James Family Bakery for the last five years without my family stepping in to help. It would only matter that I hadn't been there for the last four days making sure everything ran smoothly. Although five years ago when I started managing the bakery, I knew I could do it all by myself, but now after the last four days, I knew there was more to life than just working. I wanted a future that looked more like the last four days.

'Tomorrow, I'll go with you, and it's not up for negotiation.' I felt his chest rest on my back and his arms wrap around me, then in my ear he whispered, 'You can tell your family about your last four days, lay it all out for them how you want things to change. All I will be is in your corner the whole time, and I promise I'll let you handle this. I won't overstep this time.'

Zach kissed just below my ear, before he spun me around and picked me up. I guessed this conversation was over for now. Zach had something else on his mind.

He carried me into his bedroom and when he had lain me down, my robe fell open. He made short work of the jeans, boots and black tee-shirt he had dressed himself in this morning before going to get breakfast.

Zach stood over my nakedness in his boxers. I felt exposed, but I knew Zach liked what he saw. My body wasn't like Zach's, lean and full of tight, tanned skin. My body was my own, what you saw was what you got, and it was curvy from top to toe. Zach's eyes flashed with desire, and he moved onto the bed to lie on top of me. His body covered most of mine, and I liked the feel of our skin on skin. I loved the feel of his cock pressed against my naked pussy.

Zach kissed me, deeply, making my head spin. Then he teasingly moved his lips down my body from my head to my dragonfly tattoo. I shivered all over and felt my sex juice start to flow. I loved the way he made me feel, aching with desire.

He reached past me into his bedside table for a condom, and as he leaned back to peel off his briefs, I reached my hand out and took the foil pack from Zach's hand. I tore it open and as soon as his cock had sprung free, I moved to sheath his hardness. Zach gasped as my fingers lingered, and I couldn't help but feel him. My hand wrapped around his length and moved once up and down before Zach placed his hand over mine to stop me.

'Your hand feels amazing, and you'll get your chance to play, but today it's my turn.' Zach's voice had gone hoarse. He was losing his control, and I liked that I had that effect on him. I wanted to be the only woman who could bring this man to his knees.

Zach then pushed me down until I was flat on my back and pushed inside me in one fluid motion. Once inside, he stopped. My arms moved around Zach's neck, and I pulled him towards me, his neck to my lips as I nipped, sucked and licked his sun-kissed skin.

'Harley.' My name rolling off Zach's tongue was meant to warn me. I took my lips away from his skin, but I couldn't help but flick out my tongue and let it dance on the skin of Zach's neck. The movement of my tongue made his hips move and more air leave my lungs. My pussy pulsated a little more intensely now Zach was inside me than when only his lips touched my skin.

I moaned as I moved my hands past Zach's neck to curl my fingers through the ends of his hair. 'Please don't stop.' I tightened my grip on Zach's hair.

He reached down to kiss the tip of my nose and moved his hips once more. I felt him throb inside of me. He hadn't once moved out of me to plough back in. But at the smile on my lips, Zach was no longer motionless. His movement was so perfect, and I thought to myself, *Was this what it was like to make love?*

Zach's steady rhythm filled me, and the pleasure inside me built further until it had nowhere else to go but explode. That was when I felt his thumb on my clit, his fingers splayed across my lower abdomen. His thumb moved in a gentle circular motion.

'Come for me, babe,' Zach said as he felt my sex muscles tighten around him. He growled and I automatically let go of my hold on his hair. But my arms stayed wrapped around his body as he let out a few quick breaths that let me know his climax was close.

My breath came in quick pants just like Zach's, and as my body started to shake, I closed my eyes. I had come so hard there were white flashes under my eyelids.

Zach groaned once, placed his lips on mine, a quick kiss, and my eyes flew open. I watched him as he came undone and released his seed, pulsing inside of me. I stared as the man whose body covered mine became even more beautiful.

Zach moved off the bed to take care of his condom. A moment later, he was back sitting next to me with breakfast. When breakfast was gone, I turned on my side, laid my head on Zach's shoulder and traced my fingers along the edge of Zach's armoured tattoo. Now I was up close and personal with Zach and his tattoo, I could see the intricate details inside the armour that I hadn't seen earlier. My fingers danced along Zach's skin, and I moved them closer to the inked fob watch, where time had stopped, then over the broken hourglass where the sand was falling out.

'Will you ever tell me about your tattoo?'

'One day.' I heard before I closed my eyes and relaxed further into him.

Nineteen

The sound of an acoustic guitar woke me from the early afternoon nap I seemed to have taken. I listened for a couple of minutes before I realised it wasn't the radio that was playing. More strums from the guitar told me they came from close by, and I smiled as I listened to the music. I pushed the covers back and searched for my robe then quietly opened Zach's bedroom door, wanting to take in the man before me without him knowing.

Moving to the end of Zach's small hall, I leaned up against the wall and watched. Zach had seated himself on the lounge, and the top part of his body was naked. I wondered if the rest of him was too, but I doubted it. The strum from the guitar didn't seem so distant now I stood a little closer. As I continued to watch, Zach shoulders tensed and he rolled his head from side to side, then let his chin rest on his chest.

Something wasn't right. The song he played didn't come out the way he wanted it to, and Zach just couldn't make his vocals fit to the cords of the song. It was then I realised the song he wanted to master was one from my phone's playlist, one of my favourite songs – Jason Aldean's 'My Kinda Party'.

Zach stopped, and the room was silent. Just when I thought he was about to turn around and catch me as I checked him out, he leaned over and wrote something down, then took a deep breath, dropped the vocals and played my song from start to finish on his guitar. The music was perfect, and on the second run-through Zach added his vocals back in. This time his voice was much smoother. It still wasn't perfect, but I knew he would always try to make it perfect.

'Hey,' Zach smiled as he saw me lean against his hallway wall. 'Did I wake you?' He put down his guitar and stood in only his black boxer briefs, looking me up and down.

I shook my head and revelled in the intensity of Zach's stare, unable to find the words to speak.

Zach moved towards me, wrapped me in his arms and placed a kiss on my lips as he reached me. His touch was gentle, just like every other touch he had given me, and it made me all warm and gooey inside.

'Your song needs a second guitar,' I said when Zach's lips had left mine.

'Maybe.' Zach walked me backwards into his bedroom.

Maybe I was right, or maybe I had no idea. It was one of my favourite songs, so you would think I'd know how it should sound.

'Have you finished your practice session?' I asked as we crossed the threshold into Zach's room. His attention had moved from his music to me.

'Babe, when you're awake, you get all of my attention, so for now, practice is over. And now that you're awake, I want to go out.'

Zach walked me straight into his shower and turned the water on. I squealed at the cold spray as it soaked through my robe. There was nowhere else to go as Zach had boxed me into the shower. I had no choice but to wait until the water warmed. I pushed my robe from my skin, where it puddled on the floor. I lathered face wash and shower gel to cleanse my skin all while Zach watched on. He didn't join me. Had he showered while I napped?

When I was satisfied I was clean enough, I turned off the shower and towelled off. Both Zach and I dressed warmly, as you could never put on enough warm clothes for Melbourne's weather. My hair was tamed as I ran my brush through it and styled it into a braid. By the time I was ready, I was caught off guard once again by what hung on Zach's bedroom wall. My necklace.

'You should wear it.' Zach reached over my shoulder, picked up my necklace and a moment later it hung around my neck. My hand immediately touched the metal on my skin, and I clutched it in gratitude.

'Babe?'

'You have no idea what this necklace means to me,' This necklace meant the world to me as it proved that my hard work had paid off.

'Tell me?'

'I bought it with my first pay-check, and I never took it off. My necklace was my reminder that if I worked hard, I could achieve anything. I never thought I would lose it and when I did, I lost a little piece of me.'

'You are the most incredible woman I know. After all you've been through, I'm glad to be able to give you back your hope.'

Zach's kiss was chaste before he leaned over the bed to grab my jacket and scarf, then he took my hand and pulled me out of his front door. Wherever we were headed this evening, it was on foot. Zach didn't reach for his truck keys or lead me in the direction of the basement to his truck. He just held my jacket out for me to slip my arms inside, then he wrapped my scarf around my neck and pulled me close to his side as we started to walk at a brisk pace.

I wanted to ask where we were headed when Zach said, 'You know Little Beats has the best karaoke?'

I knew that because I had been there, but maybe Zach didn't know that.

'I say that because I own it, that's why I have an apartment here in Melbourne.'

I was a little shocked at Zach's revelation, of the amount of information he'd offered up about himself. I had never seen Zach there any of the times I had been inside of Little Beats.

He must have heard the wheels as they turned in my head. 'I'm never here when the business is open, and I've never seen you in here. The reason I know it's the best karaoke is because the figures show it,' Zach said, and I relaxed into his side under his shoulder.

'I have to admit that because we are the best, Little Beats records everyone who sings karaoke. The good ones get passed on; the not so good ones get trashed. I think that's how Connor got a copy of your video. It was passed on to him. It's probably why he approached you. If you sang at The Groove, there's no doubt Connor wanted you to sing at his club and use you for his event-planning business. I must admit, my brother has a way of finding raw talent.' Zach inhaled deeply. On his exhale, he said. 'I know my brother also owns range of businesses and is ruthless with every deal he makes. One day it's going to get him into a world of trouble that's bigger than the beef he has with me. If Connor's not careful, he's going to find himself in a place neither my father nor I can bail him out of.'

'That's not good.' I was glad that Zach had shared something personal with me, the same as I had. I'd hoped that Zach would let down his guard to let someone like me in. After all, we were close once.

Incredibly, since the last time I'd seen Zach ten years ago, there had been a synchronistic pull back towards each other that had led us to today, with us being together again. I turned to face Zach and kissed him. 'I don't ever want to lose you again,' I whispered.

'That's not possible. I have your number now.'

It felt good to know that Zach and I would never be too far away from each other. A chaste kiss landed on my lips before he grabbed my hand, but not so we could go inside Little Beats. We started to walk and once again I had no idea what Zach had planned.

However, I knew as we moved down the street and when Zach stopped us on the footpath that The Groove was on the other side of the street. I had only been inside once, but tonight, just like the night I'd sung karaoke, it gave off bad vibes. But with Zach's hand in mine, I knew we wouldn't go any further than the footpath.

'You need to know,' Zach informed me, 'that Connor and I co-own The Groove. But we are nothing alike. Little Beats is clean, and I run a tight ship at both of my bars. Dirty deals aren't done inside either of my businesses, and my employees and patrons alike know I have a no-tolerance policy. Neither of my businesses have ever been raided or searched by police.'

What was I supposed to say to that? Zach was letting me in and showing me the kind of man he was, and that he was nothing like his smug brother Connor, in person or in the way he did business.

'Harley?' The way Zach said my name commanded my attention, so I looked up into his brown eyes. 'What started out as a joint venture with my brother ended up with me as a silent partner because I don't like the way he does business. Not at The Groove and especially not when he took on Jam. Connor has a way of attracting attention from the wrong kind of people. Attention that has landed him being arrested and being bailed out by not only me, but our father as well. And Harley, you know my father is a detective.' I vaguely remembered Zach's dad had joined the police force the year we moved in next door, but I didn't know he'd been promoted to detective.

'Did you know videos of me singing karaoke were out there? Did Little Beats hand over my video to Connor?' Did I really want to know the answer? Did Zach know about my video? That it had been handed around? Did Zach know Connor would approach me?

'Harley, I didn't know about your video or that it had been passed on to Connor.'

I could see it in Zach's eyes he told the truth.

'The videos are handled by the manager at Little Beats. He has connections that he uses when he passes on the videos, and my brother must be one of those connections.'

So Zach didn't know about me singing at Little Beats or that his brother had a copy of the video. If he had known, then maybe we would have run into each other sooner.

'Babe, when I looked into Connor, I was informed that he used The Groove and other karaoke bars around Melbourne as a way to drum up interest in his event-planning business. I asked around and found out that Connor hires out his talented employees and depending on how successful each event is, Connor promises his employees time in his recording studio. When I approached one of his employees about the time they had spent in the recording studio, they told me they hadn't spent any time in any recording studio.'

Would that have happened to me if I had agreed to the deal Connor had wanted to make with me? Would I have been like the rest of Connor's employees, still waiting to log recording time?

'Connor has a lot of businesses to his name. I know some of them are dodgy, others are dingy, but few are legitimate. That night at Jam was the first time I had ever been inside since the business opened. I saw for myself the things Connor let happen at Jam. I saw the deals done under the table, the drugs, the underage kids, so that's why the place was so dark. I knew I had to distance myself from my brother and from The Groove. I don't run my businesses like that, so I became a silent partner. Connor knows how to land himself in trouble, I know that now.'

There was a moment of silence between us. He leaned in, pressed his lips to mine, then said, 'I feel like all this time, if I were here, if I had watched Connor more closely, I would have found you sooner.'

'You wouldn't have found me, Zach. After that night at Jam, I didn't go out again for long time. I buckled down and worked my arse off.' I admitted what my life had been like for the last five years. 'Even when I did manage to work up the nerve to venture out to sing karaoke, I sang, had one drink, then I went home. I didn't spend the night out drinking or listening to the other singers. Connor is the only person who ever approached me to hand over an envelope.'

'Harley,' was all Zach had a chance to say to me as my finger on his lips stopped his words.

'We can't change what's happened,' I said honestly to Zach. 'We can't change that we haven't seen each other for ten years. We can only be grateful that life has brought us together again and move forward.'

I stood on tip toes to kiss Zach's cheek, then whispered close to his ear, 'I'm hungry. Take me somewhere yummy to eat.'

There was a mischievous look on Zach's face, and I knew exactly what he wanted to eat.

'Food.' I slapped Zach's chest. 'I want food.'

'I want you,' he whispered in my ear. His tongue wet the bottom of my lobe then he took my hand and moved us in the direction of food.

Twenty

Even as the time ticked closer to midday, Fitzroy was a busy Melbourne suburb. Finding a park at this time of day near my house should have been easy. But with my grandparents, mother and sister all needing parks as well, Zach and I were going to have to walk at least two blocks.

My family hovered on the veranda of my house as they tried to block out the chill that hung in the Melbourne air. Zach gave my hand a quick squeeze before he let me go and I made my way over to my family. I hugged everyone hello before I opened my front door and let everyone in.

My grandparents had made themselves comfortable at the small kitchen table, while my mother and sister made their way to the lounge in my living room and sat down. Zach followed me into my kitchen and reached to entwine his fingers with mine.

My grandmother was always good at breaking the ice. 'It's good to see you, Harley.'

'You too, Grandma.' How long had it been since I had seen anyone in my family? Had being stuck in Groundhog Day kept me from spending time with all of them?

No one was impressed a family meeting had been called. What had changed in our lives that we didn't spend time together anymore? Had we not spent time together since Grandpa and Grandma James insisted we move out of their house and into places of our own? That had been five years ago when I began managing the bakery. Why was I only seeing now that our family had drifted apart? Was I the only one holding us together by managing the family business? Would the dare that Addison gave me tear us further apart or would it bring us closer together? Only time would tell.

I returned the squeeze of my hand then moved my arm around his waist. 'Everyone, this is Zach. We lived next door to him in Mulwala for a year. Zach, you remember my mum, Mia, and sister Addison. The couple at the kitchen table are Grandma and Grandpa James.' I didn't need to point out who was who. Zach had already figured out who everyone was.

There was a silence as everyone looked at one another while we waited for this family meeting to start.

'I appreciate that everyone could make it today. It has been a while since this family has been under one roof.' My grandfather spoke in his usual gruff tone.

But having lived with my grandfather for five years after my father died and working alongside him at the bakery, Grandpa's temperament never bothered me.

'It has also been a while since we have all sat down to talk as a family,' Grandpa continued before he took a moment to look from my mother to Addison then to me.

I followed Grandpa James's gaze around my living room. My family seemed put off by the fact that this meeting had been called. I had never rocked the boat before and disappeared. But couldn't they see that even though I was the gel holding the family business together, I couldn't be that gel any longer. Something bothered me as my grandfather's eyes met mine. Was my grandfather hiding something? I wasn't sure, but now that the thought had crossed my mind, I was going to try to find out.

'I want to know what happened. Why have you not been at the bakery for the last four days, Harley?' Grandpa didn't waste any time with pleasantries.

What could I say? How did I explain how I got to this moment? Did I just blurt out I'd found out-of-date business terms that left me wondering who actually owned the James Family Bakery? Did I tell my family that Addison dared me to sing and if I didn't sing, she was going to find a way to take over the business and kick me out of this house? But instead, I answered honestly and told my grandfather, 'I needed a break.'

'Why didn't you just come to me, Harley?'

Maybe he was slightly offended I didn't confide in him about this earlier. In the last five years, my family and I had only caught up a handful of times, the most recent Addison, who had shown up four weeks ago when she enlightened me about her dare.

Did everyone think that because I showed up to work every day that everything in my life and at the bakery was fine? Well, they weren't, and they hadn't been for a while. I truly needed a break, one that was longer than four days.

'It's not that simple.' My grandpa knew in some way or another that it wasn't. A lot rested on my shoulders now that I was manager. He had managed the bakery previously, and if he'd wanted a break, he'd had my dad before he died and me after my dad died. But who did I have?

'Harley.' The sound of my name was meant to caution me.

But I brushed off his caution. 'If you want more information, then you need to ask Addison.' I kept my gaze on Grandpa and avoided Addison and the look I knew she glared at me.

Grandpa shifted his focus from me to Addison. 'Why, Addison, have you all of a sudden shown up for shifts at the bakery?'

'I needed a job,' Addison told her grandfather with a shrug of her shoulders as though Grandpa should have known her answer already.

'I have asked you on many occasions to come and work for the business, and every time you told me no, so why now? What's changed?' Grandpa's tone had an edge to it.

'The bartending job I have, I can't do it anymore,' Addison explained to everyone in the room. But was she willing to give up more information about herself?

'Why not?' My grandfather grilled my sister.

'It makes me sick,' she fired back at him. They haven't always gotten along. It was why she had never put in any hours at the bakery before the last four weeks. Grandpa only had to raise his eyebrow at her before Addison continued. 'The smell of alcohol makes me sick.'

'I appreciate the shifts you have done to help out while Harley has been away, but if you want to continue at the bakery then you have to start at the bottom and work your way up, just like Harley did,' my sister was told sternly.

'But...' Addison said. She would always want the easy way out.

'Addison,' Grandpa warned, 'tread carefully with your next words. I may not work at the bakery anymore, but I still have a say in the business.'

'Start at the bottom, but that's not fair, Grandpa.' Addison looked her grandfather in the eye and scoffed at him. 'I know how to manage a business. I've been doing it for two years now at the bar I work at, so I should at least be able to start with managing the three shops the bakery has.'

'Managing the shops?' Grandpa replied with his own scoff, and I wanted to laugh myself, but I didn't. I kept my laughter and my thoughts to myself. 'You may have experience managing bars, but Addison, do you even know how to bake? Anything?'

I was interested in what my sister had to say, but she didn't say anything, she just shook her head.

'Then you start at the bottom. If you want to manage the James Family Bakery then you have to learn how to bake,' Grandpa told Addison firmly.

I could see she wanted to object, and I wasn't the only one who could see the change in my sister's body language, because Grandpa then said, 'My word is final. And Harley.' He turned his attention back to me. 'What happened?'

I knew Grandpa wanted to know where I had been and why I hadn't been at work, but to tell him that I had to drag Addison's dare into it and all of my other shit too.

I couldn't contain the mess just to me anymore. It was about to become everyone's mess.

'I just couldn't do it anymore,' I began. 'The hours I put in at the bakery, the factory, and then the paperwork on top of that, it's all too much. When you retired five years ago, Grandpa, the work kept me busy and stopped me from hitting rock bottom, but my insomnia isn't the same now as it was back then. I'm tired. The bakery has been growing since I took over and it's too much for one person to manage by themselves.'

I watched as my mother narrowed her gaze on me. Surprise filled her facial features before it disappeared a moment later. Zach squeezed my hip for comfort. I guess my mother didn't know about the insomnia. Well, she did now, but I couldn't stop to explain it to her.

'You always said Addison and I would do this together, work alongside each other, but I didn't think it would take this long for Addison to come on board. It's great that she is, but after all the hours I've put in, I'm burnt out.' Relief washed over me now that what I needed to say was out in the open.

'It will be easier now Addison is on board,' Grandpa explained. 'You can start to cut back your hours.'

'But for how long? Until Addison gets sick from the smell of the bakery and finds somewhere else to work. Then what happens?' I knew I had hit a nerve and maybe it wasn't fair, but life wasn't fair. It was about time this family dealt with the elephant in the room.

'Harley, you bitch.' It was loud enough that everyone could hear it.

'Addison, I know you thought this would play out differently, but you need to fess up to what you have done,' I said to my sister, even after what she'd just called me.

'Fess up to what, Harley. What does Addison need to fess up to?' Grandpa stared between the two of us with his eyebrows drawn in.

'You need to tell them. They will find out sooner or later.' I met my sister's eyes straight on. Her eyes were green just like mine. She was pissed and so was I, but she had started this mess. I just wanted it to work in my favour. I wanted out.

Maybe she needed to fess up about the dare she put on me, but she definitely needed to tell our family about her pregnancy. She wouldn't be able to raise a child on her own, and she would need our help. Addison had always been the wild one of the family, so her news shouldn't come as a surprise to anyone. It didn't to me when Addison had shared her news right before she had dared me. I remember the night four weeks ago when I'd found her waiting on the veranda of my house. She'd blurted out, 'I'm pregnant,' and after I'd congratulated her, Addison had proceeded to lay out her dare for me to sing in a public setting or hand over this house and operations of the bakery to her.

I knew Addison's pregnancy was the real reason she wanted what I had. So, I did the one thing that she wouldn't be able to back down from. It was my turn, although the stakes weren't as high as Addison's, but then again, maybe they were higher.

'I dare you, and if you don't, I will.' My eyes stayed locked on my sister's.

'Oh my God. Enough with the dares! You two are neither children nor teenagers, you're both adults.' It was the first time our mother had spoken, and she had our attention now. 'I don't know when these dares escalated, but they need to stop. These dares have clearly torn you two apart. They were always meant to be a bit of harmless fun between the two of you, to stop you from getting bored. They were meant to be a way for you two to always stick together and have each other's backs. Now look at the both of you. You look like you want to kill each other.'

Just when I thought my mother had finished, she said, 'Tell us about the dare, Addison. What did you do?'

Addison didn't say anything, not at first. My sister and I were both staring at our mother, and it was quite possible we had both come to the same conclusion. When did our mother re-join humanity instead of being the recluse she had become?

'Mum?' Addison said.

'Don't Mum me, Addison.' Our mother said. 'I may have not been present in the years after your father's death, and I'm sorry. I was depressed for long time and getting out of bed most days was impossible. But you two had always been good girls, and thank you, Robert and Johanna, for all that you have done when I couldn't.'

My mum had gone silent, and I could tell she needed to compose herself to say what she had to say next. 'When your grandparents moved us out of their house, I knew I couldn't sleep the rest of my life away. It's taken a long time to get to a place I'd call normal, and I work on my new normal every day. I still have moments where I can't get out of bed, but I know that's okay. It took me a while to find a job that let me work from home as well as the office. But I found one, and when I have one of those days where I can't face the world, I stay home.'

Hearing Mum tell us about her struggle since my dad had passed made me realise I wasn't the only one who hadn't fully come to terms with my father's death. She had surprised me as much as I guess I had surprised her.

'Tell me, Addison, what did you do?' My mother asked, no longer wanting the silence she'd created to linger.

'I dared Harley to sing publicly and if she didn't, she would have to hand over the operations of the family business and this house to me. Harley doesn't sing anymore because the last time she did, she blacked out. So I dared her to. I didn't know she would take off like that.'

'What?' My mother was shocked our dares had gone that far.

'Why?' Mum and Grandpa's questions were a one–two punch into the tension that had built in my living room.

'Because I want everything that Harley's been given, this house and her job. So I would have stability when I had my baby.' As she dropped this bombshell, Addison looked at no one in particular but around living room instead. My sister without a doubt was oblivious to everything I had achieved at the bakery. The house was a gift, and my job was the opportunity to work hard in the family business.

'Baby!' everyone except Zach and I exclaimed, astonished.

Zach raised eyebrow as he glanced at me, which told me he wasn't impressed by the 'given' comment Addison had made, not after the conversation we'd shared in his truck on our way down to Melbourne.

'You're pregnant?' My mother questioned her youngest daughter.

'Yes,' was all that Addison said. Her one-worded answer hung in the silence that followed.

No one was shocked that Addison wasn't forthcoming with more information about her pregnancy. But that was Addison keeping her business close to her chest. We were all slow to congratulate my sister, and the thoughts running through everyone's minds were evident in the lines of their faces as they looked at one another.

Grandpa was the first to recover. 'With a stunt like that, Addison, I shouldn't employ you,' he told my sister. 'But as you have shown interest in working at the bakery, I'll train you personally, just like I did with Harley. If you aren't far too along in your pregnancy, we should have plenty of time to work on your baking before we move onto your management skills.'

'Great,' my sister huffed as she stood, her interest in our family meeting depleted. 'If there is nothing else to talk about, then I would like to go.'

We all said goodbye to Addison and watched as she strolled down the hallway of my house. Grandma slid the kitchen chair she was occupying back, stood, and followed Addison out of my house. Would Addison listen to any of the words anyone spoke to her?

'Harley, I expect to see you back at work next week,' Grandpa said as he turned his attention to me.

'No,' I said back. This new-found confidence made it easier to stand my ground.

'Harley?' Grandpa's voice had only slightly risen.

'No, Grandpa.' I didn't raise my voice. This was my chance to start to change things in my life. 'I'm sorry, but I won't be back at work next week. If you want someone to work in the office for the bakery, please hire someone or get Mum to do it, if she's interested. Now that Mum is back on her feet, she could handle it if you train her or get someone else to train her. We all know she needs to put in as many hours as Addison does.' I may have overstepped, but I didn't want to work in the bakery anymore.

'Harley, this is not like you. What's happened in the last four days that has made you like this?' Grandpa asked me.

I'd found out something: that I'd been stuck in Groundhog Day. But also, I'd found there was more to life than work. I needed balance, less work and more fun.

'I told you I needed a break, Grandpa,' I responded as we locked eyes. 'There is more to life than work, and I needed to see what life looked like when I wasn't at work.'

'This is all your fault.' Grandpa pointed to Zach. 'What rubbish have you filled her head with?'

'I haven't filled her head with anything, sir,' Zach said firmly as Grandma sat back down in her chair at the kitchen table. 'Harley needed a break and now that she's had one, she is an even more amazing woman than when she sat down exhausted at my bar.'

Did Zach just call me amazing in front of my family? Of course he did. Heat flamed my cheeks as I thought about how Zach had come to the conclusion that I was amazing. Was it my four-day break that made his statement true or was it that I had stood my ground and was finally making changes in my life? Regardless, now that I was stepping back from my job at the bakery, I realised I needed some alone time to figure out what I was going to do next.

I moved away from where I stood next to Zach and moved further into my living room. 'I know that this has all been a lot to take in, but I think this meeting is over for now. I know we'll all be in touch as we transition into this new phase, but right now, I need some time alone to work out what I want for the first time in my life.'

Mum kissed my cheek as she walked past me and out the door. Grandma squeezed my hand, and I kissed her cheek. Grandpa walked past me, and I almost let him walk out without another word between us, but I didn't.

'Bye, Grandpa.'

But he remained silent as he reached for Grandma's arm. A moment later, Zach and I were the only people left in my house.

I let out a deep breath.

'You were incredible,' Zach said.

'Thank you, Zach, for being here. But I need you need to go too,' I said softly.

'No,' Zach said as he came to stand in front of me.

'Zach.' I tried to formulate the words that I would say to him. 'Spending time with you has been incredible, and I will forever be grateful for the break I've had. But if the last four days have taught me anything, it's that I don't really know myself other than a workaholic who used work to escape actually living. I need to figure out who I am.' And I needed to do this on my own, to find my free-spirited independence the same as Addison had. 'So I would appreciate the space to do this.' I needed to prove to myself I could do this. Not rely on anyone or my job, just myself.

'Believe me.' I grabbed Zach's hand. 'If there were any other way to find what I'm looking for, I would do it.'

Zach hadn't pulled away just yet, so I brought his hand up to cup my face and kissed his palm. 'I told you, I'm a mess, and I'm going to change that. I want to be the woman you deserve.'

Zach tilted my head back with the hand that cupped my face, then he leaned in and pressed his forehead to mine. I closed my eyes and let his touch sink in. Then Zach let go of my face and walked out. I touched the necklace he had placed around my neck yesterday as I told myself there was work I needed to do. Not at the bakery, but on me.

Twenty-one

I had asked for space. Told Zach to leave. The only person who calmed me, I had made leave my house. I believed it was a good idea. What I needed to do, I had to do myself.

My first night without Zach was not the best, and I knew every night without him would only get worse, until I didn't sleep at all. I tossed and turned and thought about him all night. But as I laid in bed and willed myself to sleep, I decided it was time to take responsibility for myself.

The first thing I needed to take care of was the bakery. After today's family meeting and the look Grandpa gave me, something didn't feel right, and I wanted to get to the bottom of it. The other thing I needed to take care of was me, and that meant I needed to talk to someone about my dad's death and the accident. I needed to understand the insomnia and also why I blacked out. There had to be a better way to cope. Then I needed to figure out if Zach and I could be more than the moments we had already spent together, because I definitely wanted to spend more time with him if he'd have me.

The next day I was on a mission to find some answers. But after a shitty night's sleep and three cups of coffee, I didn't feel as brave now as I had last night when I'd talked myself into this. Butterflies in my stomach this morning told me I was almost back to how I'd felt before my break. But not quite. Today was a brand-new day and I had to accept that a lot of things from now on would be new. That different would be good.

I was about to leave my house when I heard a knock at my door. *Surely,* I thought to myself, *Zach wasn't going to come back to try and change my mind.* If he were on the other side of my door, I didn't even know what I would do. But when I opened the door, it wasn't Zach but someone just as familiar: Lex. Had Zach, like that night at his bar, sent his sister to check up on me? What had Zach told Lex? Why would she show up at my house randomly?

'If you've come here to lecture me about Zach and tell me how much of an idiot I am, you can go right ahead, but I have somewhere I need to be.' I let her into my house anyway.

'Jesus!' Lex laughed, straight off the bat. 'I'm not here to give you a hard time about my brother. Yes, Zach sent me to make sure you were okay and hadn't fallen off the deep end. He's just worried. You're back in his life, and he doesn't want to lose you again.'

'I'm fine, Lex, and you can tell your brother I'm okay,' I told Lex honestly. 'I have a few things to figure out and take care of, then I want to make a plan to be with Zach. I don't want to lose him again either.'

'Thank God!' Lex exclaimed. 'You know you've had the hots for him for like ever! And him for you. But you could talk to me. Let me help you.'

'Thank you, Lex, but as I said to your brother, I need to do this by myself. I appreciate your offer to talk, but I don't want to burden you with my shit.'

She nodded her understanding. 'I know we were never close when we lived next to each other, Harley, but if you are going to be in Zach's life, then this is me reaching out to you. I would like us to be friends.' Lex placed the business card that was in her hand on my kitchen table, then she turned to face me. 'I'm going to leave you my card, and if you need me for anything, please call me or send me a text.'

It was sweet that Lex cared. I'd never had someone like her in my corner since my dad had died, not even Addison. It was hard for me to accept. I reached over to pick up the card Lex put down on my kitchen table and found she had left another business card under her own. 'I can't call that number and you know it.' I blurted, and just managed to refrain from rolling my eyes at her.

'Why not?

'Your mother's name is on this card. Your mother may be a psychologist, but I don't want to burden your family with my problems.'

I shuddered at the thought of the conversation Mrs Black and I would have. I didn't want to reminisce about living next door to the Blacks. The whole reason to visit a psychologist would be to talk about me, my insomnia, my blackouts, my dad and why my heart on occasion would beat freakishly fast. I needed to work on my strength as an independent woman before I explored my relationship with Zach.

'It's not often that Zach talks about the women in his life, but he's been talking to Mum about you,' Lex confessed. 'She knows you're back in his life.'

So that's how Zach knew he could put me in a cold bath. But I still didn't want to talk Mrs Black; I only wanted to talk to someone who didn't know me.

'Harley, honey. No one who knows us Blacks wants to be psychoanalysed by my mother, not even her own adult children, but she has several people working for her you could talk to.' The look Lex gave me told me I should know this. 'Please tell me you will think about it?' Lex reached out and squeezed my hand for encouragement. I returned her gesture with the nod of my head.

'Will do,' I agreed. I needed Lex to go so I could get to the bakery. 'But I really do need to go now.' I grabbed my handbag and threw it over my shoulder as we both walked towards my front door.

Lex hugged me goodbye on the street, and we headed in opposite directions. The bakery wasn't too far, and that was a good thing for my legs, but not so good if I wanted to snoop around the office. We all lived about the same distance. We were all within five kilometres from the factory in our own houses. The factory, and everyone's living arrangements, were all tangled together, that much I knew. But I needed to know more.

I decided the first thing I needed to do was to find the bakery's business terms, the ones I'd stumbled upon recently, and look at them more closely. The James Family Bakery needed an overhaul because I wasn't going to be managing the business anymore.

I needed to sort through all the paperwork in the office that I could find before I went in search of a lawyer to help me with the business. Because after yesterday's family meeting, I had convinced myself that Grandpa James was hiding something.

When I got to the office situated upstairs over our factory and main bakery, I walked in the rear entrance and climbed the stairs to the second level. When I opened the door to the office, no one was there. Relieved I was alone, I got to work to find the information I needed.

One side of this square room had a leather lounge, the same leather lounge I had spent many a night on, while the other side had a bookcase with a few of Grandpa's favourite books, his cookbooks and achievements. Next to the bookcase were four cabinets which were, as far as I knew, filled with paperwork.

I sat down at the desk ready to start my search, only to find paperwork scattered across the desk. Addison had been here. I could tell she had been trying to help enter the daily figures. I tucked the paperwork under the keyboard to deal with later and opened the drawers on the left-hand side of the desk, as that was where I'd stumbled across and found out about the business terms about a week ago. But they were not here today, so they must have been filed away.

What I did find in the bottom desk drawer was a leather-bound A4 zipped-up folder that looked like the one my dad had once carried around. I didn't even open it, just shoved it into my handbag. I would look at it later when there was no chance of being interrupted.

I moved from the desk to the cabinets, and I searched each drawer in the hope that I would find something. The first cabinet of four drawers had employee records in it, two for current and two for past employees. I stopped for a few moments to check each of my family member's files, and they were pretty consistent. Nothing was hidden in them, and not even my dad's file had anything out of the ordinary in it.

The second cabinet of four drawers had the bakery paperwork in it, all of Grandpa's paper records that I'd digitised over the last five years. This filing cabinet stored years and years of invoices, receipts, budgets, profit and loss, tax returns, and assets and liabilities statements.

The next cabinet had two drawers of supplier information; the other two drawers contained special order information. The last cabinet was the one I really wanted to have a good look through as it was where I thought all the information I needed was filed.

I didn't get to look, not right now anyway. I heard voices and footsteps coming up the staircase towards me. Halting my search, I took a seat back at the desk and fired up the computer. I know I said I wouldn't work at the bakery anymore, but I needed answers and the only way to get them was to hang around.

'Harley?' My mother and grandfather said at the same time. They were surprised that I was here.

'Mum, Grandpa,' I answered in a voice that was higher than I normally used to give my them the impression they had caught me by surprise, but what I didn't want them to know was what I was doing.

'What are you doing here, Harley?'

I wondered if my grandfather was suspicious of me.

'Consider this my two weeks' notice. I'm not quitting, just going to take a little break from the family business.'

Grandpa wasn't happy but he didn't press me on the issue. I turned away from him and towards my mother. 'What are you doing here, Mum?'

'I'm here for the tour of the bakery. After yesterday's family meeting, your grandfather offered for me to take a look around. He also thinks I need to pull my weight.' My mother elbowed me before she grinned at my grandfather in jest.

'Well, if you're here for the tour, we may as well get it started.' I turned to Grandpa James and said evenly, 'I can take it from here. I know the bakery better than anyone. While I show Mum around why don't you take Grandma out for lunch.' Grandma James would love for him to show her some attention. He had, after all, put in as many hours as I had, and he needed to spend more time with Grandma. But he offered again to show my mum around.

'I know you own the bakery, but you are retired, Grandpa, and you left me in charge the day you did. I'm the manager, and I do a good job, so let me show Mum the ropes.' The words were out of my mouth before I knew it as I stood up from the behind the desk.

'Okay Harley, if you're sure,' Grandpa responded. 'Lunch out would be nice.' He said goodbye before walking out.

It would a chance to spend some time with my mother. We hadn't spent a lot of time together since the accident. With my mother's depression and my insomnia, I'd never seen her out of her bedroom. By the time my grandparents insisted Mum, Addison and I move out, I had become the manager of our family business and was stuck in Groundhog Day whereas my mother was coping with living her new normal. There were only a couple of times a year that Grandma James would make us all get together. I knew my mother would appreciate the tour I would give her.

'First of all, how much do you know about administration?' It was a question I felt stupid asking. I was interviewing my own mother on her work experience. Where did she work when we lived in Melbourne? I remembered she worked at the bakery named 'Sweets' in Mulwala for the four years we lived there. Did my mother know anything about managing a business? Was she currently working in administration? Could she handle working in a bakery this big? I had to believe the answers were yes.

'You mean can I manage an office?'

Okay, that was not the answer I expected from my mother, but I guess you learned something new every day.

'Harley, I can do this job with my eyes closed.' My mother's next words stopped me in my tracks. 'This was my job back in the day when you and your sister were little. It was actually how I met your father. He would always make an effort to get to work early when he worked night shift just to see me before I left for the day. Then he would walk me to my car, and one day after a few months, your dad finally worked up the nerve to kiss me, and we spent every day together ever since. I worked here at the bakery up until Addison were born. I moved on from James Family bakery to another office job when you and Addison started school.'

It had been a long time since I'd heard those stories, or my favourite story of how my dad had met my mum. 'When Dad wasn't telling Addison and me about his crazy days in his band, you were telling us the story about how Ethan fell for Princess Mia.' I waited for Mum to look at me. 'I know we don't talk about Dad anymore, but I want to. I don't want to forget him or the crazy things he told us he did.'

'I fell apart after your dad died. I'm so sorry I wasn't there for you girls. But we won't forget your dad, and we can talk about him and the crazy stories he told whenever you want. '

'I would like that. Will you be alright working here, Mum, with memories of Dad all around you?'

'Somehow I think I'll have to take each day as it comes,' my mother answered before she asked a question of her own. 'How do you feel about me being here now that you're stepping down?'

How did I feel about spending the next couple of weeks working alongside my mother as she transitioned in and I transitioned out of working at the bakery? I had missed my mother's recovery the same as she had missed my spiral into insomnia as I grieved my father's death. We never checked in with each other; we were just trying to get through our days the best way we knew how. Now that neither of us were living in our own dark days, my family needed to work on the closeness we'd once had before my dad died. So, I told my Mum as much.

'I know losing Dad was hard on you, and having Grandpa and Grandma James around after he died kept you, Addison, and I together, but our close-knit family fell apart. It will take some time, but we should work on being close again, especially now that Addison is having a baby.'

'I would like that,' my mother repeated my words back to me. 'I would like us to be close again.'

'Okay.' I gave my mother one of my more genuine smiles and in return received one of hers. 'Let me show you where everything is here in the office, then we can wander downstairs to the shop and where everything is made in the factory.'

I showed my mother all the cabinets I had just rummaged through, so she knew where to find all the paperwork and where to file everything. When I got to the last cabinet, the one I didn't get to look at before, I found three of the four drawers empty. Either Grandpa had left room for expansion, or some files had gone walkabout. There was one file in the top drawer, and it had all the information about the bakery inside. I took the whole file out and stuck it into my handbag, along with the folder I already had in there.

'What are you doing?' my mother asked when I had finished with my handbag.

'Do you know where Dad's Will is?' I ignored my mother's question to ask my own.

'Harley, what are you up to?' I guess my mother knew how to play that game too.

'Do you trust me?' I asked her, and she nodded her head. 'Yesterday at the family meeting, I got the sense that Grandpa was hiding something.'

'Your grandfather isn't hiding anything, Harley.'

I nodded my acknowledgement to my mother; I didn't want to worry her unnecessarily. She didn't trust me that something was wrong and as much as I wanted to believe her that nothing was, I couldn't ignore the feeling that Grandpa was keeping something from his family.

Grandpa had a hold over this family, and I didn't know why. Then a thought crossed my mind, *Had he taken advantage of our vulnerability to keep us close for some reason known only to him?* If he had, I needed to find out why.

I didn't tell my mother about any of my suspicions. I showed her around the shop and the factory floor probably quicker than I needed to, but she thanked me for the basic tour and we both left early. We would have a fresh start tomorrow and get stuck right into all things that were office paperwork.

'See you here at eight tomorrow?'

'See you then,' she replied. Then she reached for me for the first time since my father's funeral to really hug me.

I locked the office and made my way back to my house to figure out the paperwork I had stashed in my handbag. I hoped somewhere inside the files held the answers to the suspicions that were niggling me.

Twenty-two

When I got home I dropped my now-heavy handbag onto one of the chairs at my kitchen table. I kicked my shoes off and took a moment to wander around my house.

I thought about what I would take with me if I had to leave here tomorrow. The answer: there wouldn't be much. I had never been one to hold on to things. I guessed what I had would either fit into the one suitcase I owned and the one box of treasures I'd kept since living with my grandparents. The house had been furnished when I moved in, styled by my grandparents, who were only too happy to help.

I pulled the contents of my handbag out onto the kitchen table. I didn't open the files straight away. Somehow, I was a little nervous about what I would find.

My mobile chimed with a new message. I wanted to ignore it, but just in case it was bakery-related, I dug my phone from my bag. The text was from Zach.

Z: I hope you find what needs to be found. When you do, come back to me.

I thought about a response but wasn't quick enough. Zach had text me again.

Z: I just want you to know I'm on your side. I know you have to do this your way. I just wished you would have let me continue to hold your hand.

Zach's words hit a soft place inside me, and I wanted him to know that I would find my way back to him. But it was the business first, then me, then Zach. That was the way it had to be. With my phone in hand, I sat down on my lounge.

H: I appreciate your support and I would have loved for you to continue to hold my hand. But right now I want to work on being the best woman I can be for you.

I moved back to my kitchen table in front of the leather-bound folder and unzipped it. I didn't know what to expect as I opened the folder, so I took a seat and sifted through paper after paper. After the first quick look through, I wondered how my dad's folder had ended up in the office desk drawer. Had Dad left it there? Had Grandpa put it there and simply forgot about it? Why had I not bothered before this moment to look inside? I guess I was managing okay and up until now I hadn't needed to.

Dad had kept tabs on his father. That was what this paperwork told me. He had kept important papers in his leather-bound folder, and it was now time to sort through them. I took out all the papers in Dad's folder and laid them out on my kitchen table.

I didn't understand them and none of these papers made any sense. It took me a few hours to comprehend what was on them. But it all fell into place once I looked at the last piece of paper. The paper I held in my hand told me that my dad had been working towards upgrading and expanding the James Family Bakery to another factory and more shop fronts. He had wanted to bake more than bread and savoury pastries, and to expand the bakery range to include sweet pastries too. This expansion would have taken a few years while he saved the money, but his plan was to move back to Melbourne after Addison and I finished high school to focus on modernising the James Family Bakery brand.

Grandpa had kept hidden that he hadn't been the head of James Family Bakery for quite some time. My dad had been in charge before he died and the papers from the lawyers stated the change in ownership was…

Wait…

Was that right? I stared at the date while I tried to make it all make sense. The date was too familiar, and I was caught by surprise. The date the handover was effective from was the last time we'd headed to Melbourne as a family. That was the purpose of our school holiday trip, I now realised ten years later, to make the changes to the business my dad had wanted.

Grandpa had known the direction his son was going to take the family business when he'd handed it over to my dad. But the James Family Bakery hadn't expanded in the last ten years. We'd ended up in Melbourne like my dad had envisaged, but none of his other plans had come to fruition. And I wondered why that was. Had Dad's dreams been too much for Grandpa? Had Grandpa been waiting for me to take over to be able to bring my dad's dreams to life.

I needed to find a copy of my dad's Will. Was my mother the only beneficiary? Why hadn't she continued on with what Dad had planned? Was missing him the only thing that had kept my mother away from the bakery, or was it her depression, or was there something else? Did my mother think she couldn't do it – run the family business without my father? Was it easier let Grandpa maintain control?

It was time to set what my dad had wanted into motion. The first thing I needed to do was call his lawyer, but at this time of night they wouldn't be open. I made a note of the lawyer's number I needed to call. Then I crammed the papers back into the leather folder, zipped it up and stashed it in my wardrobe. I wanted to hold onto the folder until I had spoken with Dad's lawyer.

I tossed and turned and stared at the ceiling most of the night. My mind wouldn't let go of the information I had learnt. Now that morning was here, I was worse for wear. I cursed myself and wished Zach were here with his arm around me so I could let it all go. But Zach wasn't here. Soon, was all I could tell my weary self that things would be better.

I called Mum as soon as I could to tell her I wouldn't make it to the office today. She didn't question me, and I didn't offer any more information than I needed to. It would be good for my mother to be there by herself, to sink her feet in, to get a feel for being back where it had all started. And to work on her own terms without someone watching over her shoulder.

The call to the lawyers was next, and the appointment was set. Although there was a wait, I couldn't complain. The next call I knew I had to make, but didn't really want to, was to the psychologist. I couldn't deny I needed the help anymore, not after last night's lack of solid sleep, unable to shut off the outside world. I needed an olive branch now more than ever.

I called the number Lex had left me but without a referral from my GP, I knew how much this would sting me. But did the money really matter if my health deteriorated to a point that I was so mentally crippled I couldn't leave the house I lived in? I couldn't do that to myself; there was a light at the end of the tunnel, and I just needed to find it. The first availability was today, later this afternoon, so I took it. I needed to take the first step to get myself on a track that was better than the one I was currently on.

I eyed the folder still on my kitchen table and the papers inside it. I needed to sort through the folder and to try and understand Grandpa's side. I made myself toast and a coffee and sat down. The folder I stared at was a decent thickness as there were many papers inside. Most of them related to when Grandpa had first set up the bakery and were most likely useless to me. But I looked at them anyway.

Like a dog with a bone, I knew I just couldn't let this go. I couldn't help myself. I needed to understand. I took all the papers out and laid them all out just like I had done last night with what was inside of Dad's folder. The papers in Grandpa's folder were untidy and I didn't understand any of it, which was why I also needed the lawyer.

I grouped papers that I thought went together. Everything in here seemed so dated. Grandpa's papers were old-school, and the writing was almost illegible. I found the business terms I had stumbled upon hidden amongst the other papers in the folder. Once everything was sorted, I realised the business terms I had found had been superseded by my dad, who had taken over ownership of the bakery.

When I thought I had read through everything, I put all the papers back in the folder, closed it and put it with Dad's leather-bound folder in my wardrobe. I needed to hold on to these, keep them safe until my appointment when I could talk to the lawyer.

It was time to get ready for my appointment today. There was no need to see my reflection to know that one restless night's sleep and an overactive brain could turn a woman into a red-hot mess. But one could hope that a shower, the right clothes and a little make-up could iron out the wrinkles and smooth me, Harley James, out.

Only after I put myself through the wringer of my get-ready routine did I look at myself in the mirror. I could see I was tired; the makeup wouldn't hide that. But I put it on anyway and felt a little better. As I gave myself one last look in the mirror, I knew I had done enough to give me the confidence I needed to leave the house today. I may have even given myself enough confidence to get through the appointment I was about to walk into.

Twenty-three

Four weeks. That was how much time had passed since I had watched Zach walk out of my quaint Victorian terrace because I had asked him to give me some space. God damn, did I miss that man. Four weeks. That was how much time I'd had to work on myself with the help of my psychologist, where we talked about my how I was feeling and how to deal with my anxiety. Now I was ready to move on and take the next step. Four weeks. That was how much time I've had to wait for my appointment with the lawyer's office. That day had finally come.

I looked back at the last four weeks and wondered how I'd managed to do what I did. The answer was: one day at a time. It had taken longer than I'd wanted to see the lawyer. But every day I waited I was able to work on the exercises my psychologist had given me, including the calming exercise. It was a breathing technique I had been shown and was a must before bed and any time throughout the day when my heart started to race.

My life would soon be wrinkle-free. Well mostly, anyhow. There was some stuff that would take longer to smooth out, mainly my relationships with my mother, Addison and my grandparents, as I had been distant with them over the last five years. But that was okay, it was a work in progress, and I got better at opening up every day. I now had a plan in place, and I was determined to stick to it. There was also a man I hoped still waited for me.

My time at the bakery since I had told my mother and grandfather I was stepping away from the family business had come and gone. Technically I was on holidays, but in reality, I was two weeks into figuring out what I was going to do next.

My mum had settled into her office manager role easier than I thought. I'd only had to show her the new computer program I'd purchased to help manage the money coming in, how to enter the bills to manage the outgoing money and how to order in bulk when the stock levels were low. Otherwise, she really didn't need my help. I didn't mind that my mother didn't need me at work; my mind was elsewhere anyway.

Mum was so talented with her organisational skills in the office she was able to move on to managing the staff and their rosters. She even helped out on the bakery floor. She swept up flour, received deliveries, stocked up on supplies and checked the quality of our bakery products. The only thing she wouldn't do was lift the bags of flour; she made the other bakers do that. I was proud of her. She was back on her feet. It was so good to see her happy in her new normal without my dad. This was what he would have wanted, Mum working for the family business even though it had taken her ten years to come on board.

Five years to overcome her depression and another five years navigating the workforce until she'd found something that suited her. The James Family Bakery was what suited my mother best.

The last two weeks had been the worst though. I had been stuck in limbo as I waited for my appointment with the lawyer's office. I'd had no choice but to hang around. In Melbourne. For that long. To kill time, I exercised every day, another technique the psychologist recommended to me. My body was less curvy and pasty white and musclier with a healthy glow.

While I'd hoped today wouldn't be too difficult, the process consumed a large proportion of my time, and the paralegals. Why I had bothered with an appointment at the lawyer's office I didn't know. I had wasted my time.

Brad Waters, the lawyer who had been assigned to sort through the information I brought in, introduced himself when I first arrived but left me shortly after with his team of paralegals.

It made sense for me to use the same firm, Waters' Law Firm, that my dad had used to change over the ownership of the bakery. I had taken his work folder with me in preparation to ask questions about the plans he'd had for the James Family Bakery. But as I was merely a manager and not the owner, the paralegals weren't overly helpful.

I even asked the paralegals about my dad's Will, and the explanation I received was what once belonged to my father now belonged to my mother. I knew nothing about Wills, having been fifteen at the time of my father's death, but now, ten years later, I held a copy of his Will in my hands.

Exhausted from my time spent at Waters' Law Firm, I crashed down onto my lounge and dropped my head back into its cushioned arm. I sighed, wanting tomorrow to come around quicker than it was. Time dragged as I became stuck in my own head trying to find the right words to not only tell my family but what I would say to Zach as well. My phone vibrated next to me, and I almost didn't answer. But when I looked at the number I didn't know that had come up on my screen, I knew I couldn't ignore it.

'Hello,' I said.

'Harley James?' I was asked by the person on the other end.

'Yes,' I answered, as butterflies began to dance in my stomach.

'This is Brad Waters,' the voice told me. 'We met briefly earlier at Waters' law firm, and I'm sorry I was unable to sit in on your appointment.'

Why was I now on the phone with the lawyer? Was there something I had missed at my appointment? I was none the wiser, having already spent time with his team of paralegals and learning nothing new.

'What can I do for you, Mr Waters?' I politely asked in return, wanting this conversation to be over. I didn't need to waste any more of my time with lawyers.

'Please, call me Brad. I believe you asked my team many questions about the James Family Bakery, your father's Will and what will happen now that you won't be managing your family's business?'

'Yes.' I had asked those questions amongst others, not that his team of paralegals offered much in the way of answers. I just wanted to make sure the James Family Bakery could manage without me.

'I know my team weren't forthcoming with the answers that you wanted, Harley. We are bound by privacy regulations, and without your mother, we were limited on what we could tell you.'

Damn privacy regulations.

'Mr Waters,' I started, then stopped. 'Brad, at the end of the day the bakery is in my mother's hands and now that she's working there, I hope now my father's dreams can come to fruition.'

'I understand that you have planned a family meeting?' Brad's tone was professional. How he knew what my plans were was beyond me. Maybe I'd let it slip to the paralegals that I had organised a family meeting for tomorrow. An inkling in the pit of my stomach now that the butterflies had stopped told me that maybe Brad knew something I didn't.

'That's right.' I spoke as confidently as I could. Why did he want to know about the meeting I had planned? What more could there be to go over?

'When, Harley?'

Patience was definitely not this man's virtue.

'You have paid Waters' Law Firm to do a job, and I have a responsibility to talk to the rest of your family.'

Total lawyer speak. His mannerism though reminded me of Zach, which just made me miss that man even more.

'Okay.' There was no point arguing with a lawyer, who was out of my league. I was unsure that having Brad at my home was a good idea, but if the man said he needed to speak to the rest of my family, then I needed to trust it was for a good reason. I just hoped I wasn't about to be blindsided.

'What time, Harley?' Brad pushed for a time.

I hadn't yet thought about it. Was it too late to cancel the meeting I had already set up? Yes. My family needed to meet as we all needed to be on the same page.

'Noon at my house tomorrow. I gave my details to your team.'

'See you tomorrow,' Brad said before he hung up our call.

So, now all I had to do was tell my family what time we needed to meet. I leaned back into the lounge and kicked my feet up onto the coffee table. With my phone still in my hand I opened my family's group chat and texted them.

H: Family meeting tomorrow. My house, 12 pm. Please don't be late.

The message had been seen by everyone. But no one replied and for that I was thankful. This time tomorrow everyone would know what I knew, that I'd found Dad's folder and the dreams he'd planned to make come true. My phone chimed and just when I thought Brad was about to cancel on me, the message I saw on my phone wasn't from the lawyer. It was from Zach.

Z: I know I haven't heard from you, and I know you must be busy. I just want you to know you are always on my mind and that I miss you.

H: I miss you too.

It was all I could think of. It was the only response I had.

Z: I have an acoustic event on this weekend. I don't sing at the events very often but this weekend I will be. I've practised a few new songs and I would like to play them for you. I hope you can make it.

My fingers itched to type out another response, but I didn't know what to say. So, I didn't say anything. I wanted to surprise Zach when I turned up unannounced. I wanted to believe a surprise was the best way to get us back on track.

Tomorrow, I would be one step closer to Zach. Tomorrow, I could get out of Melbourne after Brad and I talked to my family. All I needed was a way to get back to Zach. I thought maybe I could get the man himself to come and get me and whisk me away. But I had so much to say to him, it didn't feel right to explain everything on a three-hour drive back to his house. Zach was also a busy man with his event coming up.

I would have to think of someone else to give me that ride, or maybe another mode of transport. I thought about Lex and that she had reached out to me offering her friendship. Maybe I could text her and ask her for her help.

I got off the lounge and picked up the business card Lex had left me with her details on it. After I added her as a new contact in my phone, I sat back down on my lounge. I hesitated for second and questioned if this was a good idea. But my fingers typed out a message anyway. Lex had said after all that she wanted us to be friends. This was me reaching out to her to apologise.

H: I wasn't very nice to you when you came to my house to see me, I'm sorry.

I hit send and before Lex could reply, I typed.

H: I don't have many friends, and I would like it if we could be.

L: OMG, I was just about to text you. Zach is having an event this weekend at his bar and I'm going to show my support. Would you like me to give you a lift?

H: I would love a lift, but I have a family meeting tomorrow.

L: I have to work until four, and I want to leave Melbourne around five. Does that work for you?

H: That would be perfect.

L: Okay. See you then.

H: See you then.

I put my phone down and took a deep breath. I smiled a big grin, even if it was only to myself. I couldn't believe this really was about to happen. I was about to walk away. From my family to a man who had single-handedly stopped my unhealthy lifestyle and helped me see the light at the end of the tunnel of my Groundhog Days.

I would give everything up for the boy I'd crushed on in high school, who also happened to be my neighbour before my father had died. The boy I'd kissed all those years ago and never saw again, until just over a month ago when my life changed for the better.

I pinched myself. Yep. I needed to get a grip. I needed to get off the lounge and go pack. I just wished the time would pass quicker than this.

Twenty-four

Another restless night. Sleep for most of the night escaped me. I knew it wasn't the insomnia as my sleep had been better this past couple of weeks. Last night was nerves and excitement. My time in Melbourne was almost over, and I could finally get out of here. I was ready. My one suitcase was packed and under my bed. My one box of treasures was packed and stowed right next to my suitcase. Today was the day I had asked my family to meet me. The countdown was on until everyone got here.

The time passed slowly. Either that or I got out of bed way too early. Now that I was ready, I wore holes in the floorboards of my house. The house was already tidy, and I was already packed. There were no other jobs to pass the time. I could make something, a batch of biscuits I thought to myself, but I didn't want to get my family's hopes up.

It had been over four weeks since I had been anywhere near dough of any type, and I liked that I wasn't under the pump.

That there wasn't any pressure. So, I didn't make the biscuits. Instead, I walked the two blocks from my house in George Street, Fitzroy, to Smith Street to get morning tea for my family. After Addison had revealed that she was pregnant at our last family meeting, I wanted morning tea to be a celebration of my sister's news, not just from me but from my mum and grandparents.

Somewhere close to the time I said we should all meet, I heard the doorbell ring for what would be the first time of many until my family were all here. I opened the door to my mum, and we exchanged hellos.

Mum dropped her handbag onto the lounge and when she turned to face me, she said, 'Harley, what is this all about? This meeting?' The look on my mother's face said she was a little worried. There was nothing to worry about, but I couldn't tell her that. We had to wait for everyone to get here. It was only fair.

'All in good time, Mum. How's the bakery?' I was curious how the bakery was going without me.

'The bakery is running well. There are a lot of things I remember how to do and a lot of new things I'm still trying to get the hang of.'

I could tell things with my mum were good because she looked healthy and vibrant.

I was so pleased my mother was back to the way I remembered her when my dad was still around, now that she was on her feet.

The doorbell rang again. This time it was Addison. After more hellos, Addison walked down to my kitchen and greeted our mother.

'How's work at the bakery?' I was also interested as to what her answer would be. Addison wasn't allowed in the factory and had been relegated to shifts across the bakery's three shops.

'Great.' It was a sarcastic answer, but I'd take a short answer over the silent treatment any day.

'I purchased morning tea for you.' I waited for Addison to make eye contact before I continued. 'To congratulate you on your pregnancy.'

'Thank you.' Addison's reached for one of the biscuits I'd purchased, sarcasm still present as she spoke.

Our sisterly love may never be the same again, but I was okay with that, for now anyway. Addison made her way over to the lounge and plopped herself down into the cushions.

'How far along are you, Addison?' I wanted to know.

'Almost twelve weeks.'

My sister hadn't started to show yet, but that didn't stop her from rubbing her hand over her belly. I poured my mother and sister glasses of water and sat them down on the coffee table in front of the lounge.

'Again, I can't believe you're going to be a mum and I'm going to be a grandma.' I watched as my mother leaned in to hug my sister.

The doorbell rang again, but it wouldn't be the last time it would ring. If my grandparents were on the other side, then Brad the lawyer was yet to arrive. Or vice versa. When I looked through the peep hole, I could see my grandparents on the other side. They didn't look impressed but at least they'd bothered to turn up and hear me out. I opened the door and let them in. It wasn't until I entered the kitchen that my grandparents greeted everyone in my living room.

'So, why are we here?' my grandfather asked.

The words came out of my mouth before I could stop them. 'To congratulate Addison on her pregnancy.' Whether my grandfather believed my words or not, I would never know.

Everyone was here for a reason other than to congratulate Addison. I was just waiting on Brad to arrive before I said anything. My grandparents sat down at my kitchen table, the same as four weeks ago. I poured two more glasses of water for them and offered biscuits to everyone.

The doorbell rang again, and I hoped Brad was standing on the other side of my front door. I sighed in relief as I opened my door to let the lawyer in.

'Everyone's in the living room,' I said. Brad followed me down my hallway and stood next to me before we began.

Everyone turned their attention to Brad, but nobody spoke. Were they perplexed as to why he was here? I opened my mouth to start this family meeting, but no words came out. What was I meant to say anyway, to get this meeting underway. Somehow it didn't matter that I hadn't spoken as Brad had stepped forward.

'Mr and Mrs James. Mia. It's been a few years since we last saw each other. You all look well.' Brad said before he turned his attention towards Addison and moved closer to her. 'You must be Addison. I'm Brad Waters. I was your father's lawyer.'

Brad outstretched his hand for Addison to shake. When she had shaken his hand, he made his way back to stand next to me. A momentary glance around my silent living room told me my guests were waiting for me to start. Waiting for me to explain why I had asked everyone to meet only four weeks after our last family meeting.

'I don't know what happened at the reading of my dad's Will, or after his funeral, but our family fell apart. As hard as it is to admit, it has taken a long time for me to realise that this family is broken. We all have drifted into our own solitary lives, and we can't keep going on like this, not now that I won't be managing the bakery anymore.'

No one was staring at Brad anymore; their attention was solely focused on me. I even had Addison's attention. 'Dad wouldn't have wanted us to drift away the way we have, but we can't change that. We can only move forward. Dad had taken over ownership of the James Family Bakery before he died, and if he left everything in his Will to Mum, then the bakery is Mum's to manage.'

The bakery had always been my mother's to manage, and why for the last ten years she hadn't, I may never understand.

'Oh, Harley.' Hearing my name had me turning to look at my mother. 'What you have to realise is that your father was the love of my life, and carrying on his dreams while he wasn't here was too much to cope with at the time. Your dad had grand plans, which I'm sure you know about if you've read through his work folder. I noticed it as I walked in.'

I nodded my head but didn't say anything.

My mother spoke again. 'Your dad wanted you to follow in his footsteps, Harley. To be his apprentice and one day take over the business. Your father wanted to pass on the family tradition.'

'But you let Grandpa continue to manage the bakery?' Not once had I thought that the reason I couldn't upgrade the James Family Bakery was because I needed Mum's approval to sign off on everything. But I hadn't known the ownership of the bakery was Dad's before I'd read through his work folder. I'd thought Grandpa still owned it. Nor had I known my dad's dreams were exactly what I'd wanted to do with the bakery: the upgrades to the factory, the expansion of our brand, more shops and another factory.

'Yes, Harley,' my mother replied. 'I wasn't the baker in the family. Your father was, because his father had trained him.

In my mother's silence, I realised she had a point.

'Allowing Grandpa to manage the bakery while he trained you allowed part of your dad's dream to come true. I also wasn't in a position to manage it.'

'When you took over managing the bakery,' Grandpa James said, 'I told your mother it was time she joined us there, but she disagreed and told me she needed more time. Mia said she was still getting back on her feet and that you were doing a great job of managing the bakery in her place.'

So had Grandpa James kicked us all out of his house because Mum wasn't ready to work at the bakery? Or because I had begun to manage the family business? Or had we all simply outgrown each other and needed our own space?

Addison had reached out her hand and placed it on our mother's knee. 'What was Dad's plan for me?' Addison asked with sarcasm, questioning where she fit in with a family of bakers.

When Addison made eye contact, Mum replied, 'Addison, your father knew you had his mile-wide wild streak and carefree nature that couldn't be tied down to any one spot. He knew you were more likely to run away and join a band than you were to help with the bakery.'

'Oh,' fell out of Addison's mouth before she commented. 'But Dad settled down eventually.'

'And he knew eventually you would too.' My mother squeezed Addison's hand. 'And if you want to work at the bakery and one day manage it, you have to be trained the same as Harley.'

Addison nodded in understanding but didn't say anything else because the moment she was sharing with our mother was interrupted. Brad had spoken.

'Ethan James knew that if anything happened to him, his wife would be devastated. Unfortunately, no one knew how long Mia would be devastated for. Which is why when Ethan took over ownership of the bakery, he came to me to set up a family trust. Every asset Ethan owned at the time and planned to own in the future would go into that trust. For the last ten years, I have overseen the James Family Trust, and now that you're managing the bakery, Mia, you can manage the family trust as well.'

'Family trust? What assets?' Why was this the first time I was hearing about my dad having set up a family trust? Were the details of the trust explained when the Will was read and because I was underage, was never told? And did Mum never say anything about having a family trust because of her depression? A family trust was not something you forgot about, even if Brad had been overseeing it. How had the trust my dad set up over ten years ago survived all these years? Had it survived because of me? Because of my effort to get up and go to work every day?

I had spent a whole day with Brad's paralegals talking about the plans in my dad's work folder and there was never any mention of a family trust. Why had my mother not mentioned there was a family trust? A trust that singlehandedly survived because I had been managing the family business.

I now needed to work out if being a baker and working at the James Family Bakery was what I really wanted. As I had singlehandedly kept the family business operational for the last five years, my break from the James Family Bakery would be indefinite.

'The family trust was never meant to be a secret,' my mother replied defensively.

And before my mother could say another word, abrupt words came out of my mouth. 'Then please tell us about it.'

But my mother wasn't the one who replied. The voice that spoke was deep. Male. Brad's response to my question was, 'When the ownership of the James Family Bakery was in your father's name, he came to me with his intentions to hold the family business in the trust and reinvest the money from the trust to acquire a residence for each member of the family. If there was any money left over after paying the bills then each beneficiary would get a share.' Brad paused to let what he had said sink in. 'As of today, the trust holds four houses and the James Family Bakery, which includes the factory and the shops.'

'Beneficiaries?' Who was a beneficiary of the James Family Trust? Just my mother or did my father include Addison and me?

'The beneficiaries of the James Family Trust include Mia, Addison, and you, Harley.' Brad advised, as I tried to recall if I had ever received anything other than the wages I'd paid myself. Nope. Nothing came to mind. But that wasn't true: I had been living in this house and hadn't needed to worry about the bills. No one had ever explained why to me.

'And the houses?' There were four houses in the James Family Trust, and I wondered which four houses they were.

'Yes.' Brad answered again.

Did my mother not remember the details of the family trust my father had set up? Or did she only know my father's intentions for the trust?

'This house, your mother's house and there are two houses in Mulwala that make up the four residences in the trust.'

'Mulwala? What houses?'

When I heard Brad read the two addresses out loud, they sounded familiar, but I wanted to check their location. I reached out for my phone, then stopped myself. I recognised the street name and that the houses were next door to each other. I had been driven down that street. Attended a party there. Spent a few quiet days there. With Zach. He lived in the beautiful house that neighboured the rundown bungalow I had seen on my walk.

My head was spinning. So much had happened since I had returned to Melbourne. I closed my eyes to find my centre. Breathed in to a count of five then out to the same count. I repeated the same breathing technique the psychologist had taught me a few more times.

Two hands then cupped my shoulders.

'Harley, honey.' I opened my eyes to see my mother in front of me. 'We were going to retire, your father and I, in the house we were building in Mulwala. Your dad was going to purchase the bakery in the main street and we were going to live there. And Grandma and Grandpa James were going to come up from Melbourne and stay in the bungalow next door.'

Mum took a deep breath then continued. 'We were going to move back to Melbourne when you girls finished high school and your dad was going to teach you both the skills that his father had taught him. Once you were both trained, you were going to be given the opportunity to stay in Melbourne and manage the family business.' My mother's eyes watered with the tears she tried to hold in. I knew it must be hard for her to talk about her and Dad's broken dreams.

'I'm proud of you, Harley, and your dad would be proud too, even if it didn't unfold the way he planned it.' My mother let go of my shoulders and returned to the lounge and sat down.

'On top of what I have already mentioned being a part of the James Family Trust, there is also one other business you need to be made aware of.' Brad looked around my living room, and he held everyone's attention.

'What business?' I asked.

'Sweets.' The name of the bakery sounded familiar. Then I remembered Mum had worked there while we lived in Mulwala.

'Sweets had come up for sale around the time of the change in ownership of the James Family Bakery. Ethan had told me about it, and I made sure all the paperwork that was needed was signed.' What Brad had just explained seemed to be news to everyone.

'We never went back after the accident,' I stated changing the topic of conversation. 'To our house. To get our things. Whatever happened to them?'

Grandma spoke up for the first time today. 'Your grandfather and I paid for all your belongings to be packed up and stored in the bungalow until the three of you were ready to cope with the memories of losing a husband and a father.' She held in tears as she looked at first my mother then Addison and me as she talked about her only son.

'And the house next door to the bungalow?' I said out loud as I thought about how Zach had come to live in the house owned by the trust my dad had started.

'The house was to be rented out until it was decided what I wanted to happen with it. But without your father, I was never going to retire and live in it,' Mum admitted.

'Zach lives in that house,' I told the members of my family, and waited to see their reactions. Their eyes widened slightly. They didn't know Zach had been renting out our house. Did Zach know the house belonged to my family?

'What happens now?' Addison asked.

'You will start training to be a baker, and I will continue what I started four weeks ago managing the bakery,' my mother replied.

Addison spared a glance at me, then asked her question. 'What about Harley?'

'What about me?' I asked as evenly as I could.

'What will you do? With your indefinite break? Where will you go?' My sister seemed genuinely interested.

'Zach's sister Lex is driving to Mulwala tonight and I'm going with her. You remember Lex? You two were inseparable when we lived next door to the Blacks.'

Addison nodded and smiled.

And I would be okay, as soon as I saw the man with the armour tattooed over his heart. My pulse quickened at the thought of how much I missed Zach.

'You're not coming back, are you?' my family asked in unison.

No. Not permanently, but I would visit. There was something about spending time in a little country town with a man named Zach. 'I don't think so. I have some money saved up, so I'll be okay for a little while. But I'll be back to visit, especially with a little niece or nephew on the way.' But would all be well when I saw Zach again? My fingers were crossed.

'You swore you would never go back. That it would be too painful. You said you didn't want to walk around in reverie bumping into old family memories.' Addison had called me out on something I said a long time ago.

But she didn't know about the things that had happened since I'd said those words. Of course she didn't. Her dare had changed everything. I had fallen in and out of Groundhog Day and had been diagnosed with anxiety. I'd reconnected with Zach because her dare had driven me straight past the point of pain where our car had spun out of control all those years ago. Now I was on the other side, and I was going to be okay.

'I've made my peace.' I needed tranquility, and a little country town could give it to me.

'Because of Zach?'

My sister would always push the boundaries of my comfort zone. Something told me that I would always need her to do that for me.

'Yes,' I told her, because it was the easiest answer. I couldn't deny how I felt about Zach anymore.

'You always did have a thing for him.' My sister and I both giggled the same way we did when we were younger.

'Yeah. I always did have a thing for Zach.' And I wasn't too scared to admit it in front of everyone.

Twenty-five

As our family meeting came to an end, my mother came up to me. 'You did good, Harley.' My mum squeezed my hand. 'You helped bring this family back together. You were right, we did fall into our own solitary lives. I realise now after my few short weeks how much I've missed not only working at the bakery, but also missed you and Addison as well.'

'I love you, Mum.' The words slipped out, but my mum deserved to hear them. She had been through a lot and even though she hadn't always been there for me, I hadn't been there for her either. There was a lot of wasted years to make up for, and it started right now by telling my mother I loved her.

'I love you too, Harley.' It had been a long time since I'd heard those words, and it felt good to hear them. Would our family meeting change the solitary lives this family had fallen into? I didn't know, but with each conversation and interaction

I planned to have from now on, I could only hope my family, grandparents included, would continue to grow closer together.

There was a moment's silence between us before my mum said, 'I'm so proud of you. Thank you for all the years you put into the bakery.'

'You're welcome,' I whispered as I reached out and squeezed my mother's hand.

My mum returned the squeeze of my hand, kissed my cheek, then said, 'Now go get your man.'

Before my mother left, I handed over the leather folder that had once belonged to my father. She was going to need it to implement all of the dreams my father had planned.

Brad shook my hand we exchanged 'take cares' before he left, and I wondered if we would ever cross paths again.

Both my grandparents kissed my cheek. My grandmother reached into her bag and placed a set of keys in my hand. 'Now you have some spare time, the bungalow next door to Zach's is where you can sort through your memories. Maybe find someone to give the bungalow a little love. I can only image the amount of work that needs to be done after ten years.'

'It needs some work on the outside from what I have seen, but I'm not sure about the inside. I'll see if I can find someone to bring her back to life.'

'Then find someone who would like to rent it.'

'You don't want the bungalow for when you visit?' Would my grandparents visit me in Mulwala?

'It's not that we don't want to visit you, Harley. Your grandfather and I would love to, but for the time we would spend in the bungalow, it would be better for someone to rent it out. We can always stay in a hotel.'

'Okay,' I said, when my grandmother hugged me.

'I should have told you a long time ago about this family's tradition of teaching the next generation to be bakers. I just couldn't seem to let go of the business I had built after your father died. You have been quite capable of managing every aspect of the bakery. You are like your father in many ways, and I'm sorry, Harley. If I could, I'd guarantee that things would be different at the bakery from now on. And I would beg you to stay and help me with your sister, but I understand why you need a break.'

I reached for my grandpa and the affection he hardly ever gave. I took it and hugged the man. They too needed to find their own new normal. Their lives changed all those years ago too when they lost their only son. But they would be okay now, we all would.

'Thank you for everything you have done. You rescued Mum, Addison and me from a black hole, but we can stand on our own two feet now. This is how Dad wanted everything to be.' I told my grandparents, glad that everyone was on the same page. 'You don't need my help with Addison, Grandpa, just don't be as harsh on her as you were with me. She'll make a good baker if you let her.'

'We don't want to lose you out of our lives, Harley.'

'You won't,' I told them as they left my house. I would make the time to call them and catch up whenever I was in Melbourne. I hoped one day my grandparents would also visit me.

When I walked back down the hallway, I realised Addison was still here, seated on my lounge. Maybe she just wanted to talk. Just her and I. Sister to sister. Maybe I needed to talk to Addison too.

Before Addison could say what she needed to say, I made my way closer to her and said, 'The last ten years of our lives may not have turned out the way that we wanted, but we have this opportunity to change how the next ten years of our lives turn out.' I reached for Addison's hands to squeeze them. When I let go of them, I told her, 'I may never come back to live in this house or Melbourne, and rather than leave it empty, I'd like you to turn this house into a home for yourself and that niece or nephew of mine.'

'I know I haven't always been there for you.' Addison's words had caught me off guard. With tears in her eyes, she continued. 'As your sister or friend or when you really needed me. You held us all together while you fell apart. I never knew. Never wanted to know. I'm sorry we fell apart. I'm sorry we grew distant. I'm sorry our dares spiralled out of control. But after that night at Jam, you stopped visiting me at work, and we didn't sing karaoke anymore. I thought if I dared you to sing, you would reach out again. Thank you for the house. As for taking over your job at the bakery, I will never be as qualified as you to run the family business. But at least now working with Mum and Grandpa, I can try as per Dad's wishes.'

'I threw myself into work after that night at Jam, and it took a long time to work up the courage to go out just to sing karaoke myself.' I confessed to Addison. 'Your dare, though, may have just saved my life. I got to reconnect with Zach for the second time since the accident.' A blissful sensation filled me as I thought about Zach and the time we had spent together recently. I couldn't wait to see him again.

'What?' Addison mouthed, and her mouth hung open, stunned.

'Yeah, that night at Jam,' I told her. 'He picked me up off the stage floor and took me to his apartment. Only I didn't know it was him until recently. When I walked out the next morning, his apartment was empty. I never remembered his face that night, as Jam was dark, and I was not in a good place.' I was glad Addison and I got to have this moment. This might be the moment we got to reconnect.

'Oh my God. That night. I was so selfish, all I cared about was me. Sure, I wanted to check out the new karaoke club and get up and sing. I didn't know "Flame Trees" would do that to you. In the commotion of you collapsing on the floor, Marcus pulled me from the stage to calm me down, then he took me home. I didn't even see you leave. Marcus told me that you were safe, that one of the owners was looking after you. I'm sorry I wasn't there for you.' Addison's words came out in a rush. Her ramble sounded exactly like mine. She was even breathless like me too.

'We're okay, Addison.' I reached out and offered my affection. 'As long as there will be no more dares between us.'

'No more dares, I promise.' Then Addison pointed to my chest. 'You found your necklace?'

'How did you know I lost it?' Maybe there were times my sister did pay attention.

'You always wore it, never took it off.' Addison reached out to touch the chain. She spoke of the time we still lived at our grandparents and had seen each other every day.

'I lost it that night we went to Jam,' I admitted to her. 'I found it though at Zach's. He'd had it this whole time. I found it hung up on the wall in his bedroom.'

'I know how much that necklace means to you. I'm glad you have it back.' I could see Addison reminisce about the way it was before everything changed.

'I'm glad too.'

When I heard a knock at the front door, I knew Lex was here to collect me. I let Lex inside and we exchanged our hellos. Seeing my sister, she then screeched, 'Addison! How long has it been?'

'Forever and a day,' Addison replied.

'You're not wrong.' Lex's voice had returned to normal.

'I'm going to be an aunt, can you believe it,' I told Lex, sharing my sister's news.

'Congrats to both of you. That's so exciting.' Lex leaned in to give her old friend a hug.

'Thanks,' both my sister and I said simultaneously.

'So, who's the lucky man in your life?' Lex sure did know how to grill people, my sister included.

'No one special.'

I didn't miss the shiver that ran through my sister.

'Addison you're having a baby. You're going to be a mum.'

'A single mum.'

'You won't be alone. Mum and I will help you whenever and wherever we can. Grandma James will help you too if you need her,' I reassured.

Addison didn't reply. There was more to my sister's pregnancy than she wanted to let on. Maybe one day she would be brave enough to tell me her story. 'If you ever want to talk, I'm here.' I pulled my sister into my hug before I said, 'I really am happy for you, Addison.'

Addison lips tipped upwards ever so slightly. Her half smile told me she was over talking about her pregnancy.

'So, Lex.' I changed the topic of conversation. 'Mum has taken over managing the James Family Bakery, and now that I won't be in the city, I know she could use someone with your experience in her corner. Would you mind reaching out?'

'That's great that your mum's managing the bakery.'

I'm sure Lex thought her face was unreadable, but I saw a slight twitch. 'I'll reach out when I get back.'

Did Lex already have enough on her plate and now I'd just added more to it? Maybe I shouldn't have asked. Surely Lex would have said if she couldn't help.

'Let me grab my things and we can go.' I made my way to my bedroom to pull out my box of treasures and my suitcase. I laid my suitcase on my bed pulled out an oversized tee-shirt and a pair of leggings and left them on my bed. My sister could wear them or not.

I handed the box over to Lex and headed for the front door with my suitcase in tow. As I turned back for my handbag, I caught Addison's eye. 'Will you be okay? I left some clothes for you.'

'Harley, you don't need to worry. I'll be fine. I too need to find what my new normal looks like.'

Even though she didn't want me to, I would still worry. I would reach out to her often, more often than before anyway.

'Call me.' I squeezed my sister's hand. 'If you need anything, I'll be there.' I then handed her the keys to my house. 'Take care, sis.'

'You, too.' Addison hugged me her goodbye.

'Bye,' Lex said as she followed me out.

'What's up with Addison?' Lex questioned me as we walked out to her car.

'It's been a long time since there's been more than dares between us,' I told Lex. 'Today felt like we could be close again. So much has happened in the last ten years, but my family is trying to find a way to reconnect. Addison has to find her new normal while being pregnant. Maybe she thought I would stay longer, but I have my own new normal to find.'

'Your sister didn't like it when I brought up the father.'

So I wasn't the only one who'd noticed my sister was a little off.

'Yeah, she hasn't said much.' In truth, Addison and I hadn't had a chance to talk, but once I was settled, I would reach out. 'I haven't had much of a chance to talk to Addison about her baby. I've been a little busy with the bakery and therapy,' I confessed of my own situation.

'You went to therapy,' Lex said excitedly, her face happy. 'That's great, Harley.'

I laughed at how contagious Lex's vibe was as we walked down the footpath.

We reached Lex's car, a souped-up black V8 Commodore wagon. This family and their cars, they sure loved to make a statement. Name, colour and noise.

Then I noticed that the last person I felt like seeing was leaning up against the passenger door. I hadn't seen Connor Black since that night at Black's Bar and Grill where Connor had manhandled me.

'No way, Lex.' I shook my head. I didn't want to be in the same space as Connor.

'Wait, you two know each other?'

'It's a long story.'

'And we have a three-hour drive, so you can explain on the way.'

I was surprised when I heard a deep voice say, 'I'm sorry.' Connor had spoken.

'I'm sorry,' Connor repeated. 'I should never have manhandled you.'

I moved closer towards Lex's car and locked my green eyes with the brown eyes that ran in the family.

'It's going to take time to forgive you, Connor, but the apology helps.' Connor gave a slight nod of his head, then I called shot gun.

I dropped my handbag at my feet and before I even had my seatbelt clicked in place, Lex had taken off. Connor had already made himself comfortable in the back of Lex's car. He laid out along the back seat. His eyes were closed and for all I knew he had gone to sleep.

Lex made her way to the freeway, setting her cruise control to the speed limit, and we settled in for our three-hour drive north. We chatted the whole way and caught up on the last ten years. Both of our lives had been less than uneventful. Mine with the bakery, the accident and lack of sleep. Hers with her overprotective family, her brothers included, her move to the city to find herself and the sassy independent two feet she now stood on.

'Are you playing at Zach's event?' I was curious as to why there were guitars in the boot of Lex's car. I'd noticed them when putting my suitcase in.

'Don't be ridiculous,' she said. 'Zach only allows the locals to sing at his events, and Connor and I aren't exactly locals. We were, but we both now live in Melbourne.'

'But why the guitars?'

'Stress relief,' Lex told me.

I didn't believe her but maybe I shouldn't knock it until I tried it.

'I usually travel with my guitar. Sometimes I get to play it, and sometimes I don't.' Lex turned off the freeway, and there wasn't long to go now.

The glimpse of Lex's face that I caught as she turned her head my way briefly gave me the impression she was up to something, despite what she'd just told me about only locals being able to play tonight. After all my family's drama, I hoped Lex knew what she was up to.

After arriving in Mulwala, Lex pulled her car into the first spot in the Black's Bar and Grill carpark she could find. I hugged her across the centre console and thanked her for the lift. With only my phone in my hand, I took off. There was someone I needed to find. Someone I needed to give a little bit of love to.

Twenty-six

I walked into Black's Bar and Grill and moved to where I could hear the tail end of a song and the sound of cheers. I knew that song, 'Blacked Out' by Chris Young. I turned to the stage to see who could sing like that. I was only a little bit surprised.

A crowd had built up in the Carbon Bar. There was a small silence then the man I stared at spoke into the microphone. 'Thank you. I'm grateful to everyone who came out this evening to celebrate our annual acoustic shindig. It was a pleasure to perform for you tonight, and soon some of my friends will get up here and play for everyone. I have a couple more songs to play for you, and I just want to say that these songs go out to the woman who has my heart completely. I just wish she was here tonight to hear me sing them to her.' It was Zach who had spoken to the crowd.

Frozen to the spot, I hadn't taken my eyes off him on the stage. Tonight, he looked tired, maybe a little worn out, and I wasn't sure if it was from sleepless nights or this event. I knew I had contributed to his stress, but up on stage with a guitar in his hand under the stage lights, to me, he looked incredible, totally edible. From the way he wore his hair and the beard he hadn't shaved to the way his casual clothes fit over his lean body. There was no doubt that he was the man I loved.

There was another silence before Zach started to move his fingers over the strings of his guitar. I knew this song too. When Zach started to sing the first verse, my heart melted. I sang quietly along to 'Break on Me' by Keith Urban as I let Zach's voice wash over me.

He didn't know I was here, but I knew in this moment that this was where I wanted to be, right next to the man on stage. I wanted what he was singing to me, to lay my head on his shoulder, fall part in his arms and love him for the rest of my life.

As the song finished, Zach moved straight into his next song. Without an introduction, I wasn't sure if anyone here this evening would know this song. But Zach played it anyway, and I knew the only reason he knew this song was because of me. Because he'd found my favourite playlist from the night I'd stayed in his hotel, the playlist I had sang along to.

Somehow throughout the time we spent together, Zach had managed to copy the list of my favourite songs, and it didn't surprise me that he had learnt every one of them given the recent time we had spent apart.

'I Ain't Going Nowhere, Baby,' by Cody Johnson, were the words that came of Zach's mouth, and in that moment, I knew I had to let him know I was here.

I walked over to the sound desk to ask for the microphone, but the guy behind the desk just looked me up and down. Then

I saw Brock approach from behind and relaxed. After telling Brock exactly what I wanted him to do, I hugged him then took the microphone and waited for my favourite part of the song. And when it was my turn, I sang about changing our plans.

From the moment his microphone was turned off and he heard the female voice come out of another mic, I knew that he knew it was me. I walked towards him as I sang, climbing the stairs to stand next to him. I didn't face the people who had come out tonight to enjoy this event, but just gazed lovingly at Zach and sang. When I got to the chorus, he joined me. His mic had been turned back on so we sang the last part of the song together.

As the song ended and our audience cheered for us, Zach removed his guitar and put it down on the stand. He turned to me, took my hand and pulled me towards his body, then wrapped me up in his muscular arms and dropped his lips to mine. It was a kiss I never wanted to end, but this wasn't the time or the place for our reunion.

Zach and I both thanked everyone with a bow, then we both left the stage. Brock and Shea had made their way to the stage to take part in this event, but Zach didn't want to hang around to watch his friends perform.

No. He had other plans. Ones that involved me and only me. With a firm hold of my hand, he was on the move, and he was in a hurry. As Zach pulled me along, I didn't have to guess where we were headed. And as soon as Zach pointed us towards the stairs, I knew the only place down there that he wanted to take me to was his office.

Behind the closed office door, Zach pushed me up against it. As he reached down to turn the lock, I wrapped my arms around his neck.

'Tell me you're here to stay,' Zach whispered into my ear, and when I nodded ever so slightly, he added, 'Tell me you don't want me to stop.'

All I could do was shake my head, and with this movement, we had our hands on each other and our clothes on the floor. Our lips pressed together for the longest time, and it was the neediest kiss we had ever shared. It said I missed you and I want you so much. As Zach's hands cupped my face, he tilted my jaw ever so slightly upwards to get better access for his mouth to devour mine. Our lips and our tongues danced together with a need that I never wanted to let go of.

Zach picked me up with an ease I could get used to and laid me down on the leather lounge in his office. He reached for a condom and rolled it on, and all I could do was watch. I stared up at Zach as he stared back at me, our eyes locked. I guess four weeks really did affect a man. I felt a shiver run the length of my body. My desire was obvious. I squirmed a little against the coldness of the leather lounge, and one side of Zach's mouth lifted in the sexiest smirk I had ever seen on a man.

Zach ran a hand through his hair, and I found the movement so erotic as it stretched out all the muscles on his torso. He moved closer to me and stood over my body then kneeled down to check if I was ready, his tongue running the length of my pussy, and I squirmed again.

'Zach,' I moaned.

Zach moved up my body, his tongue flat against my skin as he licked in a straight line from my pubic bone over my belly button, through the gap between my breasts to my neck. My head fell backward to make room for him to continue the movement of his tongue up my neck and over my chin, where he came to a complete stop at my lips.

Zach kissed me again as he manoeuvred his body to lay on top of mine. I loved the feel of his nakedness against me, and my flesh tingled and shivered as I waited for the shock of electricity I got when we were passionate this way. Body to body, skin to skin, his lips covering mine. Our mouths moved together as we licked, bit, sucked and tasted one another, and I hoped this never got old between us.

Zach rocked his hips up and down, pushing his cock through my wetness, and I opened my thighs wider for him. My arms had already found their way around his neck, but he took my hands in his placed them over my head. One hand took a hold of both of my hands. I was stretched out for him, and I knew he liked the view. Zach's lips left my mouth and moved over my face along my jawline and down my neck. His whiskers brushed my skin, and I arched into him.

He made several passes with his lips, tongue and whiskers along the skin from my ear to the tip of my shoulder. The movement of Zach's jaw and the hair on his face only added to the sensations I felt right now. Small sparks of electricity where Zach's tongue left a trail felt magical.

'I need you,' I breathed against Zach's skin.

My words were the ones Zach wanted to hear. And as he wrapped my leg around his hip, he filled me completely. Zach kissed the tip of my nose, then began to move, thrusting his length inside me.

I knew it had been four weeks without him, four long weeks as I'd tried to figure me out. But right here, right now, I knew I needed this man in my life forever.

'Make me feel good,' I said to the man on top of me. 'For keeps.'

'There's only ever been you for me.' Zach continued to move in and out of me. 'I got you.' He hadn't told me he loved me, but I would take 'I got you' as the next best thing.

I pulsed on the inside, and maybe my happiness showed on the outside too. Zach had no idea how those words made me feel. I needed to tell this man I loved him and soon.

Our movements were quicker as we chased our own bliss.

'Babe?' Zach groaned, and I knew he was close. I was almost there too. I just needed a little more friction, and it would send me over the edge. When I felt Zach's finger rub my clit, my body shuddered, and I moaned with the strength of my orgasm.

'Oh my god, Harley.'

I felt my pussy clamp down around Zach's length, and I knew he had come. I had milked him dry for now.

Zach let go of my hands and gently moved my leg away from his body so he could withdraw. I moved my hands up to his face and cupped it. My lips chased his as I wanted to express to him without words that I didn't want this moment or what we'd just shared to be over yet. I wanted to continue to build on what we had.

Twenty-seven

God only knew what time it was when I heard a bang on the front door. I wanted to get up and answer the door, but I couldn't. I was still wrapped up in Zach's arms like I'd always hoped one day I would be. There was a growl from the man in question and I could tell he wasn't very happy he had to get out of bed. We had left Black's Bar and Grill after watching the remaining sets on stage. Unbeknownst to Zach, Lex had organised for her and Connor to sing, and he hadn't been too happy about seeing Connor in his bar. But he didn't cause a scene. We went home, made love and fell asleep in each other's arms.

'Let me get the door.' I made a move to leave his arms but he only tightened his hold on me.

Zach sang the lyrics of last night's song before he dropped a kiss on my shoulder and got off the bed. I thought about the lyrics he had sung to me now and last night, and I understood why he now called me baby, not babe. I would take either one as long as they came from his beautiful lips. Happiness spread throughout me.

Zach had slipped into dark grey track pants and a black tee. I guess he didn't want to show off his muscles to whoever was at the door. I rolled over and listened to the conversation unfold.

'You're not the only one who can play the guitar, Zach. Lex and I know how to play too. You could have at least stayed for the whole three songs. We just wanted to show our support. We didn't do it to piss you off.' It was Connor.

I had known Lex was up to something yesterday, and here was Connor apologising. Was it just for last night or was there more Connor came to apologise for.

I couldn't see Zach's reaction, only hear his words. His tone was sharp. 'Is there a reason why you have dragged my arse out of bed this early this morning? I really did want a sleep in today. It's my day off, and I could use a quiet one.'

There was silence for a moment. Then Connor said, 'I sold them. I sold every single one of them.' Another silence. 'Every single business I ever owned, dodgy and legit.'

'Connor. Are you serious?'

I could tell Zach was caught a little off guard. So, I got up, got dressed in last night's clothes and wandered out to stand by Zach's side. My fingers entwined with his.

'You're right, I am an arsehole.' Connor breathed deeply as he tried to get his next words out. 'To you, to Harley, to everyone and I'm sorry. My family deserves better from me. I want to try and be better.' There was another silence, but it seemed that Connor hadn't finished as he turned his attention to me.

'I didn't know you were my brother's woman.'

I stared up at Zach. I didn't know I was Zach's woman either. But before either Zach or I could speak, Connor continued. 'Your family moved in after I'd moved to Melbourne. I didn't know you then, and didn't know you and Zach were close. You were going to be my ticket, Harley. You and I, we could have been so rich. But I only ever thought about me and no one else. I'm sorry for every arsehole thing I've ever done, to you and my brother.'

Connor had made an effort to apologise to both of us, to mend the bridges he had burnt. It wouldn't happen overnight, mine or Zach's forgiveness of Connor, but it was a start to see him want to try to be better.

'I know I deserved the punch you gave me,' Connor confessed. 'For what I'd done to you over the years, and for not considering Harley's needs about a music career. It was the wake-up call I needed. I don't want to be that man. I sold everything for a clean slate.'

There was a moment's silence before Connor spoke again. 'Lex let me borrow her car to come here. I'd better make a move so she can head back to Melbourne. Thanks for the chance to apologise. Sorry I interrupted your personal time.'

'You're not going back with Lex?'

'No.' Connor shook his head. 'If I want my clean slate to work, I need to stay away from temptation, and Melbourne is full of it.'

'Connor, if you are serious about your clean slate, don't be a stranger.' Zach shook hands with his brother. 'If you're done being a dick, it'd be nice to have my big brother back.' Then the front door closed and there was the faint sound of an engine, a rumble as it started and moved away from the house. Connor was gone.

'Coffee?'

I nodded then followed Zach into the kitchen and made myself comfortable at the breakfast bar. 'Your brother apologised.'

Zach sat next to me as he passed over my coffee. The man knew how to make café quality coffee.

'It's a start. Let's see how serious he is about not being an arsehole and getting into trouble.'

We both knew there was a long way to go.

'I didn't think Connor had it in him to apologise to you or to me, but yesterday before I got into Lex's car, he did.'

'Harley,' Zach uncurled his fingers from his coffee cup and stood up. 'It's great my brother apologised to the both of us, but he's not who we need to talk about.' The words left Zach's lips to land in my ear on a whisper.

'Who do we need to talk about?' I knew full well who Zach wanted to talk about. Me. Harley James.

'Harley,' Zach warned.

I knew he wanted to know all about the last four weeks. My absence. But we were interrupted by my phone ringing. I'd been gone a little more twelve hours, and someone in my family was already reaching out to me. It was my mother.

'Is everything okay?' I asked after saying hello.

'Everything's fine. I wanted to let you know I've made some changes to the family trust your dad set up.'

I went into Zach's bedroom for some privacy. 'Our family meeting was less than twenty-four hours ago and you're already making changes to the James Family Trust? Why?'

'Your dad is why. Brad is on his way to see you at Zach's, and he'll be able to explain everything better than I can.'

Oh, I thought to myself, but didn't say it out loud. 'Grandma gave me the keys to the bungalow. She thinks we should rent it out, but I think we should sell it.'

'Have you got a buyer in mind?'

'No, but I can get Zach to ask around.'

'Talk to Brad,' my mother said before she told me she had to go.

As I hung up, I saw a message on my screen. Grandma James had sent me a text.

GJ: I've organised a removalist. He'll be there soon. I'll leave finding storage up to you.

I tossed my phone onto Zach's bed and walked back into the kitchen.

'Everything okay?' Zach asked me.

'Mum said dad's former lawyer, Brad Waters, is on his way here, and he will explain everything when he gets here.' Brad wasn't the only person on his way as the removalist for next door was as well. But I couldn't tell Zach that because there was more to explain than a lawyer and a removalist. There was the last four weeks to tell Zach about. I just needed the right time to share everything.

Our family meeting had been less than twenty-four hours ago, and my mother had already made some changes. Wasn't it too soon to be making big changes to my father's trust? Was the bakery and the trust too much to handle for her? Is that why she was sending Brad?

Zach's jaw twitched, all he wanted was for us to talk. But we kept being interrupted. With the way this day was unfolding, everything I wanted and needed to say to Zach would be told before I had the chance to do so in private.

I swivelled on my stool when I heard a knock at the front door. As I made a move to answer it, Zach gave a slight shake of his head. For some reason, Zach wanted to be the one to answer the door. I wondered if it was Brad.

'I'm Brad Waters from Waters' Law Firm. Is Ms James here?' I heard as soon as the front door opened.

'What is this about?' I knew Zach was as curious as I was to know what this was all about.

'Mia James has sent me. I need to speak with Harley.' There was an urgency in his voice that made me walk over to stand next to Zach.

'Brad, this is Zach. Zach meet Brad Waters, my late father's lawyer.' Zach and I filled the space of the open front door. 'Why on earth did my mother make you come all this way to see me?'

'Your mother made some changes to the trust.'

What changes? 'Yes, Mum just told me she'd made changes and that you would explain. It hasn't even been a day since our meeting, so what changes could she have made?'

'Can I come in so we can talk about this?'

Zach and I shared a look. He raised his eyebrow at me, and I knew he wasn't completely happy his day off had started out like this. But what could I say? I was less of a complete mess, but there were still a few things that needed sorting out.

Zach and I stood back from the door and let Brad in. He took a seat at Zach's kitchen table and pulled a file from his briefcase.

I took a seat at the table across from Brad. Zach grabbed his coffee, but he didn't sit down next to me. He hovered somewhere behind me. I knew I needed to talk to Zach, but I also wanted to know why Brad thought it was so important to travel all this way to tell me in person about the changes my mother had made.

'Brad, I'll just let you know that Zach isn't privy yet to our previous discussions. I would rather it was me and not you who told him everything.' Brad had a way of getting straight to the point, like ripping off a band aid, but that couldn't happen today.

Brad nodded his acknowledgement.

'Can you please tell me why these changes my mother has made are so important that you had to speak with me in person and not over the phone?'

'I have paperwork for you to sign.' Brad pulled a pen out of his front pocket. 'Harley, when your family first moved here, your parents were thinking about and planning their future. Your father had purchased two blocks of land and had a house built on each.'

My dad's grand plans. The plans I'd known nothing about until recently.

'Your father had purchased the local bakery about three months before his accident. Your school holiday trip finalised the James Family Trust and your grandfather signed over the James Family Bakery to your father. With the assets from Mulwala, the house you grew up in Melbourne and a newly acquired investment property, your house, the trust was set up to take care of you, your mother and your sister if anything was to ever happen to your dad.'

'Yes, I know all this.'

'If your father hadn't passed away, he would have trained you and Addison to become bakers just like him. At the end of both your apprenticeships, your father was going to make the decision whether or not to split the family trust. You and Addison would be partners in the James Family Bakery, and your trust would look after the business and the two Melbourne properties while your parents would have Sweets Bakery and the two properties here in Mulwala.'

'But my dad did pass away,' I said softly.

'Yes, and your mother has decided to split the family trust as your father suggested.'

Wow, this was a lot of information to take in.

'Harley, your mother would have told you herself but there is paperwork to be signed, that's why I'm telling you all of this.'

Zach took my coffee cup and moved towards the kitchen to make more café-quality coffee for the three of us. I knew this was Zach giving me space to look over the changes my mother had made to the trust and the paperwork that needed to be signed.

When I finished reading through the paperwork for the new trust Brad had put together, I faced him and asked, 'Is this correct? Is this what my mother wants?'

'Yes,' was Brad's simple answer.

My mother had set up a new trust in my name with this house and Sweets Bakery in it. All I had to do was sign and Brad would make these changes.

'There's just one thing.' I looked up at Zach, then turned back to face Brad. 'Before I sign, Mum said to talk to you about selling the bungalow next door.'

'I can get some papers drawn up.'

'The house needs to be emptied. It also needs some work done. I won't know the extent until I check the house out.'

'You haven't been inside?'

'When my father died, Mum, Addison and I moved in with my grandparents. Someone packed up our things and stored them next door. I haven't been inside.' I had only seen the outside of the house on the afternoon I went for a walk, and that was four weeks ago.

'Harley, you should take your time, think this over and talk to Zach. Work out what needs to be done next door.'

I shook my head. 'This is what my dad wanted then, and it's what my mum wants now.'

'If you're happy to go ahead with the changes your mother has made, you can sign the paperwork. When the bungalow next door has been sold, I can finalise all your trust paperwork.'

I nodded. There was a moment's silence before I said, 'Brad.' I wanted his full attention for what I was about to say next. 'I'd Alex Black as the accountant for my trust.'

'Alright, I'll set it up and reach out to Alex when your paperwork is finalised.' Brad stood and made his way towards the front door. 'My card is on the table if you have any questions, so please call me.'

'I'm going to read over this one more time, and when I've signed it, I'll let you know.'

Twenty-eight

'Why is there a mover's truck in my front yard?' Zach asked after I had showered and changed my clothes.

Zach stood by the bay window in his lounge room. I moved to stand in front of him and stared straight into his eyes, then told him the one thing I wanted to say. The one thing he wanted to hear. 'I love you. The truck isn't for you.' I pressed my lips to his cheek. 'It's for me.' I was calm as I moved past Zach, and out the front door. I knew I had stunned the man with the words that came out of my mouth.

'Wait,' Zach said, and the way his voice reached out across his front yard stopped me in my tracks. I turned around to see Zach leaning up against the front door. 'Lex left your things here on the veranda last night after she dropped you off. Your suitcase, handbag and box of treasures. How much more stuff could you possibly have?'

'Everything I owned I brought with me.' Then I surprised Zach with, 'The truck is empty, and I'll be next door. I've only got the removalist for the day.'

I made my way over to the mover's truck as he stared at me quizzically.

When the driver jumped out of the truck, I said, 'I take it my grandma sent you?'

The driver nodded.

'This isn't the house that needs to be packed up. The house that does isn't far from here. I'll direct you.'

'Okay,' the driver said. 'Jump in. Name is Jack.'

'Harley,' I told the mover.

I gave the driver directions to the house next door, and he manoeuvred the truck along the dirt track towards the neighbouring home.

The keys jangled in my pocket, and I placed my hand over them as I walked up the steps to the front door. I had never been inside this run-down weatherboard bungalow. I didn't know what to expect. I opened the door, and I wasn't surprised by the musty smell that hit me first up. I moved through the bungalow to open as many windows and doors as I could. Anything to air this place out.

After the smell started to disappear, I took a proper look at the home that was once meant to be a holiday retreat for my grandparents. But it had been used as a storage facility for all of my family's treasures instead. Now that the bungalow was to be sold, it didn't change the reason for it to be emptied. It had been ten years since I had seen what was once inside our family home, which was stored here.

The house was scattered with furniture and boxes. What a day to have to sort this out. Not the best time to deal with this but I had to work with what I had. I wanted this bungalow emptied today, then would find a builder to sort out what needed to be fixed both inside and outside.

There was furniture scattered everywhere with packed boxes in every room. I didn't realise how much our small family house had held back then. Maybe this wouldn't be so bad, I told myself, but how did I know. I'd never had to organise a move before, but I would figure it out. Every box would need to be sorted through, and I would get to it eventually now that I had nothing better to do.

I walked through the rooms and assessed what was inside. The mover, Jack, needed to know where to start, and I didn't have a clue. I didn't even know what to do with all of this, as I knew I had nowhere to store it. I stood just outside the kitchen deep in thought when I felt two arms wrap around me. I breathed in cedar and coffee.

'Zach?' He would never know how much this moment meant to me. I looked down and saw Abby at my feet. She sat and gave me her puppy-dog eyes. That told me she had definitely missed me. 'Can you help me figure this out, the bungalow I mean?'

'So, what's your plan?' Zach squeezed me tight.

'Get the bungalow sorted quickly before we talk,' the words rolled out of my mouth.

'Where do you want to store everything?' he asked me like I had a plan. There was no plan. Zach turned me around to stare into my green eyes.

'I haven't figured that out yet. I'm still trying to work out how to fill you in on everything that's happened,' I admitted. I knew we had to talk, and we would as soon as I figured out this bungalow.

'Okay, baby, let's get it all in the truck. I have an empty container you can use for storage.' Zach kissed my forehead and slapped my butt. Time to get this show on the road.

So that was what happened. Zach and Jack moved the furniture from the house to the removal truck. Abby found a quiet spot on the veranda to lie down and watch while I packed the back of Zach's truck with as many boxes as I could fit in it. Half an hour in and half-way through a load out to Zach's truck, I heard the sounds of a vehicle as it approached. Abby barked once but didn't move from her spot.

'Harley?' I heard an unfamiliar voice say as I placed the box I had in my hands on the tailgate of Zach's truck.

'Brock.' I was surprised as I didn't realise the men needed help. 'Did Zach call you to come and help?' The question had caught Brock off guard. He was here for another reason.

'Zach called.' Brock stepped closer to me. 'But I'm here to see you, actually.'

'Oh?' I leaned up against Zach's truck.

'Zach mentioned that you want to sell the bungalow,' Brock explained as to why he was here.

Zach hadn't wasted any time. 'You're interested in the bungalow?'

'I am.'

Something in Brock's voice told me he was still hesitant. 'I hope you're not disappointed?'

I'm not sure why Brock would think I'd be disappointed. It would be nice for Zach to have a neighbour and for someone to look after this bungalow.

'No, why would I be?' I leaned forward and hugged Brock. 'I'm surprised, I must admit. How did you even know about the bungalow?'

'I've had my eye on the bungalow since Zach moved in next door,' Brock told me as he leaned up against the side of Zach's truck.

'Wow, that's a long time.' I shook of my head and wondered how much Brock knew about this home. It would need ten years of maintenance to bring her back to glory.

'I couldn't believe it when Zach called to tell me about it.' The look on Brock's face said he couldn't be happier.

'I'll get my lawyer to contact you.'

Brock handed over a business card with his details on it. A quick look at his card told me he was a builder. The bungalow would be a perfect project for him.

I put Brock's card in my pocket as Zach made his way over after another trip to the removal truck. 'Congratulations, Brock,' I said.

'Congratulations are in order?' Zach's eyebrow was raised in question.

'Yeah.' I turned to Zach. 'Looks like you'll have a new neighbour soon.'

'Is that right?'

I tipped my head towards Brock and waited for Zach to catch on. Zach turned to Brock like he had read this moment right then stuck out his hand for Brock to shake. 'Man, that's awesome. I told you not to worry about asking Harley.'

'I'm just glad someone will finally get to look after this place and appreciate her.'

'Well, that's a relief,' Brock said. 'And you won't mind if I'm your neighbour, mate?'

'It will be fantastic to finally have a neighbour.' Zach pulled Brock into a man hug.

'Come on.' My words had broken up their man hug. 'There's work to do.'

'Do you know what you're in for? You'll have your hands full with this one,' Zach bantered with Brock.

'Come on, man,' Brock scoffed back. 'You do know what I do for a living, right?'

'I do.' Zach reached over to slap Brock's shoulder. 'Come on, there's plenty to do.'

We all followed Zach back into the bungalow. Zach and Jack picked the next item to haul out to the removal truck while I showed Brock around the small three-bedroom bungalow. I'm not sure if Brock realised how much work there was to do around the place, but it would be his soon, and he could do as he pleased. It would definitely keep him busy. But I think he knew his way around a house or two, as he was a builder after all. He could rip down a wall, build a wall or change the entire layout of the bungalow. He could do whatever he wanted to if this was his dream house.

It took another hour to get my family belongings out. Now there was a mess on the front lawn that needed to be cleaned up. Ten years was a long time to leave possessions unattended. Not everything was built to last that long.

I stared at the mess as Zach carried out the last box. We had let Jack go after the last of the larger furniture was packed away.

'Come on, let's get this last load into the container.' Zach tugged on my hand to pull me closer to him then whistled for Abby, opening the passenger door for her to jump in.

'Okay, but what about the mess?'

'I'll text Brock, and he can load it into the back of his truck.'

'He won't mind?' I wasn't sure if that was okay.

'No, Harley, Brock won't mind.' Zach started his truck and made his way to the container.

'Okay.' I stared out the window to think. There was a lot on my mind, and now I had to text Brad to let him know there was a buyer for the bungalow.

'What are you going to do with all this anyway?' Zach asked.

'See if Brock wants any of it, donate the rest of the furniture.' Maybe I had this all figured out after all.

'Your family won't want the furniture?'

I guess Zach genuinely wanted to know. 'I don't think so, all their houses already have furniture.'

'And the boxes?'

I didn't answer. I wanted to be the first to sort through everything. Separate the boxes into who they belonged to. When it was time to sort through Dad's stuff and our family photos, maybe Mum, Addison and I could go through it together.

What I really needed was to figure out what to say to Zach. Was this where I wanted to be? Here with Zach in a house that was meant to be my mum and dad's. To live in their house the way they were meant to? Did Zach even want me here? Living together so quickly? Zach and I really did need to talk.

If I'd paid more attention to the man next to me, I would have known he was up to something.

As soon as Zach opened the passenger door, Abby was off to her favourite place on the back veranda, leaving Zach and I to unpack the last of the boxes from the back of truck. Then Zach closed the door to the container, and I moved towards the passenger door of his truck. 'I don't think so.' I was spun around so quickly I felt dizzy.

Laughing, Zach slung me over his shoulder fireman style and carried me around the back of his house towards his back yard bar. The man had gone total caveman. 'If you move, you will pay.'

I was almost tempted to run just to play games with him. Zach's hand moved from holding the back of my legs to slap my butt, before he set me on my feet. I smiled as Zach pulled me closer to him and his lips moved closer to kiss me.

'Zach,' I said to get his attention. I had to find the words I needed to tell him. Start our conversation. But he pressed his index finger against my lips while our eyes met.

Then he grabbed an esky in one hand and mine in the other and we were off again. Down his man-made path to the river. As I looked up at him, I think I had finally caught on to why Zach had been silent. There was a look in his eyes and a hint of smugness about him that told me he was up to something.

Twenty-nine

Zach led me along the sandy edge of the river to the same spot he'd brought me to last time. Bringing my hand to his lips, he kissed my fingertips. I melted a little inside from his touch and the anticipation.

He dropped the esky into the sand and laid a blanket down. I dropped the towels he'd given me onto the blanket.

Zach had a plan – I just didn't know what that plan was.

'Whatever you're thinking about, Harley, just stop. It can wait!' When Zach noticed my stance, he stepped closer to me and whispered. 'Right now, this moment is about you and me.' The next words that came out of Zach's mouth were the lyrics from last night. He had sung them to me again. 'I ain't going nowhere, baby.'

'Is this our song now?' I was unsure of what else to say as Zach reached for both of my hands.

'What do you think?'

I guess he wanted that song to be our song. *It was perfect for us,* I thought.

'Our reunion, the last four weeks, last night and today have all been a whirlwind, baby.' The words Zach had spoken were the truth. 'We both need some healing, baby.' Zach and I shared a smile at the words I had sung to him, before Zach continued, 'Yeah, take my hand and I'll lead the way.'

Zach pulled me into him then dragged me towards the water. Just before our toes reached the shore, he picked me up. When the water was deep enough, he crocodile-rolled us until we were soaked.

'Now we have a reason to take our clothes off.' Zach's smile was sheepish on his way-too handsome face. His beard scratched my skin as he planted kisses along my jaw, and I knew he wanted to get under my clothes to my naked skin. He grabbed my legs, pulled them up and wrapped them around his waist. I could feel him, his hardness pushed up against my sex as he carried me out of the water.

This time Zach didn't dump me down onto the sand; this time he was gentle as he placed me on the blanket. A chill ran through me, maybe it was the water, maybe it was the man that hovered above me.

His hands roamed my slightly less-milky coloured flesh after he'd torn off my tee-shirt, and his touch left goosebumps on my skin from my neck to the waistband of my pants. I loved how this felt a little too much. My pants were next. He slowly peeled them down my legs and wrung out the water. All that was left was my underwear.

Zach stood in front of me and peeled out of his own clothes, quicker than I thought humanly possible. He stood butt naked on the edge of the blanket, and I had to admit I liked the view. Zach kneeled down and leaned in, reaching around me and unclasping my bra then it was gone, added to the pile of wet clothes. He stared, enjoying the view of my naked body. I will still curvy, but I now had a little more muscle. I couldn't help but smile. I liked that Zach liked looking at me.

The moment his hands landed on my hips, I felt the electricity run through my veins. It made me move my hands over my breasts, not to cover them and hide them away, but to massage them, to show Zach I liked to play. It felt good to touch myself, and I know that he liked it too. When I looked up into his eyes, I saw his hunger for me, and before I knew it my panties were gone.

Zach moved closer to me, lowering his lips to mine as his body covered me in the most delicious way. I would always want this man and only this man.

'Tell me again the words you told me earlier?'

I wondered what words from earlier Zach questioned me now about. Of course, I would be stupid if I didn't know. But I wanted to take this moment to toy with him.

'What words were they, Zach?' I pretended to think about the words Zach wanted.

'Don't be coy with me, Harley.' Zach reached for my ribs to give them a squeeze.

'It wasn't how I wanted to tell you for the first time,' I admitted to Zach, but I wasn't at all sorry that I had said them.

'Would now be a better time to say them?' Zach wasted no time and pressed his sex into mine. I gasped out loud at how good this man felt against me.

'Now would be a better time,' I whispered in agreeance.

'I love you,' Zach whispered into my ear as he lined himself up between my legs and pushed his way inside me.

I moaned, unable to say anything as I wrapped my arms around Zach's neck. I just wanted to enjoy this. Enjoy this moment. Enjoy and not worry that Zach was bare inside me. He pulled out and slammed back in. He did it again, and my body started to tingle. Another moan left my lips, the same way it left his. The tingle built each time Zach repeated his movements, in and out. More moans left our lips until we were close enough to fall off the edge and into our own bliss.

'Say it again,' I whispered as I wrapped my legs around Zach's hips. I wanted to hold him close while he said those words again.

'I love you, baby.' Zach stilled and leaned in to whisper his words into my ear.

'I love you. I love you,' I whispered back to Zach. 'Please make me come.'

They were the only words that Zach needed to hear to start his movements again to make me come. His hips pumped into mine and I knew by the way I felt inside that I was close to my climax. My muscles tightened around him. My legs squeezed around his hips. My body shook underneath him, and I always wanted our sex to feel this way: incredible.

'Come for me,' Zach said softly against my skin, and in that moment, I knew we could both feel my release. 'Again,' Zach murmured near my ear. 'Come for me again.'

Zach's forearms surrounded my head and stopped any movement I wanted to make. He took my hands from around his neck and pushed them over my head, where they landed in the sand. I felt the stretch in my body as my back arched off the blanket and into Zach's torso.

Zach's body skimmed against mine, and his hips moved out then in. He pulsed inside me. My sex muscles that were still clenched against his length started to spasm again. Orgasm number two rocked me just as much as the first, and that was when I felt Zach come inside me and fill me up.

He wasn't prepared for my bite to his bottom lip that started out gentle and ended up clamping down hard when he became more aware. And he reacted. Boy did he react, with a pinch to my nipple, the sting of which my body enjoyed way too much. It sent a current of fire through me that reached my fingers at one end and my toes at the other. My pussy felt it too, my muscles crushing Zach one last time.

He took control, manoeuvring his lips over mine and pushing my head back down on to the blanket. He devoured my mouth, slowly at first then harder the longer the kiss went on, and I thought I had gone to heaven. There was no way I ever wanted to push this man out of my life again. This moment was pure ecstasy.

'Damn, woman.' Zach pecked my lips then let me go and withdrew from my body. 'You make me feel so good.' His words made me feel gooey inside.

'So good.' I pressed my lips into Zach's skin. He still hovered over me so I kissed his chest.

After a moment's silence, I looked into his eyes. 'I want to know about your tattoo, Zach.' I said as I reached for Zach to wrap my arms around him.

'And I want to know about your last four weeks, Harley,' Zach responded as he too put his arms around me.

'You first.' I pointed at his chest then danced my fingers over his tattoo.

'Okay, my tattoo. The armour is to guard my heart.'

'Why?' Was there a reason Zach needed to guard his heart?

'To protect it from being broken.'

Had someone broken Zach's heart? 'Did it work?'

'No.' Zach shook his head. Armour hadn't stopped Zach's heart from breaking. Had I broken Zach's heart or were there other women that had broken it?

'Did I break your heart?' I couldn't help but ask Zach if I was the reason for his tattoo.

'You never came back after you kissed me so maybe my heart did break a little.'

'And the broken hourglass and fob watch?'

'That time is precious, and you never know when it's going to run out.'

'I love your tattoo.' I reached up and put my lips on Zach's chest, right over his heart and the intricate details of his tattoo.

Zach's next words though took me by surprise, but really, I should have known they were on their way. 'Talk to me. Tell me what happened after I left your house.'

I reached for a towel to wrap around myself as I sat up. Zach also covered up as he sat up beside me, and I was almost sad at the view I just lost. But what I needed to tell Zach, I couldn't do lying in his arms. I wanted our conversation to be more than just pillow talk, as he had waited all day for me to talk to him. It was also the price I paid when my man was about to feed me. Zach pulled the esky closer and reached inside to the picnic he had put together. Sandwiches, biscuits and cheese, water and chocolate. What more could a woman want? Apple pie and muffins. I was overjoyed. He'd found the goodies I'd frozen.

'The psychologist from your mum's practice was a big help with the mess that was my life.' I know my words surprised Zach, but I had to start somewhere. Why not at the place I went to for help?

'You went there?'

'Your sister recommended I go there,' I said honestly. 'Where else was I supposed to go?'

'Baby, it's okay.' Zach's words were calm as he reached out to push my chin up and brush his fingers over my cheekbone. 'I'm just glad you didn't talk to my mum.'

'I didn't want to talk to her when I didn't know what we were, especially after I sent you home that day at my house. I've been living with undiagnosed anxiety since my dad died. I wanted my therapy to focus on me, not my love life.'

'Anxiety?' Zach asked.

I nodded my confirmation. 'The psychologist is helping me deal with my anxiety. I haven't blacked out since your birthday.'

'That's great, baby. I'm proud of you.'

Zach was proud of me. I blushed and felt my body almost turn to mush.

'Did you talk about me with your psychologist?' Zach asked, and I nodded with a cheekiness on my face.

'I feel like you saved my health from a downward out-of-control spiral, and now that I'm a mostly organised mess, I feel like I'm right where I need to be.' At the light at end of the tunnel. 'Right here next to you.'

Zach grinned, and the look in his eyes trapped me. I knew this was where he wanted to be, too, with me. But there was more to say. There was a reason why we were apart for weeks.

'It took four weeks to get an appointment about my dad's Will with the lawyer's office,' I told Zach. 'Then I had to sit there in the same room with Brad's team of paralegals, and the whole time I was there all we did was skirt around answering each other's questions.'

'Ah, paralegals, how fun,' Zach joked.

'Not really. I wasted my time.' I let out a huff as I remembered how long that day was, wanting answers and not getting them.

'I know,' Zach said quietly. 'Is everything sorted now?'

'I think so.'

'Come on, you need to fill me in.' Zach reached over to try and coax out of me the information he wanted.

'My mum is where she belongs, working in the office of the bakery she now owns.'

'That's great.' Zach's words felt like there was something else he wanted to know about.

'It's going to take some time for my family to get back to the way we were before my dad died, but we'll get there. And thank you for the use of your container. It means a lot that Mum, Addison and I don't have to rush through sorting out our old belongings.'

'Harley.' My Christian name from his lips would always warn me not to play with him. I had avoided talking to Zach for long enough. 'Why was Brad here?'

'My mother made some changes to the James Family Trust.' I told Zach. 'In fact, my mother created a new trust just for me, and before my trust is finalised, the sale of the bungalow has to be settled.'

'Your trust?'

I nodded my head. 'All I have to do is sign the paperwork Brad left and send it back to him.'

'What's in your trust?'

'Tell me, Zach. Did you know your house belonged to my family?'

'Only when I signed the lease agreement.' Zach took my hand. 'When I was looking to move out of my parents' house, I wanted somewhere quiet after a long day at work, and this house gave me that.'

'My trust gives me my parents' happy ever after. This house and Sweets Bakery in the main street.'

Relieved, Zach grabbed my body and rolled us around in the sand and tickled my body. Our laughter was music to my ears as it filled the air around us.

Thirty

Three months later

Today was another of Zach's events. Today, like all events Zach put on, was a showcase of local talent. Of course I was stupid enough to allow myself to get dragged into this event and had agreed to sing. To think I was ready for this. With all the time in the world to practice, the songs I had learned for today were easy enough to get through when it was just me and the guitar. But in front of a crowd, nerves would be involved, and it wouldn't be as easy to get through the songs. There was still a chance I could get emotional and fail miserably. But I couldn't pull out now. I didn't want to let Zach down.

My name had been called, and it was time for me to get up there and do my thing. I had three songs to play just like everyone else who would play today. So here I was, on stage and under the spotlight at Black's Bar and Grill in the Graphite Bar with a guitar in my hand.

I was finally at that place where I thought I could do this and not fall apart. Not lose control and black out. The visits and phone conversations with the psychologist had helped me take one giant leap forward. With Zach's love, support and shoulder to lean on, I now had minimal stress in my life. Lex was right about the guitar being good for stress relief.

I took a couple of deep breaths to settle my nerves then stepped up in front of the microphone. 'My name is Harley James. I hope everyone is having a great time today.' The crowd cheered as I positioned the guitar over my shoulder. 'I heard this song recently and I wanted to play it for you today. This year will be ten years since I lost my dad. Dad, you were taken from me too soon, and I wasn't ready for how life was going to be without you. I love you and I miss you. Even though I'm not now, there was a time when I was drowning. I would like to dedicate this next song to anyone who has ever lost someone close to them. This one's for you, Dad.'

There was a big crowd here today packed in like sardines, and they were silent at the words I had just spoken. I pushed past the silence so it wouldn't get to me and strummed the guitar I'd borrowed from Zach. I played the cords I had practised since I'd come back here in the lead up to this event.

I stood in front of the microphone and sang the song I'd dedicated to my dad, 'Drowning' by Chris Young. While things were better now, there was a time when the lyrics to this song were very true.

I let the tears fall at the end of the song. I got through it, and I was okay. I wiped the tears away as the crowd applauded. It was time for my next song.

'I know some of you here tonight,' I said through the microphone to the crowd, 'have heard me sing the first couple of lines of this song, and if you don't mind, I'd like to sing the whole song for you tonight.'

My fingers moved along the strings of the borrowed guitar and played from start to finish my version of 'Dumb Things' by Paul Kelly. The crowd applauded, but the loudest cheers I heard were from Zach and his friends, the ones that had said 'wow' the first time. Their cheers brought happiness to my face, and my tears were almost gone.

I had one more song to play, and I didn't know if I could do this. I sent the biggest smile I had out to the crowd, and they threw more cheers back at me. I enjoyed myself. I had fun. But it took a lot of energy to be up here. I took a moment, closed my eyes and took a deep breath.

'This is my last song for you today. I hope you like it. The song is called "Here Tonight" by Brett Young.'

I worked my fingers through the cords of the song, and when it was time, I sang. I got through the first verse, then the chorus, and I could see the crowd start to sway with the rhythm. They liked my song choice.

I didn't know what came over me, but I could feel my control slip away. Too much energy had been zapped from me. I wasn't used to this much adrenaline. My fingers didn't stop, they didn't get the message, they knew exactly what to do and I was grateful. They continued to play through the cords of the song, but somehow my voice didn't want to work anymore.

I panicked a little inside, and that was when I saw movement from the corner of my eye. He was here with a microphone in his hand, and he moved it towards his lips. He sang the next verse for me while I caught my breath. I was mesmerised by the man who was on stage next to me, and I believed I could rein in this anxiety and pull off the song.

By the time the chorus came round again, I felt I had recovered enough to finish the rest of the song. Zach and I did it together. His voice had just the right amount of gruffness for this acoustic version. My voice, like nothing had gone wrong, was now normal as I sang along with Zach. His roughness fit with the smoothness of my voice like a glove. But if it weren't for Zach's presence, I would have run from this small stage.

I wanted to believe that Zach and I sounded perfect together. I wanted to believe that our voices had the right mix together and we could always do this. Sing together up here on the stage of his bar. But that was just a dream. Our song was over, and we said our thank you's. The emcee invited the next local act to the stage to play their songs as Zach and I left the stage to the partygoers who still cheered. I was grateful the crowd today liked my act.

'Thank you,' I whispered to Zach, who was beside me. He took the guitar from me to rest it on a table next to the stage.

'Did you really think that after the stunt you pulled at the last event I would pass up an opportunity to get up there and sing with you?' Zach asked as he wrapped his arms around my waist.

'I love listening to you sing.' I pressed my lips to Zach's. 'Did you know…?' I couldn't help but ask. My lips were still close to Zach's before my words drifted off into silence. I tried to take a step back, but Zach wouldn't let go of me.

'Hey, you did a good job, baby,' Zach whispered softly in my ear, then he cupped my neck so we could stare at each other. 'There was a moment where I thought, "This doesn't look good".' Zach brushed his hand over my plaited hair. 'I'm proud of you, Harley. You got it together and finished the song. Finished all three of the songs you picked.' This time Zach kissed my lips a little longer.

He grabbed his guitar in one hand and my fingers in the other. We walked away from the stage through the crowd and headed towards the exit. Everyone who saw us walk past praised my performance, and I was amazed at how good I felt. I couldn't help but relax now that I had sung my songs.

'You sounded so good up there,' I heard a voice say and it stopped me in my tracks. I would know that voice anywhere, but I was just stunned to see her here in person.

'Mum?' I let go of Zach's hand. He knew I wasn't right behind him anymore. My man was a busy man with a business to run. But I knew he would be back to find me. Zach wouldn't leave without me.

'Your dad's voice was as just as smooth as yours with those husky undertones when he sang. I could hear him in your voice. The song you dedicated to your father was beautiful, Harley. I'm really proud of you.' My mum wrapped me up in her tight hug. It lasted longer than it should, but I didn't care. She was here to support me. She came all this way, and I didn't even know.

'I can't believe you're here.' I had spoken to my mother every week since I'd been here. It was my way of continuing to reach out to my family.

'We wanted to surprise you.'

'We?' I questioned who else was with my mother. But I should have known Addison was with her.

'Yes, we.'

I knew that voice too. I was amazed my family was here to show their support.

'Addison?' I was surprised that she was also here, given she was six months pregnant. Her belly was in the way as she wrapped me up in her hug. 'How?' My eyes moved from one face to the other in question.

'Zach sent us a text to let us know you were going to dedicate a song to your father, and we wanted to see you sing,' my mum said. Why was I not surprised that Zach had set up this little reunion?

'Singing suits you more than a baker ever did, and you're a natural with the guitar.' It was nice to hear Addison compliment me.

'It's called work–life balance.' I explained. 'As for the guitar, practice makes perfect.' With all the practice I had done in preparation for today, I was more singer than baker lately, and I was happier than I had ever been.

'You did a good job up there,' Addison told me, and we exchanged chuckles. She reached for my hand. 'Your voice gives me chills. You and Zach should have a regular gig here. You sound so magical together.'

Just when I'd started to feel at ease with my voice and who heard me sing, Addison found a way to stretch the edges of my comfort zone a little wider.

'Thanks.' To hear her say I should have a regular gig after she had now listened to my voice, not our voices together, was a comfort I never knew I needed. I couldn't help but reach out and return the squeeze of her hand.

We stood together and stared at each other for the longest of moments before moving towards the bar for drinks. I felt two arms wrap around me, and I knew immediately who had enveloped me.

'I love you,' he whispered into my ear.

I couldn't help but turn in his arms and whisper. 'I love you too'.

The kiss Zach left on my temple made me feel warm inside. Addison coughed and I had momentarily forgotten my family was here. I turned to face them while Zach's hands stayed wrapped around me.

'Addison reckons you and I should sing here together regularly. What do you think?'

'Maybe,' was the only answer he gave.

There was something in his eyes, a sparkle, which made me think that Zach liked the idea. Maybe he wanted to work together. I liked the idea too. It would be good for business if we could draw a crowd like today. Maybe we could test the idea at the next barbeque Zach planned at home, and I knew just the song I wanted to sing with him. He was already learning the song that I'd told him needed a second guitar.

Mum and I took the wine we were handed, Zach took the amber liquid he had been given, while Addison took her iced water. For the first time in a long time, we had a reason to celebrate: We were a happy family.

'Cheers,' we all said in unison as we toasted our glasses together. And I knew, in this moment, that this was exactly where I wanted to be.

ACKNOWLEDGEMENTS

Thank you to my editor and independent publisher Dr Juliette Lachemeier at The Erudite Pen, who helped smooth out the rough edges of my first novel. To my book cover designer Judith San Nicolas for bringing my dream cover to life. To my wonderful family and husband Craig, who encouraged me to pursue my writing dreams. To my mum Susan for being my sounding board. To my brother-in-law Blake for all your design inspirations. To Kerrie, Cheryl, Rhonda, Kristian and Lindsay for being brave enough to read the first draft. Your insight has been invaluable and your support is truly appreciated as I work towards being a published author.

ABOUT THE AUTHOR

Kimberley Anne was born and raised on the border of New South Wales and Victoria. The small country town she grew up in is the inspiration for the fictional town in her novel. Kimberley completed her Bachelor of Arts in 2001 where she majored Professional Writing at Victoria University, Melbourne. She began writing her debut novel in 2018 after her husband gifted her a Kindle.

With life experience on her side, Kimberley moved on from her country-town beginnings and is now based in Brisbane, Australia. When Kimberley isn't looking for her next book idea or having her nose in her Kindle, she can be found kicking back with a margarita in her hand and her German Shepherds at her feet.

Blackout is Kimberley's first Make You Mine Romance novel in the Acoustic Series, where she blends romance with real-life challenges, music, passion and plenty of heat.

A Make You Mine Romance

Book 2
Coming Soon

Black Eye

When Morgan Campbell feels a sexy stranger's eyes on her, she wonders if this man can save her from recent torment. Could this chance encounter be her salvation?

From the first time Connor Black lay eyes on the hazel-eyed brunette, he feels an instant connection. Something he has never had before, and he dreams of another encounter. Will he do what it takes his pursue this beauty, get to know her and find a way to hold onto their relationship?

Follow Connor on his journey as he navigates a clean slate, a change in pace and a new lifestyle in the small country town he grew up in. But when Connor's past as a ruthless businessman catches up with him, does he have what it takes to get back on his feet and chase his happy-ever-after back to the woman who holds his heart and soul in her hands?

Enjoyed the book? You can follow the author at:

Email: info@kimberleyanneauthor.com

Facebook:
www.facebook.com/profile.php?id=100092983862271

Website: kimberleyanneauthor.com

If you liked the book, please leave a review on Amazon, Goodreads or with the author directly. Reviews are invaluable in supporting an author's hard work and are greatly appreciated.

www.ingramcontent.com/pod-product-compliance
Lightning Source LLC
Chambersburg PA
CBHW030531120726
47904CB00005B/1729

* 9 7 8 0 6 4 5 7 8 4 5 0 3 *